NO RHYME NOR REASON

NO RHYME NOR REASON

Alison Theaker

To Alison —
Enjoy the seventies!

Alison!

September 2007

iUniverse, Inc.
New York Lincoln Shanghai

No Rhyme Nor Reason

All Rights Reserved © 2003 by Alison M Theaker

No part of this book may be reproduced or transmitted in any form or by any means, graphic, electronic, or mechanical, including photocopying, recording, taping, or by any information storage retrieval system, without the written permission of the publisher.

iUniverse, Inc.

For information address:
iUniverse, Inc.
2021 Pine Lake Road, Suite 100
Lincoln, NE 68512
www.iuniverse.com

ISBN: 0-595-28230-X

Printed in the United States of America

For Rod, Aaron and Ella

Acknowledgements

Firstly, I would like to thank my family, my husband Rod, my children Aaron and Ella, who tolerated my endless clattering on the computer to write this.

I would like to thank Meriel and Lindsay Pritchard. Lindsay wrote the poem, *Breathe,* which appears at the front of the book by his kind permission, and remains his copyright.

Grateful thanks to all of those friends who read endless drafts and gave me quality feedback and encouragement: Dede Tower, Mary Lyski, Elizabeth Roll, Liz Hiser and of course my long suffering husband, Rod.

Thanks to Richard Honey for the cover, and to his partner Clare Wigzell for her critique of my own poetry. Thanks to both of them for their hospitality and friendship.

Thank you to Fiona Morris for being my long standing friend and introducing me to Julia Cameron's *The Artists's Way* and to Theresa Lenarduzzi for being my roommate at university and still being my friend even after reading the storyline.

Also to my sister, Joy and mother, Audrey, just for being there.

Salutations to the INS who prevented me from working in the USA for the first year after we moved there and so gave me the time to sit down and write this.

Alison Theaker
Newton, MA
June 2003

Breathe

How strange a beginning
Trapped underwater with someone breathing for you
Until it's time to breathe alone
That first sharp, searing inhalation
The air pumps the blood, fires the bone
And turns the soul.

We take our pocket of air with us
Everywhere, inexhaustible
We use it for
Laughing inspiration
Misting grief
Exhaled exasperation
Sforzando of anger
And a slow, slow pulse of dreams.

And you shared my bubble for a time
With the rise and fall of slow afternoon
The delicate synchronicity of a kiss
And then a sigh, a heavy sigh

But I always knew you were out there
In your own open air now
Breathing, breathing, breathing.
Just sometimes I think and catch my breath
And thinking too much can leave me
Breathless.

Sarah   Now

Beginning

Like all complicated things, it began very simply. But then, it's complicated trying to work out when exactly it all began. Was it the moment when I ran out of biscuits? If I'd had a packet of custard creams in my cupboard that day, would none of this have happened? Because why I did what I did when I found that the biscuit tin was empty had its roots far far back, somewhere before I even came to York.

I was the first in my family to get a place at university. My mother was probably much cleverer than me, she'd won a place at a girls' public school in the 1930s. Being a scholarship girl she got by with her richer, dumber peers by doing their homework as well as her own. She passed her matriculation with flying colours. The headmistress wanted her to try for a scholarship to Oxford, even coming to my grandparents' house—something unheard of for Mrs Brumby to do—to beg my grandmother to let her daughter stay on at school. But my grandmother was adamant. She had no time for some college miles away, and in the south of England at that, and Margaret's wages were needed at home. So my mother went to work as a bank teller.

My Dad was bright too, he had been the only one of his family—a huge crew of eight boys and seven girls—who'd passed the exams to get into the Civil Service. A secure career was his—"It's a job for life, Jeffrey," said his father—which turned out to be more of a curse than a blessing as he got passed over for promotion again and again by more well connected colleagues. My grandfather had been thrown out of the Masons for not paying his dues, which seriously impaired any member of the family ever making a career in the Civil Service, but my Dad was never able to get rid of the conviction that you stayed with the same employer for life. So he watched his brothers who'd gone into altogether more lowly and risky jobs—a shop assistant who went on to manage a chain of chemists' shops and eventually emigrate to a mansion in South Africa; a bank clerk who became the manager of the branch and then the region—overtake him in the earning stakes whilst he toiled at his desk for little pay and less thanks.

My brother, Noah, wanted nothing to do with university. He left school at sixteen, determined to be a pilot in the RAF, but they wouldn't have him. Some kind of heart beat syndrome stopped him, not serious and nothing that you would notice in ordinary life, but possibly critical if it happened at the wrong time when he was at the controls of a fighter plane. But he had an unerring talent for making money, although we never quite knew how he did it. He bought and sold cars, then houses, then moved into property development. "When I grow up," he confided to me when he was leaving home and I was a wide-eyed five year old, "I want to be a rich old miser". He's certainly on track for that, and has managed to shed the rest of us along the way when it became clear that none of us would assist him with this ambition.

My sister, Deborah, is an artist. She gritted her teeth and hung on at school until she was eighteen, but then it was off to London, to art school, to eventual critical acclaim and commercial success. She married Nigel, a successful management consultant with shed loads of money, eventually settled down in a huge rambling converted barn in the country near Bath, and produced two children as well as an array of vast abstract landscapes which sell for six figures.

So it's not as if my siblings weren't successful. But still, hanging in the ether was the thought that I was my parents' last chance to make it to the mystical world they'd never got to try, somewhere you could better yourself, and experience and achieve things they never had.

It was lucky that I wanted to go. I did, really. I can't remember any instances where they forced me to do my homework or fill in my application forms. I had the misfortune to find my school work reasonably easy and to be clever. I knew I was clever because the other kids called me "swot" when I handed my homework in on time and got good marks for it. I also knew that clever was not something I wanted to be, I would rather have been thin and pretty like Jennifer Adams, but I was neither of those things. I was lucky that Jennifer allowed me to be part of her gang, intermittently, as long as I didn't say anything too clever or disagree with her. I earned my entrance by being the clown, the butt of all my own jokes. It was hard work. So university seemed like a good place to go to, a fresh start, away from all the other kids who knew me as Fatty Martin, a place where I could reinvent myself as anyone I wanted to be.

Even though they didn't make me go, still I felt the weight of all that unfulfilled ambition. I was the youngest, the afterthought. I had to prove to my parents that I really wasn't just a contraceptive failure, I could do something for them that my brother and sister had failed to do. So I hope you get the idea of how important it was for me, once I had got the place at York University to do English, to make a success of it. I couldn't get thrown out, you see. Can you imagine how I must have felt, looking at the bottom of that empty tin, that awful sense of looking over the edge of a precipice, as though things are further away and closer up all at the same time? So I didn't have any alternative.

Sarah   October 1977

Meeting

That first morning, the lobby was full of trunks and suitcases, piled around the makeshift desk where two young men sprawled artistically, watching the new arrivals. A tall young woman with an impressive mane of long dark hair and equally impressive amounts of black eyeliner perched one buttock on the edge of the desk. Sarah approached them with what she hoped was a confident air, not reflecting the reality of the swirling fear in her stomach that threatened to expel this morning's breakfast and the little voice in her head yelling "Run! Get out of here now!"

She had made her parents drop her off at the entrance. Unbeknownst to them, she had decided that today was, in the words of a popular poster at the time, the first day of the rest of her life. So the last thing she wanted was for her parents to give her away, to let slip that she'd always been shy, found it hard to make friends, had spent most of her life, even to her mother's biased eyes, on the tubby side. This was the new Sarah, slim, confident, the kind of girl everyone wanted to be seen with. She felt a pang of unexpected and unplanned homesickness as she watched their blue Ford Sierra turn out onto the dual carriageway that ran through the middle of the campus (artfully landscaped into a cutting), as though her lungs had suddenly been stapled to her sternum. Then, blinking away the moisture at the corner of her eye, she walked into the lion's den.

The man in the middle, ugly handsome with a huge nose, countered by the bright blue eyes either side and a mass of pre-Raphelite curls cascading over the collar of his denim shirt, looked up and smiled. The effect of this was to make the swirling in her stomach reverse direction. "Name?" he asked.

"Sarah Martin", Sarah replied, mildly surprised to find her voice sounded fairly normal. Wasn't it supposed to come out like an embarrassing croak when you found yourself in the presence of some guy you fancied? All the romantic fiction she'd come across suggested that was what happened to women.

The Nose, meanwhile, after consulting a typed list, announced, "You're in D Block. Do you need a hand with anything?" He accompanied this with a repeat performance of the smile. Definitely a charmer. And he knew it.

Sarah indicated the largest of the trunks piled in the hallway, obviously brand new and bright blue. Her mother had supervised its purchase, its packing and its dispatch by road so that it would be waiting to greet her. Sarah didn't quite know on what basis her mother had decided that a trunk was necessary for someone going to university. After all, she'd never been there herself and didn't know anyone who had been either.

Until now, she had only had eye contact with the Nose. As he opened his mouth to volunteer to help her with the trunk (she hoped) the man on his left leapt up before he could get the words out. "I can sort that out, Dick," he said, striding towards a set of removal wheels. Had he put that emphasis on the last word on purpose, Sarah wondered. By the Nose's expression, probably. "I'm Sam," by the way," he said, "Welcome to Derwent. What are you reading?"

Sarah hadn't believed until that moment that that was how people asked what subject you were doing for your degree. "English", she said. This one really was ugly. Dark haired again, but brutally short, looked like someone had cut it with garden shears. Brown eyes above a nose that looked like he had walked into a tree. She just managed to stop herself asking him whether that was what had happened to him. Probably a bit soon to expose the residents of the College to her humour which one of her teachers had described as "ascerbic, and never funny". A red checked lumberjack shirt, drainpipe jeans and Doc Martens, the whole ensemble finished off with the largest bunch of keys that she had ever seen hanging from a broad leather belt. Social politeness kicked in. "How about you?" she asked him, though she didn't care at all, except perhaps to make sure he wasn't doing English as well.

"Economics," he said, looking pleased at her interest. Damn. The last thing she wanted to do was to be lumbered with some adoring swain, a guy that no one else wanted. She'd had enough of that with Johnny. Come to think of it, this Sam looked rather like Johnny. Although she had been quite grateful to Johnny for taking care of the embarrassing matter of her virginity in the back of her parents' Saab, she hadn't counted on the fact that he would see this as tantamount to a declaration of eternal love and an intention to get married, settle down two houses up the road from his Mum in Grange over Sands and produce a brood of children while he ran his Dad's garage and came home for his lunch every day.

Even Kirsty, sixth form bitch and loudmouth had felt sorry for her in the end, and taken Sarah on one side to give her some friendly advice on how to ditch him. "You're quite pretty now you've lost all that weight," she'd told her. "You can get something better than Johnny Manfredson. He's such a dork!" Sarah, who had lusted unsuccessfully after Daniel Palfreyman for two years, agreed with her. But no matter how clear she was with Johnny, he never took the hint. And then there was the matter of his best friend, Ged, a man mountain who kept telling her that she was the best thing that had ever happened to Johnny and he was sure he'd "top" himself if she ever gave him the push. Johnny's one advantage was that her parents had hated him.

Her father had greeted him with "My God, which stone did you find this one under?" when Johnny had called for her the first time. Her mother had started muttering about homework and the A level results she would need to get into university, and tried to take her front door key off her so that she couldn't get in after the 10pm curfew. Sarah had a spare cut just in case. In the end she'd got three A grades and passed the S level in English too, satisfyingly proving her mother wrong.

But Johnny was not a mistake she intended to make again. She had chosen to come to York because no one else from her school was coming here and she was determined to reinvent herself. "Is there a good Gay and Lesbian Society here?" she asked Sam, almost causing him to drop her trunk, which he had skillfully loaded onto the wheels, onto his boot, though luckily it looked like it was the steel toe-capped version.

"Dunno," he muttered.

"Oh, sorry, my mistake," she said, "but, you know, the keys and everything...." Sam gaped at her, aghast that his macho badge could have been so misinterpreted.

"Er, no, er, we need to go across here," he said, just managing to master the wheels with their load of everything that Sarah's mother had regarded as essential equipment to survive in York for the next three months as they threatened to take off down the ramp at the side of the stairs.

Sarah managed to suppress her bark of a laugh and effect an unconcerned amiability as they walked across to the concrete block that was to be her home for the next year. Sam's tense dumbstruck silence enabled her to realise that it was, in fact, a beautiful day. The sun was still warm on her hair, and she could sense the beginnings of autumn in the warm air, full of the scent of leaves about to turn Glancing up, the stark lines of the grey rectangles where the students were housed were softened by the brilliance of the sky, ice blue with high mare's tails of cloud.

Sam manoeuvred the trunk through the double doors and up the two flights of stairs to the first floor, mumbling his refusal of her offer to help, obviously still desperate to prove his manhood even if it resulted in a hernia. "This is your room here," he said, after they had walked down a corridor and through the shared kitchen, already full of curious neighbours. He wheeled the trunk in, deposited it in the middle of the room and beat a hasty retreat.

"See you at the Freshers' Reception tonight," she called after his rapidly vanishing back.

"Er, maybe, yeah," he replied.

Sarah closed the door and leant against it before she allowed herself to indulge in a yelp of laughter which turned into a sobbing fit of giggles so that she had to stuff her fist in her mouth and bite hard to stop it. Well, hopefully that had sorted the Sam problem out, although she would have to watch out around him. Persistent swains were quite capable of only seeing what they wanted to see and he might have rewritten the conversation before tonight. The other problem, she reflected more soberly, was that he might pass on the information to Dick that she was not available. Still, she could deal with that if it came to it.

She took a deep breath, looked around her cell and smiled. The room was about ten feet long and five feet wide. It was so narrow that the bed was pushed under a plastic covered and padded cupboard that made it possible to use the bed as a settee but not for sleeping in. When the bed was pulled out, it would sit right up to the legs of the desk on the other side of the room, making it necessary to fold up the chair that sat underneath it. A tiny built in wardrobe flanked the door on one side, on the other a stainless steel sink and a mirror was concealed in another cupboard. Lockable lockers topped both these structures. She found out later that that was where you were supposed to store your belongings in the holidays when the university made a substantial addition to its income by renting out the accommodation to conferences and tourists. Cuts in the education budget gave rise to rumours amongst the student body that the university was going to cut the length of terms so that they could make more money from their supposed sideline.

Cork boards wormholed with the drawing pins of the previous occupant lined both walls, and the far wall was almost entirely a sash window framed by sludge blue curtains. The view was of the side of the next wing of the college, featureless grey concrete. But Sarah experienced a rush of pure pleasure looking at the room and drinking in its musty cardboard smell. It was all hers, it was lockable and she held in her hand the key not just to the room but to the person she wanted to be from now on.

Within an hour she had unpacked the contents of her trunk, spreading her books on the bookshelves, putting up her posters of Yes album covers, to the accompaniment of one of those same albums, the first of the Yessongs set, at full blast on her ancient record player. It might have valves but it had a good bass tone, one which she had employed to good effect at home to annoy her mother by playing a variety of 45s which had different drum rhythms to the insistent thrum of the washing machine. She recalled that Young Gifted and Black had worked well in this regard, as well as Spirit in the Sky. She stood with her back against the door and surveyed her efforts. Bright satin-covered cushions inset with tiny mirrors softened the lines of the bed. The trunk was squeezed in next to the desk and had been transformed with an orange batik throw into a surface which held her kettle and toaster so that she could indulge in breakfast in bed without having to venture into the communal kitchen. It was cold enough to keep a pint of milk outside the window, she thought. Buying that milk would be her next adventure, the start of her independent living, buying what food she wanted with her own money, well her student grant anyway, eating what and when she wanted, not to her mother's timetable.

For now she was content to sip her Formosa Oolong black, resting back on her cushions, feet up on the end of the trunk, letting the complicated synthesiser music of Rick Wakeman with Jon Anderson's vocals fill her space and spill out the window. She could feel her body becoming liquid, spreading out across the bedspread, leaving the persona of Fatty Martin behind as it had done in weight terms some time previously. Here she was in a place where no one knew her or who she had been, where there were no expectations that she would be shy and diffident, grateful for the attentions of the sixth form dork, dressed in frumpy sweaters which disguised her body. She put a hand up to her hair, to enjoy the feeling of its velvet shortness at the nape of her neck overlaid with the silkiness of the blonde highlighted bob, instead of her natural mousy beige in the long lank style she had worn at school. Even without the Nose, she had spotted at least a dozen good looking men in the college lobby on her arrival. From now on, she resolved, she was only going to talk to handsome men.

Then there was a knock on the door.

Suzanne   4 October 1977

Diary

The first day of the rest of my life!

Today I met my best friend and the man I'm going to marry. Pretty good for my first day at uni! Sarah is brill, I can tell already she's going to be great fun. I'm lucky that she's in the next room. Was scared that there would be all these boring, booky types here, even though this is the best place to read biochemistry. Even though she likes Yes. Can't believe it. In fact that was the reason why I knocked on her door in the first place, all this psychedelic hippy music pouring out, yuck. She was lying on her bed, she'd made her room really nice already, it looked so warm and welcoming, all oranges and reds. She looked really sophisticated and confident, new Levi's, I felt a real mess and was beginning to regret knocking, even though the music was so loud it was doing my head in. But then she smiled and I knew it was going to be alright, and offered me some tea even though she didn't have any milk, and I forgot I'd gone in there to demand she turn that awful row down and we sat on the bed and chatted for ages.

And then there's Dick, he's so yummy. I knew straight away when I saw him sitting at the welcome desk that he was the one for me. Gorgeous eyes and long curly hair, and he's doing biology too, even offered to help me with my assignments when he carried my suitcase up. Seeing him later at the Freshers' Reception. Can't wait. Uni is shaping up to be the best time of my life already.

Sarah   1973

Lizzie

I'd had a best friend once before I met Suzanne. I'd known Lizzie since my first day at school, and we were in the same class all through Allithwaite Primary. She had short dark curly hair and big brown eyes, and like me she was dumpy and gauche. She lived up the road from us with her mother and elder sister, Rosie. Lizzie's father had left them when she was a few months old, and she never saw him. Occasionally a card with a five pound note would arrive for her birthday, but she never seemed to feel his absence. "What's to miss?" she would say with a shrug. Lizzie's mum had to work full time to support them all, and sometimes Lizzie would come to our house for tea.

I'd overheard my mother telling my father, "Gina's so brave and capable, it's the least we could do to help."

At first it didn't seem like anything special. We liked each other, but were thrown together by circumstances rather than from choice. She enjoyed playing with my Sindy collection, and on the rare occasions I got to go round to her house, I loved climbing the apple tree in her back garden and the swing that hung from its branches. Eventually, what began in necessity grew into a firm friendship. As we got older, we got closer, so that by the time we were ten we'd walk to and from school together, spending an hour or two every afternoon at one house or the other. At my house we pored over my copies of Bunty, full of pictures of doll-like girls and ideas of how to make unlikely items out of socks and sticky backed plastic, and later, Jackie, full of photo stories about first kisses and how to deal with bullies at school, and tips on hair and make up which we had neither the means or the inclination to follow.

It was the afternoons at Lizzie's house that I liked the best. Her mother was much less restrictive than mine in the boundaries which she placed on our behaviour. Most of our time was spent outside. We progressed from climbing the apple tree to climbing over the dry stone wall at the back of the garden and wandering the fells behind. At one end of the village was Wartbarrow, named after the knobbly tussocks scattered across the face of the hill. We would scramble over the remains of old walls which spilled onto rain exposed outcrops of limestone, weathered into chalky skeletons. At the top we would hide behind the stunted black hawthorns, bent over against years of wind, their warped and twisted branches swept sideways, watching to see whether the bull in the next field was preying on golfers who had overshot the green on the seventh hole of the Fell Golf Club. Southwards we could see out across Morecambe Bay, on a clear day we could even make out the dark grey matchstick of the Blackpool Tower on the horizon. To the north, the hills of the Lake District marched away up to Coniston Old Man. It was a place where I could understand whoever wrote that psalm that starts "I will lift up mine eyes unto the hills," could almost believe that there was some kind of grand design behind all of this and that I was reassuringly insignificant in it.

One day we reached the top breathless after a buffeting by a sudden summer wind, which sprang up as we climbed in brilliant sunshine. Lizzie yelled out, "Windmills!". We spread our arms wide like sails, letting the air currents whirl us round. I looked up at the clouds scurrying across the high dome of the sky, spinning faster and faster. Suddenly my view changed to the walls and trees as my foot caught in a stray root and I crashlanded onto the grass.

Lizzie joined me on the ground, "Turn over," she commanded. We flipped over to watch the moving sky. The grass infiltrated itself under my T-shirt, prickling the back of my neck and my back just above the waistband of my shorts. It was the summer holiday before we were due to go to the big school down the road in Cartmel, the biggest step we'd taken in the six years we'd known each other, a sure sign that we were Growing Up.

We talked about all the things we didn't know. "What are the teachers going to be like, not like Mrs Morris, I hope," said Lizzie.

"What's wrong with Mrs Morris?" I asked.

"She smells," pronounced Lizzie firmly. I'd never noticed.

"Smells of what?" I wanted to know.

"Sprouts!" This was so unlikely as to be hilarious and we sniggered in unison.

"Why do they make the girls wear those baggy blue knickers for gym," I worried.

"I'm not going to wear them," pronounced Lizzie.

"Be a bit cold without them," I laughed, and then we were giggling again, until Lizzie raised the most worrying thought of all.

"Do you think we'll ever get to like boys?" That stopped the laughter. Neither of us could envision being attracted to the likes of Brian who lived over the fish and chip shop, or Sidney who lived with his gran on the new estate at the edge of the village.

So we didn't notice that the day was changing, purple banks of rainclouds building behind the hills, until the first outriders of the storm fell on our hands and faces.

At first we tried sheltering under the trees. I could see our house in the distance, small and white. My mother was getting the washing in, a tiny figure swamped by acres of billowing sheets. The rain was like a slate barrier, moving up the wide valley, curtaining the view. Water started to trickle down my neck. We looked at each other and nodded—we had to make a run for it.

"On three," Lizzie shouted. Then, "Three!" I let my legs carry me down the hill, faster and faster, leaping from wart to wart, my eyes full of wet hair. I couldn't see, and unsure of my footing, it felt almost dangerous. The wind was like a steel comb, liquid ice on my face. We reached the road, still running, the hardness of the tarmac shot up through my heels. We fell through the door of Lizzie's house, drenched and laughing, and, carried along by adrenalin and the impetus of our flight, stumbled through to the bathroom, shedding clothes as we went. I can't remember any kind of conscious thought which resulted in the two of us ending up in the shower, naked and still gasping from exhilaration.

There was a moment, just before Lizzie reached out and turned the water on full, when I realised that this was not like all those times we'd had a bath together as we'd grown. I closed my eyes, tipped my head back to feel the hot needles massaging my scalp, breathing in the steam, surrendering to whatever was just about to happen. Lizzie started to wash my hair, then I could feel her fingers sliding down my neck, over my shoulders, her thumbs moving down my spine. She stood close behind me, I could feel her chest and belly pressing against my back and bottom, her head resting on my shoulder, so that both of us stood in the same spray. Time slipped away, there was only the sound of the water, the heat, and Lizzie's skin against mine.

After a while she turned off the shower, and we dried each other off with the towels that were hanging on the rack, patting and stroking, turning so that the other could reach every part. Lizzie reached out and stroked the hair on my arm with her fingertips, then took my hand and led me into her room. Without words we got into her bed, folded our bodies together and fell asleep.

Which is how my mother found us. She'd come to Lizzie's house because we hadn't returned, it was more than an hour after the storm and she couldn't raise Lizzie's mum on the phone. The door was open, Lizzie's mum was cooking in the back kitchen, she hadn't noticed that the phone was off the hook, knocked by our precipitate progress through the hall. My mother saw the trail of discarded clothes, and went upstairs, expecting to discover us poring over homework or comics, as so often before.

I surfaced from sleep to find her standing over the bed, with an expression of horror and shock. Then she was gone, there were urgent murmured voices from below. "Have you seen them? What on earth did you think they were doing upstairs all that time? Disgusting!" A confused time of waking and dressing, Mum pulling me from Lizzie's bed, being hurried down the road in silence, more muttering with my father. "Couldn't believe it! Bad influence."

I never saw Lizzie again after that. My mother refused to talk about her, Dad would shrug and return to reading his paper. On the rare occasions I managed to try and call her, her mother would screen my calls. "She's not home," she'd say, but I could often hear weeping in the background. No one ever answered the door when I called round either. The house soon sported a "For Sale" and then "Sold" sign, Lizzie never came to the big school, I don't know where she went. She was ripped from my life, leaving a gaping hole that was never filled, it just healed over so that I could carry on, disguising the void beneath.

Sarah   October 1977

Jules

The Freshers' Night party was held in a large room on the ground floor of the College, called the Junior Common Room. "How affected," thought Sarah, as if they were at Oxford or something. It served its purpose well, with a stage for the DJ and his rig, as well as an impressive set of lights and of course the mirror ball hung from the ceiling. The party was sparsely populated as yet, so she decided to get a drink from the makeshift bar which had been set up in the next room. She'd dressed carefully, a pair of skin tight drainpipe Levi's to show off her slim figure topped with a collarless white cotton shirt, minimal make up and brilliant blue long dangly ear drops that matched her eyes.

Where was the Nose, she wondered. Waiting at the bar for her pint of lager she was aware, with a tightening of the skin at the back of her neck, of his entrance, followed a split second later by Suzanne. Shit! They were holding hands. My God, that woman was a fast worker. You'd never think it to look at her, frail enough to be blown away, wispy red hair, white skin and enormous green eyes.

Disappointment sat in her stomach, making her view the freshly pulled pint with nausea. She grasped it anyway, and took a large gulp to quell the feeling that someone was shifting the scuffed parquet floor beneath her blue suede boots. Why was she so disappointed? She'd seen a fair crop of good looking men this afternoon, he was probably the ugliest of the lot. But she wanted him and now it looked like he was unavailable. With a mild shrug to herself she turned away from the bar, only to be greeted with the sight of Sam lounging against the far wall, watching her. With only the slightest hesitation she continued her turn, hoping he hadn't noticed and guessed the truth, that she was deliberately trying to avoid him.

She took a step forward and collided with the dark-haired woman who'd been sitting on the reception desk that afternoon, spilling lager on both their jeans. "Shit, I'm sorry," she apologised, looking up to see the other woman's appraising stare.

"Never mind, the jeans'll wash and there's plenty more of that at the bar," said the woman. "I'm Jules, how are you settling in?"

"Fine, thanks, I'm Sarah," Sarah introduced herself. "Yes, I know," said Jules with a smile.

"Sam tells me you were asking after the GaySoc?"

"That's right," replied Sarah, thinking, damn him, hadn't taken him long to put the word around, making sure that she didn't succeed with anyone else. Maybe that was why the Nose had thrown in his lot with Suzanne. Over Jules' shoulder she could see Sam, watching them both closely. She turned back to Jules. "Know anything about it?" she asked.

Jules was looking at her intently. "I'm the Chair," Jules said. "The first meeting's on Friday, over in Vanbrugh at 8 o'clock." Sarah felt disoriented, she took another mouthful of the chilled lager.

"I don't really know, I'll probably see you there…" her voice trailed off. Then Jules reached out her free hand and softly stroked the hair on Sarah's arm with her fingertips, keeping the eye contact.

"I'd rather hoped I'd see you before then," she said. Her thumb circled Sarah's wrist, and Sarah caught a faint echo of a steam filled shower, the scent of shampoo. The room fell away, she swayed and, putting out her arm to steady herself, connected with the soft denim of Jules' shirt. The circle was complete.

Jules removed Sarah's pint and deposited it and her own on the nearest table. Taking her hand and weaving their fingers together, she drew her through the bodies on the dance floor to the strains of "*Tainted Love*". Sarah was aware of Sam pushing himself off the wall and slouching out of the room.

Later, in Jules' bed, having been kissed from her neck to her nipples and back again, stroked and caressed and rubbed with oil, she felt as though the hole left by Lizzie's brutal removal from her life had started to heal. The two women lay spooned on the mattress which they had dragged onto the floor to avoid falling off the narrow bed, the covers piled in sweaty heaps, the smell of incense and oil and sex filling the room. Sarah stretched out so she could feel the smoothness of Jules' flesh all along her back and buttocks. The other woman murmured something in her half sleep, curling her hand around Sarah's breast. Sarah sighed and slipped into sleep, with the satisfying thought that her parents would have been grateful, at that moment, to have seen her safely married off to Johnny Manfredson.

Sarah   Now

Friendship

It wasn't a very auspicious start to a friendship. I mean, I was just lying there, enjoying playing the music really loud and she'd come to complain about it. Not the volume, but the fact that it was Yes! At this distance I can't remember quite how we seemed to get into talking about home and schools and A levels and parents and boys.

She wasn't my type either, whatever that was. I'd never really made friends at Cartmel, still bewildered by Lizzie's forced ejection. I was always the barely tolerated outsider. I was envious of the friendship that Jennifer Adams had with Denise Welsh, they went everywhere together, they sat together in all the classes they took apart from Latin, which Jennifer's parents had made her do because she wanted to do languages at Oxford. Then she condescended to sit next to me, because I was the only other girl in the class, and "None of the boys here are remotely fanciable," she confided. Jennifer wouldn't have had to put up with some dork who took Latin anyway, she had her pick of all of the sixth form boys. They used to start talking slightly louder about their successful exploits on the football field and preen themselves discreetly when she went by.

I did have a brief period of friendship with Jennifer when Denise's family moved to Scotland and Jennifer's bereft eye fell on me. I'd managed to turn from one of the shortest and fattest in the school to one of the tallest and thinnest, by the simple fact of growing three inches in one year. Thank God for puberty. I continued to benefit from my body's changed metabolism by being able to eat not only my own food at lunchtime, but being able to ingratiate myself with all the other girls on my table, who even then had acquired the need to ostentatiously refuse all food of any nutritional value, by eating all of theirs as well, without putting on any weight at all. "Pass them down," I crowed gleefully, managing on one occasion to eat our entire table's ration of roast potatoes.

I'm the same height now as I was then, but about thirty pounds heavier. Even then I used to complain about the shape of my stomach, which had the temerity to be naturally curved, I hope from a sense of having to fit in with all the other moaning about the shape of our bodies which all the sixth form girls seemed to indulge in. Looking in the mirror now, I find it hard to skim all that weight off my body and imagine that I actually found it attractive to look like that. Snapshots show a skinny girl with acres of mousy hair, adopting a kind of James Dean glower in an attempt to look cool and hide the fact that I was still camera shy, not used to my suddenly fashionably thin body shape being captured on film.

Anyway, the fact that I was thin made me a suitable companion for Jennifer. Added to this was the fact that I was flat-chested—the butt of the boy's jokes. "I'm not flat chested, am I?" Alan Garner would say loudly behind me.

"I don't know, turn round and I'll tell you!" his sidekick Wesley Pittfield would snicker. For some reason the adolescent development of my body didn't get round to filling in that bit until I was in my mid-twenties and had already had one child. So there was no danger of me upstaging Jennifer in that department. She certainly had no need to stuff her bra with socks, as I was tempted to do until I saw the degree of ridicule to which Jennifer subjected Jane Simpson when she was discovered having done just that, one gym lesson when an unusually large number of us had actually remembered to bring our games kit.

Games was definitely not cool and to be avoided at all costs. I think there was one time when Mrs Gargoyle—we always called her that and I can't even remember her real name now—was enraged that only three of the sixty sixth form girls had actually brought kit. She even kept a register which marked in all our periods. Having a period was the only acceptable reason (apart from having a verucca and they were impossible to fake) for missing showers, so some girls had relied on Gargoyle having a patchy memory of exactly who was on and when, resulting in some claiming to be bleeding constantly before the introduction of the register. Showers were embarrassing because you were supposed to take off all your clothes in front of every other girl in the class, attempting to cover your breasts and bottom with a towel so that the Gargoyle couldn't see, then parade through a line of lukewarm showers which had no curtains for any kind of privacy.

It amazes me that I am so easy with my naked body now. My mother used to only partially unclothe in order to wash a particular bit of her body at a time. The privacy she felt was so important for herself was not afforded to me however. I was so ashamed of my blubbery puppy fat that I too would wash whilst keeping at the very least my vest on, and spent time in the bath rarely and with the constant fear that someone would have to come in to use the only toilet in the house. My mother saw no reason to inform me if she wanted to come into the bathroom whilst I was in the bath, and even had the lack of sensitivity, when I was about seven, to invite one of her friends in to view me when she called round. It wasn't anything important, it was just that Clara had asked, "Where's Sarah?".

She'd got the reply, "She's in the bath, go in and say hello".

I suppose it's yet another thing I have to thank Jules for. Not only did she show that she loved and lusted after, even celebrated my body, but she took me to

Greece that one summer we were together. She found out where all the lesbian nudist beaches were, so we spent six weeks slumming around the Greek islands, getting deep all over tans, lying around on the sand surrounded by women of all shapes, sizes and ages. Jules taught me to appreciate my own body and those of other women for what they were.

So when Suzanne stuck her head round the door to ask me "Could you play something else if you're going to play it so loudly—like Fleetwood Mac for Christ' sake?" it was not a match made in heaven by any means. She was a redhead, but not one of those who possess a shining mane of deep chestnut orange and toss it around often to make the rest of us jealous, she had a strawberry blonde feather cut which framed her pale and pointed face. Fantastic green eyes though, which she knew were her best feature and used to good effect—on me, on Dick, on her lecturers, on barmen and the waitresses at Betty's Tea Rooms. She was about three inches shorter than me, which she also used, turning her emerald gaze upwards through long blonde eyelashes especially when standing next to Dick.

That always used to give me a needle stab of hurt, because it showed that they were so obviously together, even though he was such a dog and couldn't keep it in his trousers for the first year they were an item. I had tried to raise his philandering with Suzanne, but even before I got two minutes into my obviously subtle and roundabout approach to the subject, had been clearly told, "I know all about it. It doesn't matter, I know that he loves me the most. Besides, it's none of your business!"

When I started to read her poems and found out the extent of how she had to suppress her anger at what he was doing, and how she justified it by blaming herself, I couldn't accept her way of dealing with it any longer, and that's when the rot set in. The fact that I was stealing her work and feeling guilty about that also meant that I just couldn't be open with her anymore. She could tell something was up, but neither of us talked about it. I know she thought it was because of Dick, and made some oblique reference to "How stupid it would be for women friends to fall out over a man, don't you think?" Then again, she didn't know that I was being far more active in destroying our friendship, in what would turn out to be an awful and irrevocable way.

She was wearing jeans, tight at the top and flared at the bottom. It was just the beginning of the shift away from the loons and flares of my teenage to drainpipes. A cheesecloth shirt, striped in green and cream, surf beads and silver hoops in her ears. I looked her up and down pointedly, and said, "And you've got the cheek to call Yes, 'Hippy music'!"

I was wearing my new straight cut Levi's and a collarless shirt that I had lifted from my father's wardrobe before leaving home. "I used to have a shirt like that," he'd said when he dropped me off at the college earlier that day. Levi's and men's shirts were to become my new uniform at university. Suzanne, thank goodness, graduated out of the denim flares pretty soon but never lost her weakness for cheesecloth and smocking.

She was already flipping through my records. "My God, you really don't have any Fleetwood Mac, do you?" she asked with surprised outrage. My extensive and eclectic record collection was to grow phenomenally during the three years of my grant funded lifestyle. She was right on the button in terms of Fleetwood Mac. Soon there wasn't a room on campus that didn't possess Rumours.

I once shared the thought with Suzanne that, "You could probably listen to the whole album just by walking from Derwent all the way to Wentworth," the furthest college at that time.

Still, after a momentary hesitation on my part while I worked out that it probably wasn't wise to annoy the woman who was going to be living in the room next to mine for the rest of the first year on the first day of term, I invited her in. "Would you like a cup of tea?" I asked. I had decided to make a statement of my dislike of coffee by stocking a poseur's variety of teas. Coffee was the staple beverage of the student body, by virtue of the fact that you could, when pushed, drink it black when your milk had evolved into cottage cheese on your windowsill. Keeping it there was the only way you could be sure that the rest of those in your corridor that shared the fridge in the kitchen hadn't been pilfering it. At worst, it was even drinkable with one of those dried confections which claimed to make you faint with pleasure at the taste when you stirred in some of it.

I'd already suspected that things could be difficult when I got to university because of my experiences in the sixth form common room, where it became clear that coffee was a big help in oiling the wheels of adolescent romance. It was lucky that I fell into a long term relationship with Jules almost immediately so that she was prepared to accommodate my strange tastes in the beverage line.

It never seemed to cause a problem when I blatantly asked guys back to my room, "want a cuppa after the lecture?", in the early part of the first year when I was still managing to slip in a few illicit sexual encounters with men before I got bored with their frantic fumbling and ignorance of female anatomy.

Suzanne gamely got to grips with a cup of Formosa Oolong, one of my favourites because of its delicate peachy taste, although, as she said, "It tastes like fruity dishwater."

It was also quite satisfyingly pseud, even to the extent of flooring an arrogant waiter in a bistro I visited some years later who instead of just telling me what tea they had on offer, claimed that, "Whatever tea you want, we have it." I expressed condescending surprise as he was forced to tell me that, in fact, they had no Formosa Oolong, no Lapsang Souchong, not even any Darjeeling, just a pathetic choice between Breakfast, Ceylon and Earl Grey.

We started by checking out all the usual background details, what subject we were doing here, English for me, Biochemistry for her. "What the hell is biochemistry?" I asked.

"A kind of mixture of biology and chemistry I guess," she replied. "I mean, I don't really know, that's what I'm here to find out!" What A levels had we done? English, History and French for me, the three sciences and maths for her. Then we got into where our parents lived and where we had grown up, the Lake District and Cornwall. "Don't you just hate it when people say, oh you must be so lucky to be living somewhere where most people just go on holiday?" she said, echoing my thoughts exactly.

"Yes, because you have to put up with all the bloody tourists!" I replied. Neither of us were failed Oxbridge entrants as most of the students at York seemed to be, which made us two members of a rare breed. She was easy to talk to, she'd had even less sexual experience than I had, and confessed that she was still a virgin.

"Not for long, though!" she declared. Of course that was in the days when university was just a big round bed, not surprising when you put a few thousand people of both sexes and all sexual preferences between the ages of eighteen and twenty-three together, plus stirring in a good mix of lecturers more than happy to continue tuition outside seminar hours. Several of the lecturers in the Politics department who frequented the Derwent bar seemed to share wives and ex-wives with their fellows in the Philosophy and Sociology departments, and the majority of their female partners were alumni of the university. The English lecturers tended to be rather more circumspect, but we all knew about their lapses at the Langwith bop.

Despite the fact that she came from Cornwall and I came from the Lake District, we both shared the experience of growing up in a small town atmosphere far from any source of teenage action, where the main social activity was snogging in the bus shelters and underage drinking and driving. "Did most of your friends from school marry blokes they knew since childhood and move into a house just a few miles, if not doors, from their parents?" she asked.

"You bet," I agreed glumly.

"You're so lucky you can drive," she said wistfully.

"Well, that's the main reason I managed to lose my virginity before I got here," I reasoned.

We also shared, which was the most important thing, a tendency to speak our minds without thinking of the consequences and a sharp sense of humour. Suzanne had the ability to cut through the smoke to what was really going on, which was why it was later so obvious that I just couldn't see why she persisted in staying with Dick, a man who, I soon found out, she had set her mind on marrying. But in those early days it was just a delight to talk about everything and everyone we knew, to share bar crawls and campus bops. She was one of the most important female friendships I have ever had, and not even Jules could always keep up with the lightening leaps of sarcasm which I could spit out, especially if she was on the receiving end of my acid tongue. I still feel Suzanne's absence like an ice cube in my heart.

Sarah   1975

Haircut

The worst part about going to school in Ulverston was waiting for the train in the morning. The local comprehensive only catered until sixteen, Ulverston Victoria High was the catch-all school for anyone in South Lakeland who wanted to take A levels. Sarah and three others caught the 8.20am from Kent's Bank because it was technically the nearest to their homes and so the local education authority would not fund them a season ticket from Grange, which had a proper, heated waiting room. Kent's Bank was not staffed any more, it was merely two parallel strips of grit paved concrete alongside the north side of Morecambe Bay, with no barrier between the station and the weather that swept across from the west. There was a tiny, unheated stone hut two thirds of the way along the platform. The windows had been broken long ago and never replaced, but it did provide some protection from the biting winds and slashing rains of autumn, winter and spring.

The problem was that there were never more than two carriages on the train which was referred to as "The Bogcart," because it had only one toilet. The driver insisted on stopping right at the entrance to the platform, as near as possible to the level crossing and the signal. Sarah could never see the point of having a level crossing there anyway, the bay side gates opened out only onto sand which was completely covered twice a day by the racing waters of the Bay. He didn't stop for long either, a mere formality, as there were hardly ever any passengers waiting there, so if he didn't see you on the platform it was touch and go as to whether you could make it to the train before he drive off. Even though they caught the same train every schoolday morning, no concessions were made. So one of them always had to stand lookout in the doorway of the hut and shout, "Train!" as the train approached, to make sure they were ready to leap out as soon as it stopped.

Friends at university who had lived in London expressed envy. "Living in the Lake District, how wonderful!" they cooed. They couldn't understand Sarah's eagerness to leave it all behind, until she told them about the intermittent train service to Ulverston which was really only a small market town, no big deal.

"There was only one nightclub, but there was no point in catching the train out on Saturday, as the latest train back left at five in the afternoon". Sarah's confession would be greeted with looks of horror and condescension.

"At least there were buses in Cornwall," offered Suzanne.

"The buses were worse," said Sarah. "Apart from the fact that it took them about an hour and a half to get to Ulverston, because they went to every little piss-pot hamlet on the route, they went one way on the even hour and the other on the odd. Of course, they didn't run on Saturday afternoons because all the shops were closed then. If I wanted to go to the nearest cinema, which was a flea-pit in Bowness, I could only get there by changing buses at Newby Bridge."

By this time, southern friends' jaws were hanging open at this evidence that the Lake District was a third world country. They also had to be reminded that in order for the Lake District to be littered with all those pretty lakes was that it had to rain for a substantial part of the year. On top of that Grange over Sands was a place where people retired to, so entertainments were few.

"Feeding the ducks in the park was about the most exciting thing to do," Sarah explained. "Apart from snogging in the pavilion in the Ornamental Gardens after a Young Farmers' Club dance". She'd never been asked to go there by any of the acned youths who'd slouched against the walls and watched the women dance around their handbags.

From the age of sixteen the main social activity was underage drinking in the local pubs within walking distance, which limited the choice considerably, even more so if one of a parent's friends happened to be at the bar. This was supplemented by underage drinking further afield when one of the group passed their driving test, with the driver joining in as enthusiastically as the rest of them in partaking of illegal beverages. The first time after passing her test that Sarah had succeeded in begging her father's car to join in one of these escapades had ended disastrously. Buoyed up by the quantity of campari and lemonade she had drunk, she had agreed to participate in a race along the only straight piece of road between Ulverston and Newby Bridge. "We were neck and neck," she told Suzanne. "We were coming up to this sharp corner, when a car appeared out of nowhere ahead." The other racer had to cut in to avoid being spread across the kerbside dry stone wall. He left a Mini-shaped dent in the front wing of Sarah's father's Saab. "I couldn't believe it, the first time out!"

At the time she'd paced around the car in the pub car park, surveying the damage and muttering, "Shit. Shit. Shit!", while the other driver justified himself.

"You shouldn't have been racing."

"It was your bloody idea!" shouted Sarah. More shouting was done when she got home.

"You are NEVER driving my car again," yelled her Dad. "Never, you hear me!"

"Lucky for me he broke that promise two weeks later when I wanted to go out to the cinema," Sarah confided to Suzanne.

Having to catch the train to school was bad, but the fact that if she missed the train back that left at 3.25pm in the afternoon, ten minutes after school finished, the next one did not run until 6.30pm, meant that chances for after school fraternising were scotched unless Sarah could get a bed for the night. It also caused her to let her musical interests wither away, even though singing in the choir and playing violin in the school orchestra had been a source of pride for her at Cartmel. She couldn't be bothered to hang around for an hour after orchestra or choir practice had finished, and the grey gritstone station had neither waiting room or café that might have made the idea more attractive. She sold her violin and bought a new pair of jeans with the proceeds, something she was to recall and regret often as she got older, missing the wherewithal to make music.

Sarah had never been one of the in crowd at Cartmel, and this was emphasised by her decision to continue into the sixth form. Only three others from her fifth form group had decided to stay on, and that included wasp-tongued Kirsty, who was having to spend a year retaking some of her O levels alongside a secretarial course. The other two were the class geeks, Howard and Jonathan, who were taking maths and sciences, probably destined for careers as dot com millionaires. Jennifer Adams had gone to private school to cram for her A levels, which meant that her precarious friendship with Sarah soon shattered, Jennifer making it plain that state school attendees were beneath her. Sarah and Kirsty were thrown into a shallow alliance for the year they travelled together, with both of them recognising that they were friends of convenience only. However, this fragile truce outlasted Kirsty's leaving school, to both girls' surprise. They continued to meet at weekends, and it was through Kirsty that Sarah had met the crowd that drank and drove their way around the area, which included Johnny Manfredson.

Due to the fact that she had been overweight since a child, her mother being overly protective of her youngest hatchling, Sarah had been the butt of the class jokes about "Fatty Martin". She had managed to build an effective shell whilst at school, but she cried in private. Her mother once caught her writing out "Call me Fatty" hundreds of times on a whole pad of lined paper in a fruitless effort to exorcise the other children's taunts. She'd always felt like an outsider, never quite getting the nuances of the giggling gossip the other girls indulged in. She was never the subject of any of the swaggering approaches from the boy's side of the playground. The only time that she was asked to dance at a school disco, she found out afterwards to her hot-cheeked embarrassment, was the result of a dare from one of the boy's mates.

Losing her puppy fat and turning into a long limbed, slender teenager at fourteen never seemed quite real for Sarah. She couldn't think of herself as slim, she continued to hide herself under baggy, sloppy sweaters drab, dowdy calf length skirts at school, flared jeans at the weekend, until Kirsty told her that she looked like a blob and she should stop hiding her body. "Show it off!" she advised her. Her Saturday job waitressing in a café down in Grange funded some new clothes which she didn't have to gain her parents' approval of. Kirsty was enthusiastic about Sarah's new image which took school uniform to its limit, the grey skirt turning into a tight mini, the sensible Clarks school shoes being replaced by platforms with four inch heels. "Not bad at all," she approved.

Sarah's mother was horrified and disparaging. "You can't go out looking like that!" she would greet each of Sarah's outfits, so that it eventually became audio-wallpaper.

In the sixth form there was no uniform requirement, so they all adopted the regimen of wearing jeans of one kind or another in order to express their individuality. Sarah opted for skin tight drainpipes, standing out from the rest of the crowd who stuck to flares and loons. Having finally defeated her mother's dictat of keeping her hair cropped short all through her childhood until she was thirteen, she had taken four years to grow it until it reached down her back in a thick swathe of mousey brown.

One day, Sarah caught sight of herself in a shop window, spending her dinner money lunching on a ham roll and frothy hot malted milk at a café in the town rather than getting a hot meal in the canteen. Her hair hung lankly about her face, it was so thick her neck disappeared into its weight at the back, she kept having to push it behind her ears, then hook it out in case her ears started to stick out. She skived off general studies to have it cut into a shoulder length bob and dyed blonde. She decided to go the whole hog and have her ears pierced at the same time.

She was delighted at the reactions that she got. Classmates were shocked but mainly approving, and she even thought she caught a glimmer of interest from Daniel Palfreyman, although this was never consummated.

Her mother gasped at her hair, "My God, Sarah, what have you done! Your hair looked so nice before!" Of course, Margaret had never told her this, being far too busy disapproving about "All that hair, what a mess."

Her father was incensed by her pierced ears. "I'm not paying you an allowance so you can go and look like a tart!" he exploded.

"I paid for it with my own money," Sarah smugly informed him. All in all, a good afternoon's work and much more fruitful than snoozing through a couple of hours of general studies where there didn't seem to be any clear idea of what they were supposed to be learning anyway.

A few months later, she decided to go the whole way and had it cut even shorter into her neck, so that the hairdresser, with a worried, repeated, "Are you sure you want it shorter?" had to use the electric clippers to get the effect she wanted. By this time she had given up re-dying her roots every six weeks as her scalp hurt too much, so she changed to a variety of multicoloured blond and russet highlights for the remnants of the top layer which flopped satisfyingly over one eye. After a week or two she managed to avoid brushing it aside automatically and learnt to peer through her asymmetrical fringe in what she hoped was an interesting and mysterious way.

It was unfortunate that she had to go and waste all of that on Johnny Manfredson, but she decided to submit to his spaniel-like advances because he was the only one who offered. She drove home after he had deflowered her in the back of her father's car, trying to work out if she felt differently having endured his fumbling and thrusting. She looked into the mirror before cleaning her teeth, examining her eyes and skin. No sign of any womanly bloom, just a disappointed feeling of, "Was that it? What all the girls at school make such a fuss about?"

Sarah could only conclude that sex was just a hyped up secret, and that if anyone admitted the truth about its ridiculousness, the human race would probably die out within a generation.

Sarah   1976

Curing virginity

The first time I had sex it was with Johnny Manfredson, in the back of my father's Saab. No bells rang, no rockets went off. It was just uncomfortable.

I'd met Johnny through Kirsty, he was on the outside of the in crowd, like me. He was tolerated because he'd been the first one to pass his test, and because he could borrow his parent's car whenever he wanted. In addition, because his dad ran the local garage and Johnny went to work for him, he soon had his own motor and offered discounts to all his mates on repairs to theirs. In fact, he came in very useful when I pranged my Dad's car by racing it along the Newby Bridge road. The only way I was able to get around his threatened life time ban on borrowing the car ever again was to offer to pay for the repairs, and the only way I could afford to do that was to use Johnny. That gave him the opening he needed, and after that he would always make a point of buying me a drink and chatting me up when the crowd went out together.

In the end I just gave in. I thought I could use him to cure my virginity which had begun to seem like a disease because he seemed to actually like me. So one night I agreed to meet him for a date, just the two of us, without the rest of the group. I insisted on driving, I wanted to be in control. I picked him up from his house, where he insisted on introducing me to his parents, to my intense embarrassment and foreboding. We went through the motions, going for a couple of drinks at the Commodore, a well known haunt for teenage drinkers, then another at Royal Oak. Our stilted conversation served to illustrate that we didn't have anything in common. "Had a really nice little sports car in the garage the other day," he told me. "Red, it was. Fixed it up real good, wire wheels and everything."

"Are you going to college in September?" I asked, stifling a yawn.

"No. No point now I'm working for my Dad," he said, taking another slurp of his pint, surreptitiously looking at his watch to see if it was time to adjourn to the car park on Humphrey Head.

Humphrey Head is a weird place. It's supposed to be where the last wolf in England was hunted down. It juts out into the sands of Morecambe Bay, causing a loop in the already unpredictable and viciously changing tides and currents. There is a headstone carved into the rock under the cliffs to commemorate finding of the bodies of a mother and son, drowned in the Bay fifteen years apart but washed up at the same place, the beach underneath the Head. Those who died on the far side of the bay would be carried across the shifting sands at low tide to be buried at Cartmel Priory, and the procession would come ashore at Humphrey Head.

All of this means that, whilst during the daytime walkers and birdwatchers wander happily along the coastal path, and in the summer locals venture out onto the beach to build sandcastles with their children or even swim if the sea is making one of its brief appearances, despite the tales of drowning and disasters, at night no-one goes there at all. Unless of course you are a lusty teenager with a car and nowhere else to go. There are about half a dozen such spots in and around Grange, you just have to make sure you get to one of them first. The unspoken rule is only one car, so if anyone else is there you just have to go onto the next nearest one. One of the things I liked about my next boyfriend, Alex, was that he was very inventive at making such a space where there hadn't been one before, like the woods above Cartmel racecourse when there was a race meeting, up against a telegraph pole, in someone's back driveway.

That night, all that was still in the future. The night I drove Johnny down to Humphrey Head we were the first to arrive, so I parked and turned the engine and the headlights off. It was oppressively quiet. I felt his arm come round my shoulders, then he pulled me to him and kissed me, full on, my mouth filling with his tongue and saliva. It was horrible. No preamble, no murmuring about the stars, because there weren't any. The sky was thick and unbroken, like the silence, hot and oppressive.

The handbrake dug into my thigh, causing a bruise that was one of the few physical reminders of the event. I stuck it as long as I could, then had to beat his chest with my palms to come up for air. "Let's get into the back," I gasped, thinking it might be more comfortable. Johnny had different ideas, he slid his hand up my leg and put his fingers inside my knickers, feeling around in my bush, finding my clitoris and rubbing it hard. He was making a low sort of snorting noise. I suppose he must have read something about what women were supposed to want, but not enough. I was dry and unaroused, but he obviously hadn't got to that page.

I tried to wriggle out of the driving seat, but managed instead to hit the recliner lever and the seat went right back, almost horizontal. Johnny took this as encouragement, pulling my knickers down, then going back to his insistent rubbing, all the time chasing my mouth with his. I moaned with discomfort and frustration. As if that was some signal he'd been waiting for, he went for the buttons on the front of my dress, almost ripping them off, nuzzling my chest, reaching round and surprisingly expertly unfastening my bra. With one hand he grabbed a breast, painfully pinching my nipple and making me squeak in pain.

Then I found out what he had been doing with the other hand as something which I guessed must be his penis started to push against the flesh between my legs, searching for an opening. He started to push himself inside me, making "hoofing" sounds. I guessed that this must be "it", and waited to feel some pleasure, but it just hurt. To make it worse he'd not pushed his jeans down very far and the zip caught in my pubic hair. I yelped and wriggled, which resulted in him letting out a deep cry and subsiding on top of me.

He was so still I had a momentary panic that he might have had a heart attack and how the hell was I going to get out from underneath him? Then he gave a sort of half snore so I poked him in the ribs and told him, "I can't breathe, Johnny. Get off me, you oaf."

Then he was all concerned and wanted to know, "Sarah, are you all right? How was it for you, doll?" He didn't really want to know, he just burbled straight on. "I didn't know it would be your first time too. That's amazing. You chose me! That's something special, we were both virgins." That was how it was always to be with Johnny and me. He talked but never listened to what I said. He even asked me to marry him at some point. I think the reason he took the summer job on the oil rigs was because he was saving up to buy the ring I'd never said I'd wanted.

That opened the way for me to go off with Alex, which was the only effective way of making Johnny notice that I really wasn't interested in his chocolate box image of our life together. When he got back, he still hung around the pub where I was working, I had to give Alex a real throat bruiser of a French kiss in the car park before he got the hint.

That first night I intended that this should be a one-off. I certainly didn't want to do anything like that again. I dropped him off outside his house and drove back home, checking the seats and my clothes just to make sure that no untoward bodily fluids would give away what I had done in the car that night, before creeping upstairs to bed. Luckily my parents were asleep. I looked at myself in the bathroom mirror. I didn't look any different, just a bit untidy and my mascara was smudged.

I lay in bed and put my hand down between my legs. I still felt sore. What a let down. I fell asleep sucking the corner of the sheet, like I used to do when I was a child. My dad brought me up a cup of tea in the morning, the sun was shining through the curtains, for a moment I could believe that nothing had happened the night before. But there was that bruise on my leg, and when I got off the train from school that afternoon Johnny was waiting for me in his car to give me a lift home. I didn't want to, but it was a two mile walk home.

"Why are we going this way?" I asked, as we turned off down the back road to the Ponderosa caravan park. He was surprised.

"I thought we'd, you know," he said, gazing anxiously at me and trying to drive at the same time.

"Why would I want to do that?" I squawked. He looked so pathetic and I was in his car, now five miles from home, so I went through the motions again.

"It'll get better with practice," he promised as he smirkingly dropped me off at home. I realised that a beneficial side effect of this was that my mother's radar was immediately on alert and she disapproved.

"Who was that? What does he do? Why were you in his car?" she grilled me.

"Oh, some guy named Johnny, I think. He gave me a lift from the train," I tossed behind me as I slouched up to my room. I continued to go out with Johnny as my own kind of teenage rebellion. He was right, the sex did get better, but only in the sense that it got less uncomfortable.

I'd thought I was frigid before Alex showed me that sex could be fun, and that the fault did not lie with me after all. Of course my mother, having been loud in her condemnation of Johnny before that, the minute I took up with Alex, who looked like a heavy metal fan and rode a Triumph 750 into the bargain, started to muse about "That nice Johnny," and how upset he'd looked when she'd seen him in town one day.

My father said, "I thought you couldn't get worse than the last one, but I was wrong." I'd met Alex in the pub where I worked for the summer before going to York, and he was so outrageous in his compliments that he made me laugh.

"Your eyes are like deep blue pools," he breathed over the bar. "Your hair is like spun gold." He was much more sexually skilful than Johnny, not surprisingly, and he was totally upfront about the fact that this was not to be the most meaningful relationship in the world. He knew I was going off to university, and only vaguely seemed to entertain the thought that we would continue to see each other after I left. "Maybe at Christmas, babe, if I'm around?" he suggested, in a non-committed way. After Johnny's brand of romance, it was like being able to breathe again.

Going to York was going to be my big chance to break out of all the stereotypes that everyone had about me. I wasn't Fatty Martin any more, I didn't have to put up with Johnny and his dreams of matrimony. I didn't have to accept Kirsty's or Jennifer's subtle condescension. I was going away to find out who I really was. Then, within twenty four hours of arriving I was having a relationship with Jules, lusting after Dick and best friends with Suzanne, all of them with their own neat boxes that they wanted to fit me into.

Sarah   November 1977

Sandsend

It was a perfect day for it. The autumn air was cold and crisp, one of those bright days which looked like summer but felt like the onset of winter. The leaves outside Sarah's window were fully russet now, even starting to coat the tarmac with splashes of red, like the footprints of some outsize drunken goose. She tugged the curtains open an inch, and lay on her bed, naked and warm under the sheets and blankets, content for the moment to wake up by letting her brain go into neutral and watch the leaves shift in the breeze.

She was not allowed to relax for long. A sharp banging on the door was followed by Suzanne's voice, "Come on out, Martin, I know you're in there. We're wasting the best part of the day!" For someone so petite and fragile looking, Suzanne could certainly be strident when she chose.

"OK, OK, hold your horses," Sarah muttered, disentangling herself from the sheet which seemed to have wrapped itself tightly round her feet whilst she was asleep. In the end it seemed easier to haul the entire mess off the bed and hobble towards the door. She wondered whether this was how caterpillars felt. Wrapping the half of the sheet that wasn't imprisoning her feet round her, Sarah gingerly opened the door a crack, and nearly fell sideways as Suzanne pushed her way in.

"My God, you're not even dressed, and what have you got on your feet?" Suzanne demanded, marching in and throwing the curtains open wide, giving anyone wandering past the block opposite an uninterrupted view of Sarah's naked back and buttocks.

"Suzanne, what are you doing here? Stop making so much noise!" Sarah snatched the curtains back together, with some difficulty as she had to use one hand to grip the sheet round her so that any passer by didn't get a free flash of her front as well. Although, looking at the small alarm clock by her bed she could see that it was only 7am, and as her brain, which had now started to creak into action, came up with the information that this was a Saturday, the chances of anyone else in the entire college being awake except for the staff was minimal.

"I told you last night!" Suzanne said petulantly. "My Dad has sent me some money for my birthday, and I've managed to get Stefano to lend me his car for the weekend, so we're off to the seaside!"

"The red MG? What did you do to get him to lend you his car for God's sake?" Sarah, bewildered, slumped on to the pile of blankets on the bed. "And it's

November. Why on earth would we want to go to a beach? You may not have noticed, Suzanne, but this is not Cornwall, and it is not summer. They've never heard of the Gulf Stream up here!"

Seeing that bullying was not getting her what she wanted, Suzanne abruptly changed tactics. "Oh, please, Sarah, come on, it'll be fun! No one else will be there."

"With good reason," Sarah interrupted, darkly, but Suzanne carried on regardless.

"You've always wanted to go up to Whitby to see the Abbey, you know, where Dracula is supposed to have come ashore, all of that stuff. And I'll never get Stefano's car again. I promised I'd do his washing up for a week, by the way, not what you're thinking, dirty cow." As usual, Sarah could feel her resistance dissolving in the face of the absolute certainty of Suzanne's plans. She was not seeing Jules this weekend as her lover was away visiting her family in London. She'd been going to go out on the town, maybe pick up some townie at the De Grey Rooms, or the Disgrace Rooms as they were popularly known. She didn't think that the singles scene in Whitby would be half so exciting, but then there was the promise of the sea, and seeing the Abbey, probably eating fish and chips from the paper. Her nostrils twitched with the tang of vinegar even as she thought about it.

Suzanne could tell she was weakening as her body posture softened, slumping against the padded cushions on the wall. "Come on, then, get dressed!"

"Alright," Sarah sighed. She found clean underwear and grabbed an extra set, as Suzanne declared she was going to treat them both to a bed and breakfast. Thick green cord trousers with warm woollen socks and her rubber soled tan suede boots, layers of a silk vest, a long sleeved purple tee shirt and her favourite rainbow striped cardigan should keep out the cold she thought, plus polar fleece scarf, hat and gloves and her trusty worn sheepskin flying jacket that she had picked up in the 50s clothes shop on Walmgate. Toothbrush, toothpaste, lipstick and hairbrush completed her packing.

Suzanne, who had watched her friend get ready with increasing impatience, alternately throwing herself on the bed, then leaping up, reading the notes on Sarah's noticeboard, twitching the curtains to check the weather every two minutes, sighed dramatically, "At last!" Picking up Suzanne's own squashy blue cylinder bag from her room as they went, the two women scampered down the stairs and ran out of the building, careering over the deserted dual carriageway and into the car park. Stefano's car was clearly visible, its fire engine red paintwork gleaming with the remains of the dew. Despite the cold, the bright sun tempted them to put the top down, so they folded the hood back on itself into a neat collar around the back of the car, and wedged their bags in the tiny boot.

Suzanne had brought a bag of tapes. Sarah groaned inwardly. She hadn't packed any. This meant she'd be subjected to Suzanne's musical tastes all weekend. Sure enough, Fleetwood Mac plopped into the cassette deck as they roared away from the college, out past the straggling suburbs and onto the main road towards the coast. It gave her an excuse to slump down in her seat and try to catch up on sleep, although she was bewitched by the autumn countryside stretching away from the road on both sides, flat and open, decorated with golden trees along the edges of the burnt umber fields. Even with the heater on full, their faces tingled in the cold air as Suzanne piloted them up the A64 to Malton, then through the North Yorkshire villages as the country melted into rolling moorland.

A few miles south of Whitby, the road curved round in a broad sweep, almost a full circle, with a steep plunge down to the valley floor on their left. "Look at that," Suzanne gasped, and pulled off the road. Despite their eagerness to get to the sea, they wanted to breathe in the view. Sarah stood on the edge of the drop, feeling the wind hold her up, wrapping her jacket tightly round her. Black-and-white-headed gulls swooped and dived, using the air currents rushing up the escarpment to propel them high into the clear blue sky, before closing their wings and diving down just to do it all again, just for fun. Their white and grey bodies flashed against the background of the green and leaf brown hills. A sensation of lightness lifted Sarah up off the balls of her feet, she felt that if she launched herself off the cliff she could join the gulls.

She decided this must be what happiness felt like, a disembodied feeling of rightness, not connected to anything in particular. She glanced across at Suzanne, and in the same instant Suzanne turned her head and met her look with her emerald gaze, and both women smiled, recognising they shared the same moment. Then Suzanne broke away and disappeared over the edge, running down a narrow sheep track worn in the grass, jumping from tussock to tussock, sure-footedly finding her way at breakneck speed, her arms spread like a windmill to keep her balance.

Sarah followed, slowly at first, but then letting the momentum of the slope take her faster and faster, both of them whooping and yelping like fox cubs. Something pricked at the corners of Sarah's memory. Windmills? The thought refused to materialise and she shook her head to clear her vision.

Afterwards of course they had to climb back up, panting and laughing. "How did we get so far down?" regretted Suzanne. Flushed with effort and cold, they arrived back at the car. Sarah started to get into the passenger seat, but Suzanne stopped her. "Don't you want to drive?"

"Well, of course," Sarah replied. "But what about the insurance?"

"Oh, Stefano has it insured for anyone to drive," Suzanne said breezily. Sarah slid behind the wheel, feeling the worn leather mould itself to her body. The car was so long and low she was almost lying down to drive it. She was hit by a craving to possess it, she'd never felt like that about a car before, dismissing it as something uniquely attached to the Y chromosome. It started with a low purring roar and she pointed the bonnet at the road, spinning the tyres in the gravel as they set off. Suzanne laughed. "Calm down, Stirling Moss," she said.

They descended towards the coast, weaving down from the moors, catching glimpses of deep slate blue between the fields. The first encounter with the town was disappointing, modern semi-detached houses, petrol stations and corner shops, but as they got deeper in, the housing changed into towering Victorian terraces. Sarah followed the road into the town centre, past the railway station, over a bridge which had the ability to rise to allow ships into the safety of the river, tucked behind the granite walled harbour which was in turn protected by two outstretched arms of stone reaching into the sea. They turned into a small car park perched on the edge of the river. As the noise of the engine died, Sarah could hear the steady thrash of the waves against the outer harbour, contained for the moment but uttering its continuous reminder that humans existed here only by its tolerance.

It was only lunchtime, so they locked the car and headed into the old town, strolling along the narrow main street lined with souvenir and antique shops, as well as jewellers selling arrays of amber and jet. Suzanne lusted after the jet, "Oh look at those Victorian settings," she coo-ed.

Sarah thought it, "Too morbid. Look at the amber, it's so warm," desiring it in all its guises, from pale egg yolk to deep cinnamon. There were also several clothes shops. "Aargh, 'hippy dippy'," Sarah scornfully labelled the packed rails of fluttering tie-dyes and Indian prints. Suzanne was in heaven, flitting between the racks.

"Do you think this russet goes with my hair? Or should I choose the green to go with my eyes?" she pondered. The positions were reversed in the charity shops, where Sarah found linen, cotton and silk men's shirts, stroking the worn and faded materials, luxuriating in their softness and enjoying their history, whilst Suzanne wrinkled her nose up and muttered, "They all smell of mothballs".

Their noses drew them to the Shepherd's Purse, a health food shop of the best kind, with tubs of spices and herbs in the front of the shop and a vegetarian café in the rear which sold tongue dazzling quiches and cakes. They discovered that the place had rooms to rent, but that they were all full. They vowed to return the same time the following year. "Let's make this an annual pilgrimage", suggested Suzanne.

"Well, next time we'd better book in advance," grouched Sarah, her need for structure getting the better of her at the diminishing prospect of finding a bed for the night.

Before the climb to the Abbey they stowed their purchases in the car, returning along the narrow street and this time following it to its end, where it started to transform itself from a road into a staircase. Steep cobbles clung to the cliff, like a cross between sea anemones and limpets, rounded and slick. Fit and young as they were, both women had to stop for several rests. "Oh look at that view," panted Suzanne. "The river looks so green from here."

"What about those china dogs," wheezed Sarah, peering through the curtains of the cottages that lined the route. Above them the spars of the Abbey rose into the clouds. It was their first destination when they reached the summit, wandering through the ruins, trying to envisage the great buildings that must have stood here. "What do you think their life would have been like, with only these walls as shelter?" mused Sarah, as they feltthe force of the wind scudding across the North Sea from Scandinavia.

"Do you think the monks were allowed to wear thermals?" joked Suzanne.

After they had had their fill of the Abbey they turned right out of the car park and took the cliff path away from the town. Within a few steps they entered deserted salty meadows, the path worn to packed dry mud by thousands who had taken the way before them. The sound of the sea was louder, crashing against the foot of the cliffs and sending spouts of white high up the rocks. Around the next corner they allowed themselves to be drawn down to a grey beach of shale, perfect for skimming across the green leaden sea, calmer here as it was protected by a hidden reef of rock. "Ten jumps!" claimed Suzanne, as her stone skittered across the wavelets.

"Was not, you cheat," rejoined Sarah. "Three at the most!" Sarah allowed each sensation to fill her, moment to moment. The wind from the sea, the shushing of the water, the smell of the weed thrown up on the beach like discarded clothing.

In every moment, there was Suzanne, leaping ahead of her, leading her onto the next thing, "Come on, come on!".

They had to return the way they had come, there was nothing further along the cliff apart from a deserted caravan park, its swings and seesaw tied down against the weather, awaiting the return of the holidaymakers in the spring. Past the Abbey they veered off the main path into the church. Sarah was not really into church architecture and initially hung back, but was overwhelmed and delighted to find a hodge podge of pews at all angles, with narrow aisles between. "The wood is from old whaling ships," whispered Suzanne. Many of the bodies in the churchyard were those of whalers and fishermen. They wandered amongst the gravestones which spilled down the slope like scattered shells, noting the frequent repetition of a few surnames, mapping the generations.

"Plenty of Bakers and Fishers," said Sarah.

"No Martins or Mercers though," searched Suzanne.

"Look at that!" Suzanne pointed out the arch made from the jaw bones of a whale on the cliff on the opposite side of the river, proclaiming the town's history.

Reaching the foot of the cobbled stairs again they spotted a narrow alley off to the right which they had missed on their way up, leading along a narrow street lined with tiny cottages to an exposed narrow bridge down to the harbour wall. The tide was rising, the waves washing over the top of the breakwater with four of each five swells and there were no railings or walls to protect anyone on the top, but Suzanne was determined to reach the end. She ran down the steps from the bridge, timing it perfectly so that she reached the first of several stone benches, stepping up onto it just as the salt water lapped the stones where she had been standing just seconds before.

She turned with a triumphant wave to shout to Sarah. "Come on, slowcoach!" Sarah froze. With despair she saw Suzanne turn back towards the arm of the pier and make her way from bench to bench between the waves until she was at the end, her tawny hair streaming like a banner.

Ignoring the lump in her gut and the sensible voice in her head telling her, "You shouldn't be doing this, you don't have anything to prove, Suzanne will be back shortly, you should just wait here for her", she launched herself across the wet paving, darting between the waves, relying on instinct not thoughts. She caught up with Suzanne and passed her, reaching the final bench moments ahead, turning round to offer her a hand and pull her up beside her. They stood like naval figureheads facing into the wind, looking out across the ocean, arms tightly wrapped around each other's waist to anchor them on the narrow rock, breathing in the brine.

"Isnt this just grand?" asked Suzanne, and Sarah had to agree. After a few moments, on some unspoken signal, they broke apart and made the perilous journey back to the bridge, but this time a wave caught Sarah, soaking her tan suede boots, leaving behind enough salt to cause a white tide mark to appear later that evening.

They still had not explored the other half of the town, and the afternoon was drawing towards evening. They found it not so much to their liking, full of the usual British seaside arcades, shops selling candyfloss and rock and of course fish and chip shops. They bought bags of chips to devour, Sarah sousing hers with salt and vinegar, eating them scalding from the paper as they searched for a place to stay. None seemed right for both of them. "Too dull," said Suzanne of one.

"Too noisy," complained Sarah about another.

"Too near the sea," pronounced Suzanne.

"Not near enough to the sea," Sarah stated. The few that they agreed on were full. Tiring, they climbed the other cliff, but found themselves in tall Victorian terraces of hotels with frilly lace curtains, dining rooms peopled by nuclear families and sofas covered in overblown roses that neither of them felt fitted the bill of what they were looking for.

Slumping with disappointment on a cliff top park bench, Suzanne glanced up the coast and spotted a white house perched on the edge. "Let's try that one," she urged.

Back in the car, they found their way onto the coast road and eventually, after several tantalising glimpses of the place they were making for, arrived beside it. It was a hotel, but up close they could see that the seemingly pristine plaster was cracked, the window frames dark green and flaking. The car park was deserted, and a large sign in the window read "Vacancies". They sat in the car, gazing at it with disappointment. Neither of them felt like going in and committing themselves to spending the night here. Sarah glanced at her watch, it was already six o'clock and she was yearning for some hot water to sink into. "Why don't we drive north for fifteen minutes, and if we don't find anywhere else we like, we'll come back and stay here?" she suggested. Suzanne agreed, and they set out once more.

They were just at the limit of their deadline when the road curved round and down towards a village set in a fold in the cliffs. A stream ran under the humpback bridge that crossed it, making its way towards the sea across an expanse of pure white sand edged with tiny grey waves. They were past the pub and a tiny slate covered cottage which proclaimed "Bed & Breakfast" before they realised it, but Suzanne swerved into a parking space on the sea front just a few yards beyond them. They were at the door, and had rung the doorbell before they noticed the crushing "No Vacancies" sign tucked into the side of the sash window. The woman who answered the door confirmed the news, but seeing their crestfallen faces, suggested that they could try the hotel further along the road to the north, just beyond where they had parked the car.

Looking longingly at the welcoming lights of the pub, the two women retraced their steps, leaning into the wind. Round the corner, they came across another line of houses, with a sign for the White Sands Hotel attached to one of them. Standing on the pavement in front, it seemed to be sandwiched in between two other towering Victorian terraces, shouldering its way forward. Sarah moved forward, but Suzanne hung back, pulling at Sarah's sleeve. "I'm not sure, there's something about it," she said, but then the last rays of the lowering sun struck the windows and the brass on the door, lighting up the house like an early Christmas tree.

The door opened and a tall thin woman with long dark curls stood on the doorstep. "Come in," she said, "I've been expecting you."

Suzanne released her grip and followed Sarah into the hallway. The décor was everything they had feared—flock wallpaper, dark brown Victorian furniture, chintzy curtains with pink and yellow peonies. They could even see, through the open door to the darkened dining room, frilly white curtains. Still, the owner, who instructed them to call her Molly, led them upstairs to a pair of rooms she told them they could have the pick of.

"There's just the one twin room," she told them, "The other's a double." She showed them the twin room first, two wide single beds tucked under sloping eaves, with a tiny window looking out over a garden of tufty sea washed grass and sea pinks. "This one isn't en suite," Molly explained, but the bathroom is just next door." Sarah and Suzanne wandered about, peered into the pink and cream bathroom. Sarah looked longingly at the huge bath, garlanded with bottles of mauve and blue bath foam, huge pink fluffy towels hanging on the wooden towel rail.

"This looks great," she said.

"I'll just show you the double, then you can make up your minds which one you want," said Molly as she unlocked the door on the opposite side of the landing. I'll be downstairs in the lounge—would you like a cup of tea?" Both women "mmm"ed their assent.

Suzanne stepped through the other door first, then suddenly stopped, so that Sarah, following close behind, almost cannoned into her. Then she saw what Suzanne was staring at. A huge bay window faced them, framing the white sands and the grey sea, clouds scudding above tinged with pink and gold from the sunset. To their left, a huge, four-poster bed covered with a quilt of autumn leaves and matching hangings. The mattress was set high off the ground, the pillows were supplemented with a variety of squashy velvet cushions in russet, apple green and chocolate. Sarah recovered and moved to look through the door to the bathroom to the right. It was just as splendid, a white corner bath set in dark oak panelling, a spray of dried leaves in a Chinese vase on the cream marble counter next to the washbasin. "Suzanne," she croaked, "I think you'd better look in here too."

"Is it magnificent?" said Suzanne, not moving from where she still stood, mesmerised by the view. "Because if so, I don't think I'd be able to stand the sensory overload. Which side of the bed do you want?"

They told Molly they would just bring their things in from the car before joining her in the lounge for the promised tea, which turned out to be Yorkshire strong and served in proper china. The bitterness of the tea was offset by the homemade flapjacks, stuffed with apple and cinnamon. Molly lifted an eyebrow, feigning surprise at their choice of the front room, but smiled too because she'd known they could not resist it. Who could have? She assured them that hot water was available, and that the pub that they had seen before did meals in the evening.

Sarah allowed herself to sink into the nest of bubbles, sliding down until only her face was showing. She closed her eyes, letting the water hold her up. She could hear the humming of her blood circulating, some gurgles and hisses from the hot water pipes and the faint sounds of Suzanne pottering around the room, putting her stuff away, even though they would only be here for one night. For the second time that day she experienced that wonderful warmth and sense of well being.

She had it again as she delved into a huge plateful of homemade steak and kidney pie, accompanied by mushy peas and a pile of thick cut chips, washed down with a pint of lager. Suzanne had opted for the scampi. "My God," she yelped as her plate was set before her by the rounded waitress. "It looks like half the North Sea has just landed on my plate!" Luckily, the waitress seemed to take this as a compliment.

"I can't speak, this is just too good," gargled Sarah, though her pie. Suzanne nodded, silently setting to work on the mountain of crisp coated fishy pieces.

"Would you like to see the dessert menu?" asked their waitress, who Suzanne had got to admit to the name of Tracy, as she cleared away their plates.

"You are joking, aren't you," gasped Suzanne, clutching her belly. Afterwards they weaved back to the hotel, arm in arm. Pleasantly and thoroughly tired from the day of exploring, aided by the alcohol and the filling food, they slipped into sleep. Sarah was aware of Suzanne's light breathing as she sank into unconsciousness.

When she woke, she found they had rolled together in the night, lying back to back in the deep soft mattress which seemed to have moulded itself around them as they had slept. She could feel the warmth of Suzanne's back against hers, feel her slow breathing, still asleep. The sun streamed in through the huge window as they had forgotten to draw the curtains the night before. Despite having been convinced that she would not eat for a week after the helping of pie she had consumed the night before, Sarah found that the smell of bacon frying somewhere in the depths of the house made her nostrils twitch and her stomach gurgle with anticipation of another onslaught.

Now it was her turn to wake her friend, poking her in the ribs, shaking her shoulders when that didn't work. "Come on, we're wasting the best part of the day," she said, echoing Suzanne's wake up call the day before.

"Ohh, someone turn the light off," groaned Suzanne, burrowing under the covers. Sarah gave up and decided to take advantage of the bath yet again, pouring in tangerine bubble bath and loudly singing Yes songs or as near as she could get to Jon Anderson's high notes.

"Go-oh-ing for the one!" she squealed as she soaped herself all over, until Suzanne gave in.

"Mercy! For God's sake shut up!"

They arrived in the dining room to find a table laid in the window, the white frilly curtains drawn back to reveal the sunlit bay. A variety of cereal boxes had been laid out on the sideboard, with tall jugs of orange and grapefruit juice for them to help themselves.

Molly stuck her head around the kitchen door, "Coffee or tea?" she asked. Sarah of course chose tea, but asked if it could be made weaker, Suzanne went for a caffeine hit. "Full English, then" stated Molly, leaving no room for disagreement. Sarah looked at the huge pile of cornflakes she'd already poured into her bowl, then shrugged and set to work. She couldn't believe how hungry she was.

She was just chasing the last of the milk round with her spoon when the rest of the breakfast arrived. Rashers of bacon, crispy, just how she liked it, a runny fried egg, fried bread, sausage, black pudding, fried tomatoes and mushrooms, as well as a huge pot of tea for her and a cafetiere for Suzanne, plus a full toastrack. Suzanne looked at her own food mountain, then at Sarah, and grinned. "Definitely better than Derwent snack bar," she announced. Sarah, already mopping egg yolk from her chin, nodded.

They ate deliberately, without much conversation, savouring each bite, and gazing at the gulls swooping across the bay outside the window. The sun made the sea sparkle, catching the tops of the waves as they broke onto the sand. No clouds marred the sky, it looked set fair all day, so there was no need to hurry their breakfast, which was just as well. Sarah enjoyed each taste on her tongue, the rainbow of texture and smell meaning than she ate far more than was really comfortable. At last she could fit no more in, despite Molly's offering of more toast and tea. She leaned as far back as she could in the high backed chair. "I could just go back to bed for a little snooze," she said contentedly.

"No way, we've got to walk off all that breakfast!" Suzanne chirped. Sarah closed her eyes and groaned.

"But it's so nice sitting here, and we're warm," she protested.

"Why don't you come back after your walk for some tea, before you go back to York?" Molly suggested.

Sarah thought this might be an acceptable compromise, so they packed their things and stowed them in the car, and set off down the wide beach, washed flat and shining by the outgoing tide. Suzanne ran alongside the water's edge, dodging the waves but Sarah was still anchored by her breakfast. They had to tiptoe across the stream where it spread to a wide, shallow delta on meeting the sea, and then Sarah sat at the bottom of the cliff while Suzanne tried a small ascent.

The wind had died down, and it felt warm in the sun. She closed her eyes and leaned back, listing the sounds she could hear. Suzanne's scrambling above, the waves breaking, a faint squawking of gulls, her hair rustling against the sea grass. Then Suzanne's feet were nearer, she jumped the last few feet and thumped onto the sand. "Fancy a paddle?" she asked.

"Why not?" Sarah replied, so they peeled off their socks and boots and ran into the sea. Sarah gasped as the icy shock took her breath away. Suzanne was dancing and splashing, shouting and squealing about the coldness of the water, chasing the waves back and forth. She'd rolled her jeans up to her knees, but they were still getting wet. Her hair spun out in a ginger halo. Sarah retreated to the edge of the water, her hands raised as though trying to hold the tide back.

"Oi, Madame Canute, where do you think you're going?" yelled Suzanne. Sarah refused to be drawn from the shore, drying her feet in the sun, sitting on a rock just out of the sea's grasp. She looked at Suzanne, still in the water. How come she was always the leader and Sarah was always the follower? Yet with Jules, Sarah knew that she was setting the pace in their relationship, refusing to commit to monogamy, still flirting with men as well as women. Suzanne always seemed in thrall to Dick, hanging on his every word, gazing at him with that adoring puppy dog look. Was it all like some kind of complicated food chain? Maybe there was someone who Dick lusted after and couldn't have and so on?

Thinking was going to give her indigestion. She put her socks and boots back on, called to Suzanne, "Hey, little mermaid, it's time to move on, I'm freezing!" and set off further down the beach. Suzanne caught up with her, carrying her boots and socks, enjoying the feel of the sand squeezing between her toes.

As if reading her thoughts, she asked Sarah, "How's it going with Jules, then? Made up your mind what you want yet?"

"It's going fine, and no, I haven't. It just seems silly to pass up any opportunity at the moment. I'm still young, why would I want to settle down with someone I met on the first night here?"

"How does Jules feel about that then?" probed Suzanne. "And why not settle down if you've found the right person? I know I have," she concluded firmly.

"Do you seriously think that you and Dick are going to be together forever, then?" Sarah couldn't keep the note of incredulity out of her voice. "You'd never even slept with anyone else before him."

Suzanne shrugged. "I know he has his faults, but I don't think I'll ever find anyone better." Sarah was silent. In all other matters, Suzanne was a true scientist, she wouldn't accept things unless she had experienced them for herself, and so was scathing about both the Young Christians and anyone who claimed to have seen something paranormal. As far as Dick was concerned it was if she would not even accept the evidence that was on offer, his weak excuses for not turning up on dates they had arranged, wearing the same clothes two days running so that it was obvious he had not been back to his room the night before. She sighed.

"Well, Suzanne, if that's what you want I expect you'll get it. Just make sure you don't have to make too many compromises."

"Isn't this just a great place?" said Suzanne, abruptly changing the subject the way she always did when things got too near the mark about Dick. "We'll have to come back here with Dick and Jules."

"Not at the same time," Sarah protested. "Who would get the four-poster?" "Oh, we'd just have to take turns," laughed Suzanne. In fact, years later, when Sarah and Dick did come here, the White Sands Hotel was not to be found. Dick had remembered Suzanne talking about their weekend away and how much she had enjoyed it. Sarah couldn't even recognise the house that had once borne the sign. The landlord in the pub was new and had never heard of it, the B&B next door was shuttered and closed. They went back to Whitby and stayed at the Shepherd's Purse instead. Sarah was grateful that she didn't have to share the same bed with Dick that she had once shared with Suzanne.

Sarah and Suzanne turned round and walked back to the hotel. Suzanne paid their bill whilst Sarah took advantage of the extra tea, sipping it as she drank in the bay for the last time. As they drove back across the moors, black clouds came up from the west, and they had to stop to put the roof up, managing it just before a torrential thunderstorm hit. It was then that they found that the roof leaked, so by the time they were back in York they were wet and clammy, the inside of the car like a rain forest as they tried to combat the rain with the heater. Suzanne parked under a tree, and they had to run across the car park to the college, clutching their bags over their heads in a vain attempt to stave off the worst. Sarah threw her wet things onto the floor of her room, stripped off and went to have a hot shower, seeing the sand between her toes swirl down the plug hole. By the time she was dry and dressed and had hung her wet things up, the sea and the sun were just a memory.

Suzanne   14 November 1997

Diary

Just had a great weekend away with Sarah. We drove up to Whitby—I persuaded Stefano to lend me his car, a sexy little red topless number. It made an awful noise though, and it was so low on the ground it was like the princess and the pea—I could feel every bump on the road. It took ages to get her out of bed, she's such a slug in the mornings. The weather was great, sunny and cold, just the way I like it. I don't like summer really, it gets too hot. I can't believe I spent most of my childhood on the beach. I'd get too bored with that now.

We walked for ages, up and down these little narrow streets with cobbles, there were great shops, I bought some new dresses, green and blue with loads of embroidery. Sarah, as usual, got some old shirts. I wish she could see that she could be so much more attractive if she just wore something a bit more feminine. Still, I don't suppose Jules minds her hanging around in men's clothes. There was loads of Victorian jet jewellery too. I got Dick a signet ring, with a secret compartment in it. You're supposed to put someone's hair in it after they've died, *memento mori* they're called. I put some of my hair in it anyway, I'll give it to him when I see him tomorrow. The Abbey was at the top of this really steep hill, Sarah had to keep stopping, she's so unfit. Afterwards we walked along the cliff path, then back through this really neat church with loads of built-in pews, all higgeldy-piggeldy.

We went down onto the pier too, the sea was really rough, it was great. Sarah nearly wimped out, but we both got to the end and back again without getting wet—she's such a wuss, it wasn't dangerous at all.

We couldn't find anywhere we liked in Whitby, so we had to drive out on the cliff road. There was this dilapidated old place that we looked at first, but there was no way I was going to stay there. So I just drove on by, and then we found this weird hotel in this tiny village called Sandsend. By that time we were fed up, so we went in anyway, and I'm glad we did even though the landlady was a bit spooky. The room was amazing! We had to share a bed, which I was a bit nervous about but it was a four-poster so it was miles big enough for us both, I could almost have believed I was in there on my own. The view over the bay was fantastic. The bathroom was good too, this huge corner bath, although I could hardly get in there because Sarah was in the tub half the time. We had this huge meal at the pub down the road—I've never seen so much scampi in my life, and then in the morning there was this massive cooked breakfast. I don't think I can eat anything else for about a week.

The best bit was walking along the beach today, I took my boots and socks off. The water was crystal clear and icy, the sand was really soft. It reminded me of going to the beach in Cornwall. Even Sarah got into it in the end. Then of course the weather broke on our way home and we got soaked because we'd left the top down on the car.

It's made me think about Sarah and me though. We are so different. I know she is my best friend, but I just don't understand her sometimes. When I first met her I thought she was really confident and cool, but now I'm not sure. She just follows me around like a sheep sometimes. We do get on, but do we have real conversations? What is she doing, fooling about with Jules and then going off with men too. Why can't she just make up her mind and get on with it? Life isn't a rehearsal after all. Mind you, I've never fancied other women so I don't know anything about that either. I did wonder, when she said she wanted to sleep in the double bed, whether she would try and make a move on me, but nothing happened. Felt quite disappointed, I must admit. Even though I wouldn't have wanted to do anything about it, it would have been nice to have been asked!

But then, if she wasn't so involved with Jules and other people, I'd wonder whether she had a thing for Dick. She is always so self-conscious when he is around, she hardly talks to him. And she's started making remarks about how I shouldn't rely on him so much, he's not worth it and all that. What would she know about it? We just don't need to live in each other's pockets, that's all, it's OK to have other friends and not see each other every night. I mean, men need their freedom, don't they?

Sarah   December 1977

Christmas

Until I was married to Dick, I had always spent Christmas with my family. There have been times when I thought of avoiding it, times I've vowed, "never again", like the time after Deborah had found out what Noah did with Dad's watch and stood on the doorstep of her house, refusing to let him in, with Mum flapping about in the hallway, not understanding what was going on, and me sitting in the kitchen getting drunk and feeling guilty that I'd spilled the beans. None of us has heard from Noah since. Each year end still found me slogging up and down some train line. Now that our family has shrunk to Mum, Deborah and her crew, me and mine, we spend alternate Christmases and New Years at Dick's folks and mine.

The Christmas celebration in my first year at York was held at my sister's house in Scotland. She and Nigel were living north of Glasgow in Helensburgh, he was working on contracts for various companies in Glasgow and Edinburgh. Beth was only just three and Simon was a few months old. Somehow it had been decided that it would be easier for Deborah to have us all there rather than have to travel with the children. Of course what that meant was that she had to prepare endless beds and organise all the provisions. By the time I arrived late on Christmas Eve, all of the family had gone to bed except Debs, who was nursing a large whisky in the lounge.

At the last minute, Nigel's parents, Reg and Maureen, had decided to "drop in" as they put it, although how anyone who lived in Surrey could just happen to be passing a place thirty miles north of the Scottish border was beyond me. In addition, my father's eldest sister, Edith, had rung and made Mum feel guilty that she would be spending Christmas all alone, so Mum had invited her to spend the holiday with us. No wonder Debs looked more than a little frazzled. The only bright spark was that Noah had phoned two days before to check what Debs was getting him for a present. "I've seen this really nice leather briefcase in Harrods, I could pick it up for you myself and save you the bother of posting it" he'd suggested.

"Dream on," was her reply. Miffed, he'd casually mentioned that he was playing golf in St Lucia over the holidays.

"How are you?" I asked.

"Bloody awful," she replied, taking a swig of her drink. I wondered how Simon was liking Laphroig flavoured breast milk. At the rate she was putting it away, he must have been getting it almost neat. Probably sleeping like the proverbial baby that he was. "Today Mum and Maureen got into the amount of sex on television and how we're bringing Beth up all wrong, although, of course, they have completely different ideas of exactly how wrong we are and whose fault it is. It was rather like the run up to World War Two, without Chamberlain."

"I noticed that they've been at the vegetables," I said. I had seen rows of naked carrots, potatoes and sprouts swimming in Tupperware in the kitchen. Debs closed her eyes in pain.

"They've never heard of Vitamin C," she groaned. "And that's not the end of it. Nigel went to pick up Auntie Edith from the station, managed to miss her on the platform, although how he could miss an octagenarian with a blue rinse and a carpet bag is a mystery, she got a taxi and he sat and waited in the car park for an hour for the next train. I wouldn't have been suspicious apart from the fact that he seemed to have read the Guardian from cover to cover and done the whole of the quick crossword."

I poured myself a large port, just to keep my sister company. So when the Day itself began at 5.30am, with the slapping of tiny feet on the wooden stairs, I felt like someone had stuffed the inside of my head with old socks. Santa (aka Auntie Edith) had thoughtfully provided Beth with a plastic recorder, so the rest of us soon joined my niece in front of the tree. All except Auntie Edith herself of course, who was upstairs sleeping the sleep of the deaf.

I remember that Dad was at his best, dispensing endless cups of tea to us all. He was the only morning person in my family, and it wasn't until after he died that I realised that he'd made me into one too. I find it impossible to start the day without a cup of tea, and I'm normally awake by 6am, whilst Dick is totally inert until 7. Conversely, I want to be brought my tea, just like my father did for me, so that Dick knows that if he wants to butter me up about something, then that's the way to do it. When he was persuading me to buy the house in Roundhay that I was convinced we couldn't afford, I got tea in bed every day for a week. He trained himself to sleep walk to the kitchen I think.

Beth had managed to locate and unwrap every single one of her presents like some little cruise missile homing in on those magic letters—B-E-T-H. The rest of us tried to resist, but even at that hour greed won out, and soon the air was filled with the sound of rending paper and all those seasonal untruths, like "I've always wanted one of those," or even, "You shouldn't have!"

The first day of any family Christmas was always exhilarating, stimulating, the adrenalin pumping as we all prepared for the cut and thrust of the dinner table and the ultimate objective—to get that last roast potato. As soon as there were more than two members of my family assembled, life became a contest with constantly shifting alliances being made and broken at a moment's notice. You had to be on the ball to keep up with who was friends with who, who your allies and enemies were. Normally there were at least three different conversations going on, one in which I was directly involved, one in which I threw in the occasional aside, and another which I just listened to and observed. But at any minute the level of participation in each of the three could change. Gradually the weaker members would go under, finding excuses to leave earlier than planned or simply storming out dramatically, declaring that the afflicted person will never have anything to do with the rest of the family ever again, the effect often spoilt by having to ring up a day later and ask for one's toothbrush to be forwarded as soon as possible. It's certainly more restful now that the quantity of players has reduced, but sometimes I miss the old days.

I began to suspect that I had under estimated Auntie Edith when we found that whilst the rest of us were distracted by the present opening she had occupied the only bathroom. We crossed our legs, regretting all that tea. It was pointless to bang on the door, as she had turned her hearing aid off.

Breakfast, as always was prefixed by an exhausting interrogation from Mum. "Weetabix or cornflakes?" "Orange or grapefruit juice?" "Fried or scrambled eggs?" So many questions, so early in the morning. I'm surprised that MI6 didn't recruit my mother to debrief defecting foreign agents. She'd have had any information out of them in no time. Instead of eating her own breakfast she was always jumping up and down, fussing and interfering with the rest of us who would really rather have been left alone. I think she never realised that we have grown up, and she will still try and make me eat all of the food on my plate by making the same references to "there's children starving in Africa," that used to be made when I was under five. It didn't work then either.

The best time was when I was told that I would have to sit at the dinner table until tea time if I didn't finish all my mashed potato. I'd been going through a phase where I would only eat it after mixing in copious quantities of tomato ketchup to make a pink cement, and had just discovered that the phase was over whilst still confronted by all of that day's portion. Whilst Mum and Dad went into the kitchen to wash up I made various sculptures out of it, until I got bored and threw it out of the window. Dad came back in, saw my empty plate, and asked, "All finished, then?" I would have got away with it if he hadn't been standing at the kitchen window a moment before drying a plate, and seen gobbets of pink gloop flying out onto his prize roses.

Today Mum started on the smallest member of the assembled crew, Beth. "Would you like Granny to help you with that?" she asked her. Beth shook her head firmly.

"She can manage perfectly well, thanks, mother," said Debs through gritted teeth, trying to spoon baby rice into Simon, who seemed more interested in finger painting with it on his high chair. I wondered if he had a hangover like his mother.

"Beth likes Granny to help, don't you, dear?" said Mum, scooping up scrambled egg and making goldfish motions.

"Don't like eggmph," said Beth, as Mum took the opportunity to insert the spoon into her mouth.

"Nonsense, egg is good for you. You see Deborah, you've just got to be firm with her," said Mum, triumphantly turning to my sister, as behind her back Beth spat the egg out onto the kitchen floor, narrowly missing the cat, who started to lick it up.

There was some unformed scuffling and muttering in the hallway, which turned out to be Reg and Maureen leaving in high dudgeon about not being allowed to hold the baby as much as my parents. We all gathered in the kitchen doorway to watch, except Auntie Edith, who continued to eat her breakfast with a blissful smile, nodding at some non existent conversation, and Simon, who was still painting with his baby rice. This was unheard of, no one had ever left before Christmas dinner. Nigel was trying in vain to persuade his parents to stay, but Reg was doing a "never been so insulted in my life," speech.

Maureen stage-wept into her linen handkerchief and wimpered, "I just knew this would happen, Nigel, I had my doubts when you got married." I wondered how she had managed to be so perfectly made up before breakfast, and how she didn't seem to be leaving any mascara on the white linen.

Deborah unwisely decided to wade in and make an attempt to calm things down. "Come on Reg," she said, putting her hand on his arm, "come and have some breakfast and we can talk about this sensibly."

Instead, Reg drew himself up to his full five foot six, slapped her hand off like it was some kind of dung beetle, and retorted, "The problem is, Deborah, you're just not a good enough wife for someone like Nigel. He needs someone domestic, a homemaker, not an artist."

Nigel, who seemed to be able to take any amount of crap from his parents about himself, to his credit drew the line at them insulting his wife. He picked up their bags (matching Louis Vuitton with monograms), took them to the front door, opened it and threw them out onto the path. "That's it," he said. "Get out now." With some more muttering and sniffling, they did. Nigel slammed the door behind them.

Deborah burst into tears and was ushered upstairs by Mum. Nigel and Dad decided to be practical and started clearing up the breakfast table. I was rather put out that whilst we had been watching the amateur dramatics in the hall, Auntie Edith had eaten my toast. I resolved to pay her back at lunchtime.

"Here you are, Sarah, make yourself useful," said Dad, plonking Simon on my knee. Simon immediately stuck his hand in my tea, making oily rice slicks on the top of the hot liquid. He pulled it out again, shocked into silence at the temperature for a moment, then gathered his face up and started to wail. How do babies muster so many decibels in such small bodies? I'm so grateful that neither of my children cried very much.

I had been expecting the worst, as Mum had repeatedly told me stories of my own babyhood, which included three months of colic. Every evening, regularly between 6pm and 9pm, I yelled constantly. The only solution was movement, so she and Dad had walked for miles around the house I was born in, pushing a huge cantilevered pram with huge wheels that looked like something out of Mary Poppins. Some evenings, even that wasn't enough. They would return to the house, with me seemingly sound asleep in the depths of the pram. As soon as the movement stopped, I'd be immediately awake and sucking air into my lungs for another scream. So off they would go again.

Still, the yelling did relieve me of Simon this time, as Nigel swooped over and took him back, leaving me with the lesser task of drying up. We then discovered that the cat had been sick under Auntie Edith's chair, as it was allergic to egg only no one had thought to tell it. Auntie had then wandered into the lounge to take up her station in front of the television with the sound on full, leaving a trail of cat vomit trodden into the carpet which I was then deputed to clean up. Out of spite I muted the sound on the TV and then hid the remote control. Auntie didn't seem to notice. "She's deaf anyway," I reasoned.

Assembling a Christmas dinner in my family was always like taking part in some massive military campaign. Mum of course was the general, marshalling the troops with precision and a plethora of instructions. "Don't stuff the turkey like that, Deborah," she commanded. My sister managed to bite back an obvious crude rejoinder, but it wasn't easy for her, I could tell, her lips went white with the pressure of the invective just itching to get out. "Jeffrey, don't sit there, lay the table!" My father leapt to attention.

Nigel managed to escape by doing childcare duties, which as far as I could see meant lying on the sofa reading *Management Today* while Beth played with her Christmas haul on the floor and Simon lay supine stunned with over stimulation beneath a baby gym, transfixed by a bright yellow bird inches from his nose. Auntie Edith was still installed in front of the silent TV.

"Sarah, baste the roast potatoes". I managed to extract the potatoes from the oven, no easy task as they were hemmed in with baking tins full of turkey, stuffing, and sausages. I did try and sneak a small, caramelised parsnip out for a snack, but looked up to see Mum watching me with eyebrows raised. I regretfully returned it to the pan. It wouldn't have been wise to show my hand this early in the proceedings.

At last we all assembled at the battleground, well lubricated with sherry and wine. All except Simon, who was upstairs sleeping off Deb's last night's whisky. Dad carved the turkey, we skirmished politely about who would have the legs. Auntie Edith and I prevailed.

"Such a lovely spread," she said, "Quite different from how it was in the war."

"That's a fact," said Dad enthusiastically, scenting his favourite topic. "We were lucky to get half a chicken, let alone a turkey. Did I ever tell you about the Christmas when I was in the Casbah in Marrakesh…?"

Nigel groaned. "Not that old chestnut again, Jeffrey," he snorted. "Next you'll be telling us about when you tried to sell your cigarette ration to the undercover Military Police detail in Plymouth.". Nigel had gone too far, Dad was red in the face.

I tried to deflect him by asking, "Could you pass the cranberry sauce?", but it was too late.

"Making fun of the war, are you?" Dad was still on his feet, waving the carving knife about dangerously. "If it wasn't for people like me who were prepared to fight, what do you think would have become of lily-livered second rate arseholes like you who can't even get a proper job, then?" He threw his napkin down theatrically. It landed in the gravy boat. The gravy landed on Dad's shirt. His mouth tightened. I hoped that his teeth weren't going to fall out on the table, like last year. "I bet you belong to CND," was his final barb before slumping down onto his seat.

"No need for language like that, Jeffrey," said Mum. We weren't sure whether she was referring to arseholes or CND.

"I'll just finish off these sprouts," I said, piling them onto my plate. I was determined to get the last roast potato this year.

"Isn't it time for the Queen's speech yet?" asked Auntie Edith, continuing to eat her dinner unperturbed by the unheard warfare around her.

"Oh God, not the Queen's speech!" squawked Debs. "My husband and I," she mimicked in a high falsetto.

"There's nothing wrong with the Queen," said Mum, grittily. I managed to snag the last parsnip. It was going better than I hoped. All the activity had distracted the rest of the diners.

"She's a parasite," said Debs, gulping her wine. She'd probably had most of a bottle of Chianti by now. Simon was really going to experience a wide variety of tastes. "She gets paid millions of pounds of our money just to sit around and wave."

"I think she works very hard. I wouldn't have her job," said Mum primly. "Oh come off it, Margaret," Nigel chipped in. "Who wouldn't want a job where you get to travel all over the world, live in great big houses and have loads of servants? That's not what I call hard work!"

"I think this conversation has gone far enough," said Mum, confiscating the last of the bread sauce and heaping it onto her plate in a mountainous peak. That stopped the idle chatter as we re-grouped and reviewed what was still left.

"It's so nice to see a man who helps around the house, Nigel," said Auntie Edith, scooping up the remains of the peas.

"Yes, Debs and I have a completely equal partnership," Nigel preened. I glanced sideways at my sister. She had started to resembled a fire-breathing dragon, without the smoke.

"That's a laugh," she snarled. "You don't do half the work around here, you're always off to play golf or squash whenever there's something to be done. And you never play with the kids, either, you just want them to be quiet while you read the paper."

"That's unfair!" Nigel was stung into retaliation. "I spend a lot of my time tidying up after you, and you never get the glasses clean when you wash up, either."

"Clean glasses? Tidy up? I'll give you something to tidy up!" Debs shrieked. She flung the wine bottle at him, narrowly missing his head. It smashed against the wall, leaving a rather nice raspberry ripple effect on the wallpaper. Nigel got up to clean up the mess, muttering about artisitic temperament while the rest of us looked intensely at our plates.

"Can I have the last sausage, Auntie," asked Beth, who had maintained a wide-eyed fascination in the face of all the events of the meal. She managed to grow up surprisingly sane.

"Of course, dear," said Edith, passing it over. "You know what they put in sausages, don't you?" Beth shook her head. "Well, it's a jolly clever way of getting rid of all those leftover bits like brains and intestines and beaks and feet, all mushed up together." Beth stared at the innocent sausage sitting in front of her, then silently and deliberately transferred it back to Edith's plate.

"Can I just borrow a tissue, dear," Edith said to me. Before I knew what was happening, she was rooting about in my bag, which I'd foolishly left under the table. How did she know it was there? "There's so much stuff in here, I can't find any," she said, starting to unload the contents onto the tablecloth, beginning with lipstick, toothbrush and a spare pair of black lace knickers (in case of emergency).

"Edith, stop it!" I shouted, making a lunge for the bag and pulling it out of her grasp. As she let go, the recoil caused a small nut of cannabis resin wrapped in cling film and an open packet of condoms to fall out.

"What are those?" said Beth, reaching for the foil packets. In the dead silence which followed, I gathered everything back into the bag and shoved it under my seat.

On top of that, as I reached out for the last roast potato, Auntie Edith stabbed me in the back of the hand with her fork. "I'd get that seen to, dear," she said, eyeing the wound as she captured her prize. "Isn't there any pudding?"

Sarah   March 1978

Decision

Sarah had never thought of herself as promiscuous before she came to York. Her two lovers had been sequential, even though Johnny Manfredson hadn't quite understood that it was all over when she had started hanging around with Alex. The problem was that here sex was freely available, it was pre-AIDS and university was a place where many young things were crammed together with raging hormones and no parental control for mostly the first time in their lives. Plus of course a few predatory older things. She found that her mother, through a combination of embarrassment and sexual frustration, had not equipped her to deal with her feelings or desires. Sarah had found out about the biological facts of sexual intercourse through a very embarrassing (for both teacher and pupils) lesson from the science master in her second year at secondary school. "Can't we stop this now, sir," squirmed Howard Best.

"Shut up, then it'll be over quicker," growled Mr Masterson, Sarah later adopting his advice in her forays with Johnny. She had no idea of how to connect her physical and emotional longings, or any idea when she wanted to say no or yes. It was such a novelty to be wanted by so many that she often got herself into situations where she felt obliged to go to bed with someone just because they seemed to expect it.

Johnny had implied that having sex with someone meant that you would marry and settle down with them, whilst Alex gave her totally the opposite message—sex was just fun and there was no price tag attached. Jules was a mixture—she gave herself freely without explicit demands at first, but as their relationship progressed Sarah could feel that the other woman wanted exclusivity and commitment from her. At the back of her mind were the conflicting ideas that she should "save yourself for Mr Right", but also that she "play the field and don't settle down too early". She had no clear idea where these ideas had come from, probably a mixture of school gossip and daytime soap operas. She sometimes felt like one of the balls on the pinball table that she played between lectures, sent back and forth between the bumpers, yet without all the flashing lights and ringing bells, except with Jules. It was true that sex with Jules gave her the most physical pleasure of all her encounters, yet Sarah seemed unable to deny herself any casual opportunity that presented itself.

Sometimes it was just to relieve boredom, or to see if she could. One evening she went to the De Grey Rooms with a man who she had slept with on one night the previous week. He was good looking, blond, brilliant blue eyes, although he did have a rather droopy moustache that she found irritating when they kissed. He was a second year linguist, concentrating on Scandinavian languages having spent a year out living in Oslo, and seemed to spend his spare time translating ancient Norse poetry, which she at first had found interesting and quirky, but now realised was an indication that he simply did not have much of a life outside his studies. She had happened to meet him on one of his rare outings to Langwith bar when she was stopping in for a drink on her way to an assignation with Jules.

Sarah made a comment about the book he was carrying, a translation of Beowulf, saying, "That looks like good bedtime reading," meaning that it would soon put her to sleep, but Brian had taken it literally as an indication of her interest in Norse epics. They had chatted, Sarah found him pleasant and slightly shy, unaware of his attractiveness. He eventually asked, "Would you like to meet up again?"

"Sure, why not?", she agreed, thinking it would be at some indefinite point in the future. The next day there was a note in her pigeonhole at college asking her whether she would like to go into town for a meal that evening. He had come into the bar at Derwent at lunchtime to check that she had got it, and to suggest 6pm at the bus stop as a rendevous. Sarah had already had plans to go with Jules to see a band, but felt backed into a corner by Brian's intense glance and obvious keenness. "I had a great time last night," he told her. Sarah tried hard to remember what they had talked about but couldn't remember anything of significance. Even though Brian could not know the extent of her relationship with Jules, she found herself getting embarrassed and tongue tied as she tried to put him off without giving anything away, so ended up agreeing to go to Bibi's for pasta.

"I can always meet up with Jules at the gig anyway," she rationalised it to herself.

Jules didn't see it so calmly however. "I'm always second best with you," she shouted, when Sarah suggested her compromise and had admitted she was being taken out to dinner by someone else. She'd never been good at lying, but she resolved there and then to get better at it if it made her life quieter.

"Jules, that's not true," she tried, knowing that the other woman was right. "It's just that he was so pathetic and looking at me with these big spaniel's eyes, so I didn't have the heart to turn him down. And you know you just want to go to this gig to chat up the promoter and see if you can get a job over the holidays. I'll only cramp your style. I'll just see you a bit later, that's all." Sarah ran her finger over Jules' tense jaw and down her neck. Jules shook her off, but not before Sarah had seen the tell tale signs of her surrender.

"OK, but don't be later than 10." Sarah promised, only to break it after she had drunk a bottle of Barolo and practically fallen asleep in her spaghetti carbonara. Brian called them a taxi and manoeuvred her into it. By then, she couldn't remember the name of the pub where she was meeting Jules anyway. Back at the college, he carried her up the stairs to his room, where he laid her on the bed, undressed her and then had mild and uninteresting sex with her body, throughout which Sarah was compliant rather than active or willing.

She awoke at 5am with a splitting headache and an urgent need to pee. She scrabbled around on the floor of his room for her clothes and, after finding the nearest loo to deal with the latter problem, wandered back to her own room in the chilly pre-dawn to deal with the former by administering paracetamol and a more comfortable sleep in her own bed. In the morning she could hardly remember what had happened. There was only the evidence of a single red rose left taped to her door with a card—"All my love, B"—plus an angry note from Jules—"Where were you?" in her pigeonhole.

The result of this was that Jules refused to speak to her for a week, whilst she couldn't turn around without Brian popping up from somewhere. Hiding in her room didn't do any good either. Even when she didn't answer knocks on the door, he caught her out by throwing stones up at her window, then when she looked out, startled, to see what the noise was, stood waving and smiling below. "Damn!" Sarah thought. She ran out of essays and seminar papers as excuses, and finally agreed to go out with him again.

They went to see a showing of *2001—a Space Odyssey* which the Film Society had arranged in the cramped lecture theatre next to the Physics block. Brian seemed to feel the need to pontificate at length about the film's inner meanings. "Don't you think the whole image of the obelisk is a critique of Darwinism?" he asked her. Sarah shook her head. She had no idea what he was talking about. Already suppressing yawns by the time they got to the bar in Vanbrugh, she wondered if she could plead a headache or a period to make an early exit. She was reminded of a postcard she had seen at the Students' Union shop, captioned, Great Chat Up Lines No 63. In 1950's black and white cartoon style it pictured a couple. His speech bubble said "I'd like to go on about myself at great length if that's OK with you." His companion with a rapt smile, was saying, "That's fine, but did you know that your elbow is in your lasagne?"

There was a group of other students that Brian knew at the bar, and he introduced her as his girlfriend, obviously wanting to impress them, so that Sarah found herself becoming sulky and childishly resistant. "What are you studying?" one of them asked her.

"Can't remember. Something boring," she snapped back. The rest of the group left her alone, so that she leaned against the bar, glowering silently while Brian tried to talk enough for both of them. Then a man that she had collided with once outside the lecture hall, coming out of an economics lecture just as she was going in for one of Professor James's intense lectures on Introduction to Semiotics, arrived and joined the group. His name was Edward, he was dark haired with deep brown eyes. She could tell that there was some rivalry between him and Brian in the way they squared up to each other, puffing and strutting, each trying to be funnier than the other. "Saw the film, then, Brian," he snickered. "With Swedish subtitles, was it?"

"No, Edward, it wasn't like the films you usually go and see," sneered Brian. At school, when she was still known as Fatty Martin, she would have never thought to make a play for either of these men, they were so obviously out of her league, she'd had to be grateful to receive the attentions of a dork like Johnny. She scented a challenge, and began to practise her sidelong glances at Edward, making the most of her lashes which she had painted with some super long lasting extra-bodied mascara, pouting her lip-glossed lips, laughing too loudly at his jokes, brushing his arm with her fingertips to emphasise a point when she was talking.

She was surprised at how easy it was to manipulate him back to her college room, leaving Brian behind, wild-eyed and frustrated. "Sarah, where are you going?" he called, trapped at the bar, ordering another round of drinks.

"Bye, bye Brian," she waved, sniggering with Edward.

Once back in her room, though, as so often the exterior promised much but reality failed to deliver. He was rough and unskilled, a reference to foreplay so brief as to be less than token. He had a small penis and he certainly did not make up for lack of size with his technique, which consisted of a few humps and bucks before he came and collapsed. Sarah was reminded of her first time with Johnny and felt used and frustrated. Maybe his looks had persuaded so many women to go to bed with him that he hadn't realised he was a total klutz. He emitted a few loud snores, so that she had to poke him sharply in the ribs and slide out from underneath him.

"Sorry, sweetie," he said patronisingly. "Can't stay, darling," he said as he got dressed hurriedly afterwards, not wanting to compromise his stud image by engaging in any intimacy or closeness. "Good fuck though, wasn't it?" he announced, not concerned whether she agreed or not. "See you round, maybe," he smirked, swaggering off. "Got to be up early for a tutorial."

"Too bad you couldn't get it up tonight," muttered Sarah. She lay in bed, her clothes crumpled on the floor, the sheets mussed and sweaty, feeling in need of comfort and not knowing who to turn to for it. She wept half-heartedly but that didn't give her any relief. Her body felt unclean, and even though she knew she had started the whole process she didn't feel good about herself. She felt cheap and ashamed of how she had treated Brian, who was boring but certainly hadn't deserved such a public humiliation. In the end she got up and wrapped herself in her big pink fluffy bath towel and went down the corridor for a shower and stole somebody's milk from the fridge to make herself a cup of creamy malted Horlicks.

She straightened her bed and snuggled down into it, her body warming the cold sheets. She wished that she'd brought her old teddy bear with her from home, white and worn bald in places from being cuddled for nearly nineteen years, but she'd left him sitting on her bed in her parent's house having decided that she was a grown up. She saw now how erroneous that opinion had been.

The next evening she called round to see Jules. "I'm really sorry, I've been a complete idiot," was her opening line, which got her past Jules' initial unwelcoming frown. "Can we start again, please?" That got her past the door and back into a warm welcoming hug. Sarah sighed and relaxed. Sleeping around took up so much energy. What a relief not to have to do any of that any more.

Sarah   April 1978

Dungarees

When I think about Suzanne, I always remember the red dungarees. I'd been on at her to get out of the soppy flowery stuff for ages. "Just a pair of straight jeans would be a change, for God's sake!" I'd said. I think I must have worn her down over time, because at last she agreed to come shopping with me. Then again, it could have been because Dick was often engaged in "studying" with Alicia, another woman on his course, who wore pencil thin drainpipes and looked like a stick. I mean, God knows where she put her internal organs, there didn't look to have been enough space even for a pair of lungs in her torso so she must have been anaeorobic.

It was the end of April, we'd just come back from Easter holidays, the weather was just starting to warm up. We'd just got our grant cheques, so that made everything look better too. "Suzanne, I just have to have a pair of red dungarees," I told her.

"Mm, I could do with another tie-dye shirt," she pined wistfully.

"Try something different, for God's sake!" I persuaded her, against her better judgement, to come with me as I trawled through Dorothy Perkins, Etam, C&A and various other shops. I managed to prevent her from veering into Ruby Hearts, the 50s shop on Walmgate, although they always did have a good collection of old dress shirts which I had plundered several times. Today was strictly a high street chain store day.

We tried on everything. Jeans of various colours and cuts were in plentiful supply, but of course, no red dungarees. Suzanne looked really uncomfortable, squeezing herself into narrow fit, straight legged denims, and then because she was so short she just looked like a child dressed up in adults' clothing. The effect was made worse by the fact that for some reason she'd decided to plait her hair that day. "I look like bloody Pollyanna or Anne of Green Gables," she muttered, pouting.

"You don't have the freckles," I attempted to joke, but she was in no mood for it.

"I wish I'd never come," she sulked. I was beginning to agree with her.

At last we found a pair, just what I was looking for, in a small shop at the top of Coney Street. I wouldn't normally have gone in there, it was rather pricey, selling discontinued designer lines, but I was desperate. There they were, hanging on the rail, just winking at me and saying, "buy me!" Bright red, narrow legged but not too skimpy in the crotch. They were not in my size—they were in Suzanne's.

Gritting my teeth, I made her try them on. She looked sensational. Even her Pollyanna plaits couldn't hide the fact that the dungarees hugged her body in all the right places, and were kinder where it mattered around the hips. The colour, far from clashing with her hair, seemed to bring out the deep red highlights in her strawberry blonde. After a little tussle with her conscience, "But they cost the same as my entire weekly food allowance," Suzanne gave in. She took them off to pay and have the assistant put them in a bag.

I still hadn't bought anything, so on our way back to the bus stop we wandered through the market at the back of the Shambles, and found a stall selling jackets made of old furnishing materials. For the second time that day, something just made me gasp and reach for my cheque book.

It was orange and green. The back was a nectarine coloured satin, the front, short and cut neat into the waist, with little waistcoat points at the bottom, was a rich forest brocade. The sleeves were flame coloured linen overlaid with swirls of shiny embroidery. The buttons on the front were huge and covered in the green brocade. I reached up for it and put it on, putting my arms into the sleeves felt like slipping on an old and familiar garment. I twisted in front of the mirror, it was fantastic. When would I wear it? I didn't care, I had to have it, even though it was two weeks' food money.

Then I saw that while I had been having my love affair with the jacket, Suzanne had been trying on another one. Hers was blue and red, with a similar mix of heavy and lush finishes. The red matched the dungarees. She was parting with her cash even before I'd had time to pay for my own jacket. Then, while I was doing that, she wandered over to the shoe stall next door and bought a pair of spiky heeled red ankle boots. I was speechless. What had I done? I'd let the spending fairy out of the bag and she wasn't about to get back in. After that Suzanne's wardrobe acquired a plethora of strong colours instead of the flowery pastels she had been welded to for so long, although she never lost her fondness for Laura Ashley.

But I'll never forget her in those red dungarees, even though they should have been mine. I suppose I did get my own back, because I took far more from her than she ever wanted to give, or that I set out to get. I have this feeling that on that day we were truly friends, in harmony, although there was the usual push and pull of our different tastes and desires. Maybe that was the only day.

Sarah   May 1978

Moving in

"No, seriously, though, why don't we?" said Suzanne. Sarah sighed. She wasn't quite sure herself now why she was so reluctant. Suzanne's logic was wearing her down.

"Look, Suzanne, I need my own space, you know? I never had that at home." She still got a thrill from going into her room, small though it was, and being able to shut the door on the world.

"But you've been here a whole year now. What does it matter? And you will still have your own space," Suzanne said. "I know it's a double, but it's more than twice as big as both our rooms put together." The room on offer for next term was in one of the first-built blocks of the college, when a kind of jolly hockey sticks boarding school atmosphere had been envisaged by its Quaker sponsors, Rowntrees. The other remnant of these early ideals was the wall around parts of the college, as originally they were all to be single sex and men and women would have been housed separately. This was despite the campus being constructed with many intersecting paths to promote, as one lecturer had informed them, tongue in cheek, "accidental intercourse". Now even the corridors were mixed, leading to many cases of not-so-accidental intercourse amongst the inhabitants.

"It's got a great view out across the lawns at the back of Heslington Hall," Suzanne added.

"What, so we can watch drunken students attempting to play croquet?" Sarah responded grumpily.

"The rent's much cheaper," Suzanne tried.

"That's because the college knows that no-one wants to share a double room," Sarah replied.

"Both of us are often sleeping in Dick or Jules's rooms and so we're paying for space that we don't use," Suzanne pointed out. "And," she added," we are friends so it's not as if we've been forced on each other, like Julie and Isabel at the beginning of last year being randomly allocated to the same room. And what a disaster that was!"

Sarah could still remember the stereo wars as both women had tried to enforce their own particular taste in music upon the other. Not having the benefit of headphones, and feeling that to purchase a pair would be somehow to admit defeat, both had kept on turning the volume up on their own equipment until the whole of C block could make out every word on Led Zeppelin's Houses of the Holy, even though it was overlaid with Beethoven's Ninth.

There were two reasons why Sarah did not want to move in with Suzanne, and she didn't want to look at either of them too closely. She knew it would bring her face to face with the reality of Suzanne's relationship with Dick, which she found easier to cope with at a distance. She resented the fact that she still fancied him as much as she had the first day, even knowing his weaknesses, that he was screwing her best friend and also sleeping around. She was angry with herself for feeling that way, which meant that she turned that anger outwards, towards Dick. She couldn't express that anger without upsetting Suzanne's view of the world, that her best friend and her man got along together.

Sarah was sure that Dick knew what she felt about him, and even if he didn't he was too used to getting women into bed to acknowledge the fact that one might not fancy him. Her relationship with Jules was not a deterrent to him, in fact she was sure in a way that it aroused him. He'd even made the usual remarks, "Hey Sarah, I wouldn't mind, just watching, you know?"

On that occasion, Suzanne had not been there so she'd been able to let rip with the suppressed anger she felt. "You are a sleezeball, Dick. You're screwing my best friend and most of the female population on campus. Can't you just keep it in your trousers for once, and think with your brain rather than your prick? That's if you've got a brain that is!" After that they'd maintained a truce and neither of them had mentioned the conversation to Suzanne. So far they'd managed a reasonably balanced and superficial friendliness. Sharing a room with Suzanne would put more strain on that balance.

The other reason was the fact that it was clear that Jules wanted them to move in together, and probably get a flat off campus. Sarah could feel that their relationship was reaching a decision point. She'd agreed to go away with Jules for the summer without thinking, just for the pure joy of spending all that time together exploring another country. Now she felt that Jules had taken it as a sign of her willingness to commit further, and she was frightened by the implications of making that commitment. She'd held back from a declaration of love, and she'd convinced herself that no matter how good the relationship was, it wasn't destined to last, it wasn't the real thing. She didn't quite know what the real thing was, though the idea of living with someone who she had met the first night at university hadn't been in her game plan of reinventing herself. She knew Jules was frustrated by her adherence to beliefs based on school playground gossip, and sometimes she was herself, but somehow she wasn't willing to leave them behind.

Sarah had a sneaking suspicion that making decisions made on what was rather than what might be or should be would be the beginning of growing up for real.

Suzanne was waiting for her reply, confident that she had won Sarah over to her point of view. With an inward sigh, Sarah realised that she was right, and that she was going to agree. She pushed down the warning voices about her continued crush on Dick and the fact that though Jules would be hurt by her decision to move in with Suzanne she could now go on holiday with a safety net which would stop her taking the next step on the road to commitment. "OK, you've worn me down, you old tart," she smiled.

"Yes!" whooped Suzanne. She pulled out the application form from underneath a pile of papers and books on her desk. "Just sign here".

Sarah saw that it had already been completed and that her signature was the only thing missing. "My God, do you always get what you want, Mercer?" she grumbled as she autographed where required.

"You bet," said Suzanne, smugly. "And bags me the bed by the window." Sarah groaned. It was pointless to argue.

Sarah   June 1978

The Ball

Goodricke Summer Ball was the highlight of the year. Students dressed up in rarely seen evening dresses and dinner suits to have a sit down meal in the college dining room. Afterwards a succession of entertainments provided distraction until the morning, finished off with a champagne breakfast. At the end of their first year Sarah went with Suzanne. Jules had refused to come, saying that the whole thing was a waste of money, she'd been before and that the bands were rubbish. She wanted Sarah to come with her to see some local band in town, but the best Sarah would offer was a morning-after visit. Dick had pleaded poverty, his parents were not stumping up the cash to make up his grant and he had to work in the bar at the Spreadeagle to make ends meet. So the two women set off, tripping over their ankle length dresses in their rarely worn three inch heels.

Sarah had to admit that Jules was right. "This is like school dinners," she complained to Suzanne.

"Ugh, overcooked veggies," Suzanne agreed. "And this cheesecake tastes like it's still in the packet!" After the tables were cleared, the first act was a hypnotist of the humiliation school.

"This is so bad," Sarah sobbed, leaning on Suzanne's shoulder as she cried with laughter at the spectacle of people eating lemons that they thought were pineapples, and declaring undying love for absolute strangers.

"I know," wept Suzanne, equally overcome with mirth, "it's really demeaning." Sarah was impressed that her friend could come up with a word of three syllables given the amount she had drunk with dinner, as well as the three martinis she'd put away before they'd even left her room after a joint dressing and make-up session.

The bands were not up to much, the headline band, the Pleasers, were a kind of Beatles tribute band before such things became fashionable. They played a selection of lively danceable tunes that enabled the drunken students to strut, wiggle and pogo. Sarah couldn't remember much about the musical attributes of the rest of the bands nor the expertise of the DJ. She slumped in a corner of the bar with Suzanne as they consumed more of the grating red wine that had been barely drinkable at dinner but that became increasingly vintage as the night wore on.

"What's the best thing about going out with Jules, then," slurred Suzanne at one point. Sarah stirred uneasily, even in her drunkenness she knew this was an area which they had not traversed before.

"She knows what to do with her hands, unlike some of the bozos I've been out with," she came up with eventually.

"Mm, sounds goo-od." Suzanne looked like she was working out a particularly difficult equation. "Is it really the best sex you've ever had, then?" she asked, blearily looking up at Sarah from where her head was resting on the bar table.

"Yes," said Sarah, with a dawning realisation of where this was leading them.

"Well, then," said Suzanne, "could you show me what it's like?" Sarah was suddenly ice cold sober, aware of the juke box blaring out *Pretty Vacant*, the couples snogging with various degrees of passion and imagination around them, the fact that Suzanne's leg was pressed hard against her own and that Suzanne was lifting her head from the table and moving her lips in the approximate direction of Sarah's face.

"I can't," she stuttered. Suzanne looked puzzled.

"Why not?" Sarah ran through a list of possible replies. I don't fancy you. I'm not an experiment. You're my best friend. What about Dick? What about Jules? I don't want to. We're just about to move in together. It wouldn't work. None of them seemed useable here and now. The first one would be hurtful and even though Suzanne was pretty drunk she might not be that drunk. Although she was not a lesbian and had never shown any inclination before now to sleep with women, Suzanne would still be offended if she remembered.

She was sure that Suzanne would try and argue her out of the others, and she must not give in to her this time. Even though it was true that sleeping with Suzanne had never figured in her fantasies, just having the possibility offered made it seem interesting and attractive. She looked at the dregs of the red wine in her glass and found inspiration there.

"Because I'm going to be sick," she said, struggling unsteadily to her feet, not even having to act because although her head had sobered up the rest of her body was taking some time to get used to the idea. The stilettos assisted here also. Sarah wove her way to the Ladies, hoping Suzanne wouldn't have the ability to follow her. Once there she locked herself into a cubicle and sat on the loo seat. The music swelled and faded as someone entered.

"Sarah? Are you alright?" Damn. It was Suzanne. So she definitely wasn't as drunk as she'd made out.

"Nnnnn," Sarah groaned non-committedly. She stood up and put two fingers down her throat so that she made convincing retching noises, and spat into the toilet bowl. "Wait in the bar," she groaned, and was thankful that for once Suzanne didn't argue. Sarah sat on the seat again and waited for fifteen minutes before flushing the loo and unlocking the door. She splashed some cold water on her face, which made her mascara run so she looked like a drunken panda. She wiped the worst of it off with a paper towel which rasped her face and converted her image to that of a pink drunken panda. "Yeuch," she said to her reflection, then went back into the bar.

Suzanne was asleep in the corner, her hair draped over one bare arm as she slumped against the back of the padded bench, a small trickle of saliva dribbling down her chin, snoring loudly. Phew, Sarah sighed inwardly. "Come on, Sleeping Beauty," she said, shaking Suzanne's shoulder, which had the minimal effect of making her open one eye half way.

"Morning already?" she queried.

"Yeah, that's right, so time for you to fly away home," Sarah said as she lifted Suzanne up from the seat and draped one of her arms across her shoulders.

She managed to get Suzanne back to her room, although it was touch and go getting across the stepping stones that some mad architect had thought would be a picturesque way of getting from Goodricke past the Physics block back towards the other side of the campus. Sarah had realised halfway across that attempting this with both of them still wearing their ridiculous shoes had been a foolish endeavour. She also noticed an especially hungry carp lying in wait for any stray toes. She thought herself lucky to have made it with both of them only suffering wet hems.

After that it was comparatively easy to half drag Suzanne along the winding paths by the side of the lake avoiding the treacherous concrete mushrooms, another crazy architect's idea for supplying light in a cute way, but they didn't give sufficient light to see by and were pitched at shin height. She hauled her up to the door of her room and used the duplicate she had begged off Chris the porter, well used to seeing the inhabitants of the college in Suzanne's condition. Sarah manoeuvered Suzanne next to the bed and thankfully dropped her onto it. Suzanne immediately rolled over and began to snore again.

Sarah left Suzanne's bag on the floor, closed the door and went to make her promised call on Jules, slightly earlier than timetabled. "My God, you mean that's the first time she's propositioned you?" said Jules incredulously.

"But she's my best friend," wailed Sarah.

"What difference does that make?" asked Jules, eyebrows raised. Sarah lay back on the bed and closed her eyes. Already she knew that she would have a stonker of a hangover tomorrow morning, and all this thinking after so much alcohol was making her head ache. Her silent wish for sleep was soon granted.

The following year was completely different. Sarah went with Dick, using the ticket he had purchased for Suzanne. They got blindingly drunk, but made it to the breakfast this time. They both fell in the lake trying to cross the stepping stones. The hungry carp was nowhere to be seen.

Suzanne   Now

Before York

Suzanne grew up in a small town in Cornwall, she told me. Saltash was just over the border with Devon, near to the city of Plymouth for which it was a dormitory town. More commuters started to live there after the road bridge was built, its silvery green twin towers dwarfing the railway bridge. Before the Tamar Bridge was built, the Brunel bridge carried the Great Western Railway and its successor British Rail high above the oyster beds, and the tiny car ferry plied beneath it. Often the chains on the ferry would break, leaving workers travelling to Devon stranded on the quayside. Passengers could struggle up the hill, past the cottage of the wife of Francis Drake tucked into a narrow and neglected side street, to the station opposite the graveyard.

"I can remember steam trains going through, filling the covered bridge over the line with thick white smoke. If you got caught there your clothes smelt like you'd been standing next to a bonfire," she said. Soon, however, they were replaced by the rackety diesels with the driver's cabs incorporated, like the ones that took me to school in Cumbria.

When Suzanne started work as a Saturday waitress in the coffee shop in Dingles of Plymouth, she travelled this line, but the journey did not take her alongside the broad expanses of Morecambe Bay, like mine, but through the back streets and back gardens of the crowded suburbs, St Budeaux and Devonport, into the centre of the city. There were other trains too, huge locomotives that pulled the express all the way from Penzance to London.

"Sometimes, if I was lucky, the express would be running late on Saturday morning, and we would travel in style," she reminisced. There were several girls from school who were also doing the trip to earn extra pocket money.

"One day, Carolyn, who was always late, arrived on the platform just as the train was starting to move off. In those days there were no automatic door locks, so she ran towards the carriage where we were standing in the corridor, smoking," Suzanne told me. "She grabbed the handle and pulled the door open, trying to jump on. She'd done it once before and got away with it." But this morning, hampered as she was by her usual paraphenalia of shoulder bag, heated rollers in a carrying case and make up, and by the fact that she was wearing stiletto heeled boots, she couldn't get up enough speed to leap, despite the other girls' shrieks of encouragement.

"Suddenly, the train speeded up, she lost her footing. It was like her hands were frozen to the handle, she couldn't let go." Then they were on the bridge. Carolyn swung out over the parapet, her grip was white knuckle strong on the inside handle by now, her feet dangling over the oily olive waters of the river below, and then back towards the train, her rollers performing a slow motion dive one by one into the back gardens of the houses beside the railway line. She was sandwiched between the door and the compartment, her body half inside the train, her legs still kicking frantically outside.

"I was kneeling on the floor, trying to haul her inside. Everyone else was just screaming". At last, someone seemed to notice the commotion and pulled the emergency cord, and the train came to a juddering halt halfway across the bridge. Suzanne and the others managed to pull Carolyn in just as the guard arrived and gave her a lecture about the dangers of getting on a moving train. He said she was lucky she didn't get fined for improper use of the communication cord, and also instructed her to get herself to the buffet car for some hot, sweet tea. Suzanne couldn't even tell me the story without her hands shaking.

"I just keep thinking about what would have happened if Carolyn had dragged me out of the door with her."

Before she started to work, Suzanne spent her free time out of school at the beach every summer. She'd catch the bus with a couple of other girls from her class, Helen and Jayne, who lived in the same street. It took forever to get to Seaton, their preferred spot. There the beach, although composed of small pebbles rather than sand, ran down to the sea in a wide flat sweep, sheltered by a wooded bay. Other, nearer beaches were only accessible by navigating steep cliff paths, overgrowth with spiky heather and nettles, even though they were not so crowded as Seaton. Suzanne's mother packed her lunch with the instruction, "Don't go in the water for at least an hour after swimming in case of cramp," then waved her off at the bus stop and returned to her housework. Suzanne's asthma was not so bad then, she only got the occasional attack, mainly in pollen season. The sea air seemed to do her good, she would arrive back for tea glowing and golden, her skin nearly matching her hair.

She was not one of those redheads over-cursed with freckles, she just had enough scattered across the bridge of her nose to be attractive. Unlike me, she never had any problems attracting boys, she just wasn't very interested in any of the acned youths at her school.

"I wanted to wait for the right one," she told me. The crowd of girls she hung out with at the local comprehensive had strict rules about how long you had to go out with someone before you could kiss them, when they were allowed to go further and put their hands inside your clothing and which areas they could touch, on some kind of sliding scale. Getting to heavy petting "down below" seemed to involve at least a six month apprenticeship. Sex of course was completely forbidden unless you were at least engaged to be married. By the sixth form all of the others had broken their code of conduct, Suzanne was the only one who stubbornly remained a virgin. The accounts she heard of couplings in cars and alleys did not encourage her to try it out. She was determined that, "I wanted the first time that I did it to be in a bed."

She'd been entered for a scholarship to Grahamstown, a public school in the north of Scotland most famous for playing host to a succession of foreign Saudi princes. In fact, when Suzanne went up for the interview, one was in residence, although, "No one affected to like him much. He had to sleep in the sick room with his bodyguard apparently."

She spent two days being grilled by the science teachers to see if she came up to scratch. In between she sampled some of the dubious delights of the place, such as touring the male dorms. "One of them was furnished with those ancient fabric camp beds in something looking like a run down Nissan hut. Supposed to toughen you up, I guess."

The school had only recently decided to admit girls, and it was one of the coveted, more competitive women's scholarships entering the sixth form that Suzanne was being considered for. Consequently the girls' dorm was a modern, purpose built block with hot water, although beds were in waist high cubicles so that there was still no privacy. "The food was atrocious, the worst of English school cuisine, lumpy mashed potatoes, overcooked vegetables, stodgy suet puddings and thick tepid custard."

A military-looking obstacle course had been constructed on the front lawn of the old house which had been converted into the school. This apparently was where punishments were carried out. Instead of detention pupils would have to perform a number of circuits. "Another favourite of the prefects was to get the youngest kids to run up to the old church at dusk. On one occasion, some wag set it up with one of his friends to be waiting for them, playing some funereal dirge on the organ, with candles set out on the gravestones. I mean, they were only ten." After one of the traumatised children's parents had complained (after all they were paying thousands of pounds for their child to attend the school), the sixth formers were told to desist from this particular jape.

The school placed great emphasis on the outdoors, in a kind of "*mens sana in corpore sano*", jolly hockey sticks type way. Suzanne found the other pupils quite nice but rather naïve. So when she was offered the scholarship, she turned it down. She felt that her decision had been the right one when the second choice girl, who leapt at the chance and who also happened to be from her school in Cornwall, having been predicted as one of the brilliant Oxbridge hopes, managed to get herself expelled just after taking her A levels (in which she only achieved 2 Cs and a D), having been found smoking pot at the coastguard station.

Suzanne was an only child, her parents were attentive but distant. Her mother was thirty-eight when Suzanne was born, I think they had given up hope about ever having a child. She was certainly indulged within the limits of Suzanne's father's income, but not spoiled. Whenever they came to college to visit she would complain about her father's limited culinary tastes.

"He always wants to go to the same restaurant, he says he doesn't like foreign food, and he always has plain roast chicken." I couldn't understand what she was moaning about, but then other people's parents are always more interesting than your own. They always seemed rather quiet and rather faded. How could they have produced Suzanne? Her mother did have the remains of what must have been fairly striking red hair streaking the grey, and she looked like a much older version of her daughter apart from the fact that her eyes were blue.

I only saw them a few times, at the beginning and end of terms, once or twice in between, and of course when they came to collect Suzanne's things. They looked washed out then, stunned. Her mother stroked the clothes still hanging in her wardrobe, picked up her mug from the desk, pushed up one of the lipsticks on the washstand. Her father sat on the bed, not speaking, not making eye contact, even with his wife. It occurred to me that he was probably waiting for me to go so he could cry.

The college had moved me into a temporary room just until the end of the year, so I mumbled something about lectures and started to edge towards the door. I'd just come to let them in and see if they wanted to talk to me as I had been the one who had found her. It was the least I could do. Her mother smiled weakly and said, "Of course, we mustn't keep you," so I fled. I never saw them again. They did invite me to the funeral but I couldn't bear to go, to see them put her in the ground, then stand around eating ham sandwiches. Dick couldn't go either, he had one of his practical exams for his finals on the same day. So we both let her down in the end.

Sarah and Jules   Summer 1978

Greece

Sarah lay in the sun, her skin sizzling with Bergasol, factor 2, tan accelerator 4. She was already cooked to an even, golden brown, now her skin was turning a deep Mediterranean tan. She was completely naked, just like every other woman on the beach, so she had no pale patches where a bikini might have been. Her arms were stretched above her head, thrown back in a careless way, leaving her body open and vulnerable. She let the white sand carry her on her bamboo mat as she drifted in and out of an ouzo-induced sleep. She knew without opening her eyes that the unshaded sky above her was an ice bright blue, that the sea that lapped a few feet from her toes was a deep azure green. She revelled in the sensation of being almost without sensation, floating. Even when Jules ran up the beach and shook her hair wildly over her so that drops of cold sea water sprayed over her in a wide arc from her chest to her shins, Sarah came back to consciousness only slowly, surfacing from deep hot darkness.

"Sarah, you slug, come and swim!" hooted Jules, standing beside her on the beach, hopping from foot to foot on the hot sand. Sarah raised herself slowly on her elbows and squinted through barely open slits at her lover, bronzed and taut, her body muscular and soft in all the right places.

"You'll have to persuade me," she pouted. Jules smirked and lowered herself on top of Sarah, her body still cool but already starting to be warmed by the sun, straddling her knees and moving slowly up across her torso, her erect nipples brushing Sarah's oiled breasts, to plant a deep and hot kiss on her mouth, parting Sarah's lips with her tongue. "Mm," Sarah murmured," wouldn't you rather just nip into the olive grove instead?"

"You tart!" Jules laughed, "save it for later." Stepping back, she pulled Sarah up by her hand to sitting then standing, then both women raced across the sandy furnace to the sea, and kept running through the shallows until the water was thigh high, sending arcs of crystal flying, until they both subsided into the cooling salt water and lay back like starfish, still holding hands. "My God, this is the life!" said Jules.

Sarah mmm-ed her assent. They had been travelling in Greece for a month now, catching ferries, lying on beaches, sleeping in olive groves or occasionally treating themselves to a bed in a taverna. They ate breakfast in cafés on dusty, hidden streets, spooning clear dark honey into their yoghurt, drinking chilled orange juice and endless tea. Lunch was mostly huge beef tomatoes sliced with spongy Greek cheese or crumbly feta, fresh olives and crusty bread, eaten on the beach or under the trees. Sometimes, if they had woken in time to catch the farmer's lorry, this would be followed by slabs of watermelon, spitting out the black pips into the sand so that it looked like they were surrounded by the squashed remnants of an ant army. They ate in the evening in open air restaurants by the water, souvlaki, moussaka and kleftico with thick fried chips and Greek salad, washed down with raw retsina in a jug.

One time they bought fresh fish from a toothless fisherman by the harbour, who grinned and made obvious hand signals at them. Jules laughed and shook her head, wagging her finger at him. "We're not for you, old man," she admonished. They found a sheltered spot on the beach that night and made a fire of driftwood, cooking the fish on sticks, picking the charred flesh from the bones with their teeth.

They settled into a routine of easy going domesticity, sometimes silent, sitting next to each other devouring yet another worn and well thumbed paperback thriller, covers bent and folded back, pages yellow and stained with suntan lotion. At other times, they talked about life, their parents and childhood experiences, what they wanted to be, how they saw things, skating around the question of who they wanted to be with.

Jules would be going back to York for her final year. She was doing a music degree, she sang and played the clarinet, but she had found that her interest lay in music management rather than performance. She enjoyed the buzz of organising the music events on campus, and liked the vicarious fame of hanging out with the bands that came to play. "I want to move to London, join a management company but eventually I'm going to set up on my own," she mused, her dark eyes far away on the grey city, not seeing the beach around her.

Sarah didn't know what she wanted to do, but then, "I've got an extra year of uni to figure it out," she said. "Maybe I'll be a journalist, or a teacher, or a beach bum. But right now, I've got absolutely no idea."

"Surprise, surprise," muttered Jules, a rare sour note in their Greek idyll. It was unspoken that Jules loved Sarah and wanted to live with her. She had been upset and angry and disappointed when Sarah had announced that she had agreed to Suzanne's plan for them to share a room. After an initial furious outburst, "If you wanted to share a room with someone why the hell couldn't you have shared with me?" Jules had never referred to it again. Sarah knew that the issue had not gone away, it still hung there between them, winking from time to time like a sapphire caught in the Greek sunshine.

Coming away to Greece together had been planned before she'd told Jules she wouldn't be living with her next year. Now, as they travelled together through the golden days and velvet nights, Sarah found it hard to hold onto her original conviction that she didn't want to move in with Jules. Her reasons seemed washed out, sun bleached. Had there been something about being too young to settle down, wanting to play the field, this was going too fast, she feared that it might get too claustrophobic and spoil what they had? Why had they seemed like such strong reasons when they were in York?

She meant to raise her change of heart with Jules, talk about how she might reconsider her decision. Sometimes she'd find herself taking a breath to start a sentence, or even getting halfway through one, like "When we get back to York," or "How big is your flat?" As she fell more and more into the Greek lack of urgency, she just never got around to working up the energy to tackle it.

The days passed and somehow, without Sarah noticing, two months had flown by and they were packing their rucksacks to head north. They caught the ferry to Athens, enjoying their last day of Greek sunshine before the crispness of a Yorkshire autumn, lounging on the deck of the battered and rusty vessel as it made its way slowly and deliberately back to port. The magic of the summer started to fall away on the crowded bus from Pireaus, as they hung from the straps and bounced along the dust blown road to the airport.

An inevitable four hour flight delay stretched the journey even more, and they tried to catch some sleep on the lumpy plastic covered chairs in the airport departure lounge. "Do you think we've got enough drachmas for a couple of beers?" Sarah asked hopefully.

"No, we've only got enough for one," said Jules, counting the coins. They shared it, passing the bottle backwards and forwards, rubbing the condensation on the glass against their foreheads to cool down.

Wedged into cattle class, the two women eventually landed at Gatwick. It was raining. Still in their holiday uniform of shorts, T shirts and sandals, they had to rummage about in their packs for spare socks, jeans and jumpers unworn for eight weeks. They fought with their luggage from train to tube to train, parting at Euston. Sarah was going to her parents' house for a week before term started, Jules was going straight back to York to move into the flat she'd rented and to scour the flea markets and second hand shops for cheap furniture. Suddenly self-conscious in the midst of the stream of commuters scurrying to work around them, Sarah and Jules hugged each other, aware that the busy station concourse was not the place for a lingering farewell kiss.

At last Sarah drew back, holding the other woman at arms length. "It was a fantastic summer, Jules," she said, feeling the moisture pick at the corners of her eyes, her voice hoarse. "I'll never forget it."

"Hey, that sounds a bit serious," said Jules, her voice straining to lighten the mood. "Plenty more where that came from. And it's only a week, honey."

"Yeah," Sarah agreed, but on the train back to the north west, after Jules had waved her goodbye from the platform and she'd hung out of the window until she could no longer see the tall, tanned figure, she let the tears flow as she saw London give way to the countryside outside the window. Her indecision and failure to change had shown her that there would be no more golden summers with Jules.

Sarah   December 1978

Break-up

"We don't have to go to Emily's party if you don't want to," said Jules, although they both knew that was not why they were arguing.

"It's not that I don't want to go," said Sarah, and then added with a determination to hurt that even took her own breath away, "It's that I don't want to go with you." Jules' eyes widened, her mouth gaped. Even now, Sarah felt the need to reach out and touch her lover's lips with her fingertips, to stroke the smooth skin on Jules' cheek. But she musn't, she couldn't, not now that she had finally said the unsayable. Unable to call the words back, she ploughed on, further into the quagmire.

"We do everything together, we're never apart, I never get the time to see my own friends, I'm always hanging out with your dykey crowd." They both knew that was not true, that Sarah and Suzanne went out regularly together, that she and Jules had dinner with Suzanne and Dick every weekend, and that Sarah had many friends of her own.

Jules had recovered the power of speech. "I see," she said, her deep brown velvet voice replaced by a parched whisper, her eyes were dry too. The worst of it was, Sarah knew, was that Jules did see what was going on, she knew that Sarah was scared of the commitment that Jules offered her. She hadn't thought she would react like this. She'd expected the fiery, weeping Jules, not this concussed, wounded stranger. How could she hurt this woman so much, Sarah wondered, appalled at the visible consequences of her words as they gazed at each other, these two who had been so close for the past year. She wanted to reach out and hold her, stroke her deep, black hair, hold her head to her breast, make it all right somehow.

For a moment, a life with Jules opened before her, a life where she could be herself, where she would be loved for who she was not who someone else thought she should be, of easy conversation, making aioli together, joyous ecstatic sex and peaceful sleeping in a wide bed. She opened her mouth to apologise, to take back the words, to say she would live with Jules after all, to accept her love and to say, at last, that she loved in return.

But Jules swallowed, looked away, said, "That's that, then," and the moment was lost.

Sarah   Now

Choice

I loved Jules, but I never told her. At first, I used her to get me out of having a stultifying relationship with Sam, although why I should have felt that it was necessary to go to those lengths to avoid making a mistake I had made in the past does seem rather excessive now. To think that I was so afraid that I would be sucked into his orbit and be unable to escape, that I thought it would be better to get into a relationship with someone else who was just as needy in her own way.

It's just like watching one of those many TV soap operas where the whole plot depends on characters not speaking to each other, assuming the worst about someone they are supposed to know well, rather than just checking out a situation with them first before they get all fired up and self righteous and vengeful. It seems incredible and rather sad to me now that I never even considered that I could just have told Sam, "Fuck off," if he ever asked me out. Or told Dick, "I've lusted after you from the first moment I saw you at the registration desk." I could have told Suzanne, "I just need to borrow one of your poems," or maybe, "Could you help me write my own?". I could even have told Professor Ellis, "I just can't do your bloody creative writing assignment, I've got writer's block, I need more time, some help and understanding rather than a punitive threat to throw me out of university."

What would have happened if I'd done any of these things? Would Suzanne still have died, would I be married to Dick now? More importantly would my wonderful, amazing daughter and my handsome, monosyllabic son have been born rather than some other children?

My relationship with Jules was the first time I had ever been really involved with someone emotionally as well as physically. Lizzie was an unfulfilled possibility, Johnny had been a mere convenience, an irritation and eventually a burden. Alex taught me that sex was much more than having an orgasm, although I have to say that I never came with either him or Johnny, not once. Alex had given me the confidence to feel that I could explore sex and given me the knowledge that I could seduce others with my body. He never pretended to be in love with me, it was just "fun, babe".

With Jules it was like being on another planet altogether, an emotional roller coaster ride right from the start. She wanted much more of me and she gave much more of herself. Physically it was mind blowing. I used to have to go back to bed on my own on Friday afternoons when the college was quiet because half the first years had all gone home for the weekend, just to catch up on my sleep. I managed that for a few months, but when she found out that she could knock on my door at 4pm after her last lecture and be sure to find me drowsy, warm and naked, even that became a time of play rather than recovery. I could never say no to her then, not that I wanted to. I was as eager to be loved as she was to love me.

I loved her body, I loved to explore its smoothness and firmness and softness with my fingers and tongue. I loved the fact that I could see myself in her curves and crevices, that she was so familiar to me. Talking to Jules was sometimes like talking to myself, she seemed to know what I was thinking, knew what I meant. It had never been like that with any man, and because of how I betrayed Suzanne it could never be like that with Dick as there was always a gaping hole where neither of us could go.

My time with Jules was before all that, she was wild and open and free and she gave me the possibility to be that myself, a possibility that I knew all too briefly. Still the words wouldn't come, I could never tell her, "I love you," even though it would have avoided many tearful and angry rows, recriminations and accusations between us. I can't really say why I didn't, she gave me so much that I had never had in a relationship before or since.

It was just as well in a way that we broke up before Suzanne's death, because I would never have been able to keep a secret from her. That was really why we split, I couldn't deal with the fact that I couldn't hide from her. I retreated into adolescent sulks and tantrums, declaring that, "I need more space, you're suffocating me." The truth was that I was scared of her intensity and what it might call from me in return. I didn't see how valuable a love she offered me, and that I could just have leapt into the cool, cool, water instead of fighting against the tide. Yet, again, if I had done that, where would any of us, Suzanne, Dick, my daughter, Zanne, and son, Martin, be now?

Looking back, I can see clearly where I made decisions that seemed unimportant at the time, but which had far reaching consequences. That's the advantage of hindsight I suppose. Choosing to go to York rather than any other university, choosing Jules rather than being honest with Sam, rejecting Jules when she got too close rather than revelling in our relationship. And that other, horribly big, momentous decision which I couldn't see was the first step on the mirror glass slope to destruction.

Suzanne   21 January 1979

Diary

I just can't understand what's got into Sarah. She is being an absolute pig. Ever since she broke up with Jules she's been having one fling after another, men and women. And she's not happy and she won't listen to me. Why doesn't she just go back with Jules, I mean you can see her moping around, I'm sure that Jules would have her back like a shot. I had hoped that after the Christmas break it would be better, but she's still just as stubborn.

She's started to make funny comments about me and Dick, too. I'm sure now that she does fancy him. Well, tough luck 'cos he's mine. She's not his type anyway. How dare she try and turn me against him. She doesn't know what she is talking about anyway. I don't mind that he sleeps with other women, I know it is just a phase he's going through, men have to sow their wild oats don't they? Then when we get married he'll be able to settle down.

It's not like I thought it would be though. I didn't imagine so much waiting around for him just to get himself sorted out and realise that really, I'm the best woman for him. There was that other woman who he'd been out with for ages, but anyone could have told him that it just was never going to go anywhere, she was at a different college, and then of course she went off with someone else. It must be something I'm doing wrong, something about how I am, that is stopping him making a commitment to me. I am always determined never to question him about where he goes when we are not together, but somehow it always comes out, and it sounds like a whine. Men don't like being nagged, I don't want to do that but sometimes I just can't help myself, I want to be with him so much.

If only I could talk to Sarah about it, maybe she would have some ideas, but at the moment we just seem to be getting further and further apart. I almost wish I hadn't agreed to share this room with her, but I couldn't say no, the rent was so cheap. It was so much fun last year, now everything feels like hard work.

Sarah   February 1979

Writer's block

I can't write anything. I don't know why not. It's been like this ever since I split up with Jules and I don't want to write about that. I'm not ready to do that. I just sit here staring at this blank sheet of paper, day after day. What the hell possessed me to take Ellis' Creative Writing module anyway? The damn thing is a double and it counts towards my degree classification because it's in the second half of the year, and why it's a double module is because there has to be a major piece of creative writing completed as part of the assignment.

I'm supposed to have completed the outline plan and had marks and feedback on that over a week ago. I've managed to swing extensions so far but I'm going to run out of family members to kill off soon.

I think Ellis fancies me. The rest of the class think so, they keep sniggering that now I'm young, free and single I won't have any trouble getting through the module. Well, some snigger, but others are really angry with me and I haven't done anything yet.

My God, I thought "Yet". Surely I couldn't stoop so low as to be seduced by that dried up raisin just to get through the course. Could I?

The problem is I can't write. This is the first time in my life it's happened to me and I don't know how to deal with it. I've got no clues or techniques. This time last year I could have talked to Jules about it, but I can't do that now, she'd read too much into it. It's not as if we're talking at all, not since I picked up that woman at Jules' birthday party, right in front of her, just because I was feeling so weak and Jules looked great and I just knew if I didn't do something quick I'd end up going back with her and then we would have just fallen into bed and it would have been like it always was.

Would that really have been so bad? What is the matter with me? What am I waiting for, why am I always looking for something better to come along? Wasn't what we had so good it was good enough?

But I won't think about that. I don't want to think about Jules or why I can't just swallow my pride and say, "I was wrong, take me back."

Maybe she wouldn't have me. I know she hasn't been with anyone else since we broke up. That's one advantage of the lesbian grapevine, but the disadvantage is that she will know exactly what I've been up to, there will always have been some kind person willing to tell her that I've been sleeping my way around the first year women in the Gay Soc. None of them more than a week, most of them one night stands. I'm sure that kind person will also tell her that I've also fitted in quite a few men as well.

I'm exhausted. I don't get to sleep much, even when I'm not in bed with someone else. Moving into that double room was such a mistake. I know Suzanne was really sorry about it, when she and Dick barged in that time at three o'clock in the morning when I was supposed to be with Jules, but that was the night we'd split. Dick had lent his room to a guy he knew from school who had come to visit and some woman he'd picked up at the Vanburgh bop, they had to go to bed in our room too.

I thought they would have been a bit more sensitive, but after about ten minutes while I lay there in the dark and tried to get back to sleep they started to have sex. I had to lie there and listen to the rustlings and whisperings and suckings and moanings. It was awful and they went on for ages. I felt so alone. I had just passed up the chance to make a go of it with Jules, my first night alone for months, and then that. I just cried and cried into the pillow, I had to stuff my face into it really hard, but I could still hear them. I must have looked awful in the morning, Suzanne assumed it was because of Jules and I suppose it was partly, but I could never tell her the real reason. "Suzanne, I really fancy the bloke you're with and I just couldn't stand having to listen to you screwing him in the next bed."

Now I don't sleep so well in the room. I'm really tired and I read until my eyes are raw, but when the light goes out I lie there and listen. Little noises wake me up completely, I keep imagining that they're coming back, that I haven't made it clear to Suzanne that I'm "sleeping in" tonight.

I keep having this recurring dream, that I'm asleep in bed and they come into the room, really quietly. I start to wake up, but I can't speak, my mouth is full of thick treacle, I have to use all my energy to breathe, so I can't tell them that I'm awake. I try and move, but my limbs are numb, like that feeling you get when you've been sleeping on your arm and it's like uncooked pastry before the blood supply comes back. There's a weight pressing me down into the mattress and I can't raise my head up. Then it starts to feel really urgent that I have to wake up, I can hear them moving around, I have to stop them. My nostrils feel like they've been stuffed with cotton wool.

At last I do wake up, not just in the dream but really wake up and it's always around four in the morning and then I hear the milk float coming past, going to Heslington. Then the early buses start, and sometimes the dustcart comes into the college to take the waste from the kitchens, and I give in after about an hour and get up and make some tea. I normally doze off about half past six, then my alarm goes off at seven and I feel like death.

I've fallen asleep in lectures though, don't seem to have any trouble sleeping then. The worst time was in one of Professor Smith's when I'd got there so late that I had to sit in the front row. The lecture theatre has these fixed seats built in, benches that have high backs so that they turn into a writing desk for the people sitting in the row behind. I went to sleep and my head fell backwards and cracked onto the edge behind me, where the seat back makes a corner and turns into a writing surface. I don't know if I cried out, but it really hurt, it made my eyes water, and everyone, including the Prof, was looking in my direction. I still couldn't stay awake after that. I had to rest my forehead on my hand and look like I was writing intensely, a trick I learnt during my history A level class. I looked at the notes I'd taken afterwards and they were just a series of squiggly lines, some running off the edge of the paper.

I've always written, ever since I was a child and learnt to write at primary school. I've always loved stories and poems, the best part of the day was when my Dad would read to me at bedtime. I loved going to bed because of it. It was the only time I had him to myself. The rest of the time he was either at work, or cooking breakfast for all of us, or wanting to sit and read his paper at night. It was always him I wanted to tuck me in and read to me. So I started to write as soon as I knew how, I've still got some of the scrawls I did before I even knew anything about sentences or rhythm. I even wrote a poem about my Dad doing the decorating. Everything was a subject, even the ordinary, the mundane. I wanted to come here because the English course allowed a specialism in creative writing, rather than just churning through all the old crusty classics.

Now I sit and look at the white sheet of paper. Sometimes it seems to melt and spread out to cover my whole desk. It's so white, like snow with no footprints in it, the kind of snow that makes you want to just throw yourself into its deep powder, run up and down and in circles, just to see the marks of where you have been, the first human being to tread in it. But I can't make any marks in this snow. I've tried pens and pencils, poised over the ice lake, morning, afternoon, evening, night, waiting for the idea to strike. Propping a sheet of it up in my little portable typewriter, adjusting the tabs and margins, even though they're still the same as they were from the last time I tried to do this. Nothing, great white acres of it.

This has never happened to me before. I feel disoriented, like my feet are not connecting to the earth, I'm floating above it. Sometimes I get a second picture in my mind, just behind my eyes, running alongside what I'm seeing in front of me, a crazy uncoordinated picture show in stereo. I can see myself walking along as though I'm looking down from above. I have to stop whatever I'm doing because the strain of keeping two viewpoints in my head at the same time is unbearable. Then, as suddenly as it came, it's gone, like a bubble bursting, pop. I feel like I've woken up in the middle of the day. Are people starting to look at me, do they notice anything wrong? Or is that just my imagination, like everything else. Maybe they just think I'm the same as I always was. No one else knows, there isn't anyone I can tell. Let's not go over that again.

How long is this going to go on for, and what is going to happen to me? Am I going mad, is this what they call a nervous breakdown? The headmistress' daughter had one of those when she went to university. Tessa was always hyper about her exam marks, she'd always come out complaining that it had been awful and that she'd probably failed. Then the marks would come out and she'd have got eighty per cent or something. We stopped listening to her in the end. It was even worse for those who really had failed. She was also really pissed off that I got the same grades as her in the A levels—three As—so that we had to share the prize for Best Academic Achievement for Girls. I didn't even know there was such a thing. Apparently Tessa had had her heart set on it since she was eleven. Then she went off to Cambridge, but she was home within six months. I heard she took all her clothes off and sat in the middle of a pedestrian crossing outside her college, completely blocked up the centre of the town with traffic for an hour.

I don't feel like doing anything like that. I just feel like it's an incredible effort to keep anything in focus, if I relax my eyes then everything dissolves into a grey mass with lots of revolving white lights. The edges of the picture in my head are unravelling, like knitting without a needle in, like a photograph that's going yellow from the outside in, gradually losing its true colours. I'm drowning in fresh air.

And I can't write anything.

Sarah   March 1979

Biscuits

Sarah looked at the bottom of the empty biscuit tin in horror. She was sure that there had been some there yesterday. She was sure she had bought a new packet of custard creams on Monday, and it was only Wednesday now. She had to have a sugar rush, she just had to, she couldn't complete this assignment with out it.

One thought gave way to another, and the whole stack of dominoes started to fall inexorably. If she didn't have a biscuit, she wouldn't be able to complete the creative writing project for Professor Ellis. If she didn't complete it, Professor Ellis had threatened that she would fail her and that she would have to leave York at the end of this summer term. If she got thrown out, she would have to go back home, to the disappointment of her parents, even though they would never say anything of course. They would just look at her with those understanding eyes and tell her that they would stick by her. Who knows, if she went back home maybe Johnny Manfredson would reappear and she'd end up going back with him and they'd probably end up getting married.

She had no confidence in her university won independence, she was sure that just being back in the place of her childhood would gradually seep into her bones, she would end up falling into old patterns and lifestyles. A growing sense of horror started at the base of her stomach, creeping upwards into her chest, making her breathing tight and uncomfortable, her vision starting to go shaky in places like the beginning of a migraine.

The assignment had to be in tomorrow and she had absolutely no one she could turn to for help. Suzanne was out with Dick and wouldn't be back until after breakfast. If only she and Jules were still together, but she'd messed that up as well, and she'd told her latest fling that it was all over last week, although Emily wouldn't have been any good as a crutch anyway, nor would any of the men and women she'd been to bed with in the last few months. Sarah looked at the shiny bottom of the biscuit tin and felt a yawning chasm into which she was about to fall, taking all of her carefully built persona and its defences with her. She started to sob, clutching the tin to her chest.

Then in a flash of double vision she caught an image of herself in her mind, kneeling on the bright striped rag rug in her room, hugging an empty tin, the one that her mother had sent her with pictures of the Lake District on it through some misguided attempt to cure her non-existent home sickness. The ridiculousness of the image turned her sobs to giggles and then to gasps of hysterical laughter, tears running down her face, her nose running and adding to the general mess and moisture on her face.

After a few minutes, the noises subsided. Sarah was left looking at the tin, now the embodiment of all her hopes and investments thrown away.

"Shit!" she said, out loud. "There has to be a way round this!" It couldn't be so simple that the whole pack of cards would come crashing down owing to a few missing biscuits. Wait a minute, she thought, hadn't she seen Suzanne with a pack of those wonderful chocolate things with nuts and raisins in, just yesterday? Florentines, that was it. Normally they shared their food shopping but these were some special titbits that were Dick's favourites and Suzanne had bought them for his birthday tomorrow. Sarah winced at what Suzanne would do if she found them missing, but as long as she got this damn assignment in, like Scarlet O'Hara, she'd think about that tomorrow. Dammit, she could even go into town and get a replacement packet from Betty's Tearooms once she had handed this in to Smelly Ellis.

Now she was the hunter. Where could Suzanne have hidden them? Sarah went over to her friend's side of the room, flung open the doors and opened the top drawer in her wardrobe. She rifled through the jumble of underwear, including red and purple satin bras, tiny matching knickers, suspender belts and lace stockings. Hmm, she'd never have suspected Dick of going for such obvious stuff. She picked up one of the underwired constructions. It looked really uncomfortable. She shook her head, better not get distracted by remembering what Dick and Suzanne got up to in bed. Her reaching fingers found a packet at the back of the draw. Triumphantly she pulled it out, but it was only Suzanne's next six month's supply of the pill. "Rats!"

Neither of the next two drawers revealed what she was searching for, nor did casting about in the bottom of the wardrobe amongst Suzanne's extensive shoe collection. Sneezing from the dust storm she had raised, Sarah moved on to the shelves, the tins and jars in the cupboard above the bed and the bedside table. Nothing. She turned to the desk, feeling increasingly desperate and more than a little foolish. Still, she might as well finish what she had started. There they were, already wrapped, nestling in the bottom drawer amongst piles of lined paper, covered in Suzanne's characteristic scrawl.

Sarah pulled out the packet, and fingered the handmade paper, tied with that curly ribbon that came with boxes of cakes. There was a tag, "To Dick. Another sweet thing to get your teeth into, lover. From your one and only Suzanne". Ugh. As she felt the package to find the edge of the parchment it was wrapped in and worked up the courage to destroy the gift, Sarah caught sight of the top sheet of writing. To put off the moment when she committed herself to tearing the paper, she started to read. With growing disbelief she put the package aside and picked up the sheet.

It was a poem. More than that, it was a good one. Breathless, she picked up the next one, then the next, and devoured them with her eyes. She plunged her hand to the bottom of the drawer and came up with another and another, all of them shining and sharp. When did Suzanne write this stuff, and how could she have kept it from Sarah all the time they'd been friends, all the time they'd been sharing the same bedroom? How could a bloody biochemist have such a way with words when she, Sarah, who had got onto the fucking English degree on the strength of her shit hot poetry, couldn't write a word of the stuff anymore, not since she'd broken up with Jules.

This was a treasure trove. There must be hundreds of them in here. A worm of a thought started to wriggle its way up from that part of her brain that had used Johnny Manfredson to deflower her when her virginity had marked her out from the rest of the crowd at school, that had researched which university would be free of her former classmates, that had slept with Jules to avoid getting entangled with Sam. "What if," said that calculating voice, "What if you just took one of these and submitted it to Ellis tomorrow as yours? You even have the same initials. That's all that Suzanne has written on the bottom. There are so many poems here, she'd never miss one, surely?" Then the final justfication, "If Suzanne was here, she probably wouldn't mind, just to help you out, just this once."

"And isn't there a party on at Justine's tonight, where that tasty redhead Sally is going to be?" the voice continued. Justine had told her that Sally had especially asked if Sarah was going to be there.

Sarah stared at the poem she held. It was appropriately entitled, "Dark Ways". She looked at the bright package in her other hand. Alright then. She took a deep breath, placed the package back on top of the pile of poems, shut the drawer and went back to her own desk. Drawing out a fresh sheet of paper, she copied out Suzanne's poem and signed it with her own initials, then filled in an assignment cover sheet, clipped the two together and inserted it in the internal envelope addressed to Professor Ellis.

She left the envelope on her desk and ignored it as she showered, changed, carefully selected scent and earrings, zipped up her blue suede boots, a bit shabby now but still her favourites. Throwing on her old leather jacket, she finally returned to her desk, picked up the borrowed poem and took it back to Suzanne's side of the room, where she thrust it deep into the drawer from whence it came. After gathering keys, money and her dope stash she finally acknowledged the drab envelope.

"I'll put it in the box on my way", she thought, "Then it's done with". With that, she opened the door and stepped out, with no awareness of the fact that she had placed a far more fatal domino in line than any she had dealt so far.

Sarah   Spring 1979

Plagiarism

Of course, after that it became much more easy to take the poems again. The first one had got a rave review from Professor Ellis, though she couldn't hide her triumphant tone. She'd "known you could do it, Sarah", it had just needed "the right motivation". Was that what she called threatening to throw her out of university? Now Sarah had the added gall of having proved Ellis' teaching methods right, that all she'd needed was a kick up the arse rather than a more understanding tutor less wedded to the benefits of pressure and threat.

So of course what happened when Sarah started to lag behind again was that Ellis applied the same methods that had been successful in prising forth such a jewel of language the last time, a large dose of bullying accompanied by promises of dire consequences should the work not appear. Sarah had initially had to perform quite complicated mental acrobatics to justify that fact that she had taken Suzanne's poem and submitted it as her own and then never been brave enough to own up to its author what she had done. Befuddled by suppressed guilt, instead of seeing the professor's tactics for what they were, a constant crying of "Wolf!", she dipped her hand into the honeypot in the bottom drawer again and again.

Not there was any lack of supply, the poems multiplied and bred at an amazing rate. What was Suzanne doing studying biochemistry, wondered Sarah, as she plagiarised her friend's work repeatedly, changing a reference here, a word there, transposing a few lines.

At the same time, she learnt more about Suzanne's relationship with Dick than she really cared to, including the fact that Suzanne knew he was sleeping around but had decided to grit her teeth and hang on through some misplaced sense of fate, that Dick was her one and only soul mate on this earth. The knowledge started to creep into their friendship, Suzanne accusing her, "You're just jealous," when Sarah refused to continue to indulge in the Saturday night dinner dates.

Sarah only just bit back the words "How could I be jealous of you?", but they hung in the air, all the more awful for having been unsaid.

She couldn't confess how she had come by the knowledge of Suzanne's inner and private life. The fact that she was taking the poems rubbed against her conscience, a sore that bled at first but that with repeated pressure formed a callous so she could continue her secret burglarising of what was never intended to be known. The atmosphere between them grew arctic, neither wanting to spend time in each other's company. Their visits to the shared room became less and less frequent, stopping only to change clothes, pick up books and vanish to lectures or library. They notified each other belligerently when it was their intention to sleep in the room.

"I'm sleeping in," was the phrase they used so that the other knew not to appear that night. Sarah found herself in an increasingly sharp vice, between the aggression of her tutor and the hurt anger of her friend.

Sarah chose to stay on at York that Easter. She took a job as a chambermaid on campus for the conference season. Barbara, a regular cleaner, used to joke to the temporaries, "The terms are going to get shorter and shorter once the university accountants discover they can make more money from paying guests than from you messy students!"

Her parents felt that she should, "Get a job more worthy of your talents, Sarah," said her mother, without specifying what she thought those talents might be. Sarah listed them in her own mind. A capacity to steal and lie (especially to herself), the ability to betray her best friend, stubbornly keeping to a course of action in the face of all evidence to the contrary, inability to admit that she was wrong. She couldn't think of any particular job that would have those on the person specification.

The work was easy and didn't engage her brain, it was over by noon, leaving her free to wander along the shady paths by the artificial river from the lake by Goodricke, past Langwith and up to the old hall at Heslington. She found a spot between the trees by the croquet lawn where she could sunbathe in the unseasonable April sunshine and doze out of sight of the university administration staff in the hall.

Some days she caught the train to Harrogate, or the bus out to Brimham Rocks. Harrogate was quieter than York, it seemed like a relic of a bygone age, slightly faded and rather genteel. Betty's Tea Rooms there faced out onto the park, and she could while away an hour over a hot chocolate or a strawberry milk shake. The Rocks were a natural phenomenon, huge blocks of millstone grit perched on a hill top, softer rocks and earth washed away to leave them standing like megaliths, or towers of precariously balanced slabs. Stone age tombs and structures were interspersed with the natural monuments, ancient hill dwellers taking advantage of the materials scattered over the moor. Bracken grew thick and lush, waist high in places, and Sarah could always find a private place to lie and contemplate the insecure looking piles of massive stones, which nonetheless withstood the searching Yorkshire wind.

She didn't have to talk, to explain, justify herself. In fact, if she hadn't had to go to work she wondered whether she might have lost the capacity to speak altogether, her vocal chords drying up through lack of use.

Yet always she took with her the weight of her actions, denying her affection for Jules, destroying her friendship with Suzanne by robbing her of her secret poetry. Whilst she could keep going from day to day, and things seemed almost normal and calm, she could feel underneath the surface of her life the rushing of some mountain torrent, crashing through a ravine, white water thrashing from side to side, as it hurtled on its way towards some looming waterfall. She could feel it coming, just around the bend, she was powerless to prevent it and she feared and longed for it at the same time. The planets revolved, something inevitable was going to happen soon. The dominoes were set, balancing so that when one fell, the next one would surely follow it.

Sarah   May 1979

Ultimatum

Sarah yawned and stretched. Her eyes seemed to be glued shut. She could sense a bright light underneath her eyelashes and the waking part of her brain was beginning to suspect that it was late. Too late. Again. She tried harder to open her eyes, without success. Then one pair of eyelashes seemed to rip apart. She rubbed the other eye furiously, resulting in a sharp stabbing pain in her eyeball. That would teach her to take her mascara off before she fell into bed next time. Or maybe not. She had managed to show a remarkable resistance to learning anything for the past six months.

Her functioning eye sought out the alarm clock. "Shit!" It was 10am already and she had a tutorial at 10.15. Blinking rapidly to try and clear the mass of clogged make up in her right eye she started to grope around the bed to locate any items of clothing that might serve in an emergency. She located a serviceable bra and a shirt, which she struggled into, then noticed a beer stain on the front and its beyond-the-pale crumpled state. She crawled over to the chest of drawers for clean knickers and socks because she couldn't remember how many times she'd worn the ones that were lying on the floor next to her bed. She really would have to take some clothes down to the launderette soon. People were already showing a marked reluctance to sit next to her in lectures. She located the sink and splashed cold water into her face, which succeeded both in clearing her vision and leaving a black smudge of mascara underneath her eye and across her cheek. Damn! She had to use a few precious minutes scrubbing it off so that she didn't look quite so much like the bride of Dracula in the film she'd seen last night at the Derwent Horrors, a regular all night picture feast of B flicks. Instead she looked as though someone had scrubbed her face with a loofah, which given the state of her flannel was pretty accurate.

Opening her wardrobe she spotted a baggy sweater that would cover the worst of the damage on the shirt, and a reasonably clean pair of jeans. Where were her boots? Of course, discarded just inside the door. Just as well Suzanne hadn't come in the night before or she would have gone flat on her face falling over them. Sarah wondered vaguely if she would have been woken up by the noise, given her inebriated state. She picked up her bag and checked the timetable taped to the wall above her desk to see where she was supposed to be in five minutes time. Thank God, only in Langwith, so she could afford ten seconds to scrape the worst of the fur off her teeth and visit the loo on the way. Then a quick dash across the wet grass instead of using the picturesque but meandering path, and she arrived at the door of Professor Ellis' room only two minutes late. Knowing the lecturer's obsession with punctuality and her ritual humiliation of latecomers, the rest of her group had already gone inside. Sarah caught her breath and knocked.

"Enter!" came the imperious command from within.

Sarah turned the doorknob and stuck her head round the door, "Sorry, I'm late, Prof..." she started to say.

"Ah, Miss Martin, good of you to join us. We were awaiting your arrival with bated breath," Ellis smiled in a malignant fashion. Sarah picked her way over sundry scarves and bags to the only vacant chair in the small room, which of course was the furthest from the door, and the nearest to the Professor. She scrabbled in her bag for pen and paper, then looked up, aware for the first time of the various pitying and amused looks on the faces of her three fellow students. Shit and double shit. She should have stayed in bed and forged a medical note.

"Yes, we're waiting for your always entertaining and no doubt thoroughly researched thoughts on the imagery of the metaphysical poets," smirked Ellis.

Sarah stared at the blank piece of paper in front of her. "The chief characteristic of the metaphysicals was of course their drawing on the language of the scientific discoveries of their time," Sarah began to bluff. "This was especially the case with the more well known poems of John Donne, Andrew Marvell and George Herbert." Somehow she managed to speak for another ten minutes, drawing on some deep reserve of long ago reading from before her arrival at university. That was why she had chosen the topic, because she'd had to do a major essay for her A level English tutor. Trying to connect with the conscientious student she'd once been, she concentrated on keeping her breathing slow and even, her voice low and considered, to stave off the panic she could feel bubbling just underneath her hopefully calm exterior.

She wandered to a full stop, then looked up at Ellis' impassive face, having managed to avoid eye contact with her the whole time she had been speaking. What was going on behind those steel black eyes? Why the hell had she got it in for Sarah, and how could Sarah have ever made the mistake of signing up for a double module on creative writing with this woman?

"Hmm, very...interesting," Ellis said at last. "Well, what do the rest of you think?" The other students shifted in their seats, trying to work out from Ellis' tone whether to praise or trash Sarah's effort. Sarah didn't know any of them well and had no great expectations of support. They had long ago recognised in each other that the only thing they shared was a desire to get through this course, whether that meant stepping on each others' work to do so or not.

"I thought you could have paid more attention to Donne's background and the development of religious elements in his work," one said finally, a sandy, freckled male with his gangly legs loosely arranged in front of him. Ellis smiled approvingly, so, taking their cue from him, the other students indulged in an open season of ever more biting criticism. Sarah was now grateful for her numbed, hungover state, as most of the barbed comments passed her by. She bore them no ill will and knew that it was nothing personal. She would have done the same in their position.

At the end of twenty minutes of the assassination of her rambling thoughts, Ellis reined in the dogs and let rip with her own assessment of what Sarah had said. She pulled apart every sentence both for its content and construction. "I was surprised at the number of basic grammatical errors in your presentation, given your entry qualifications onto this course". She flavoured her remarks with some thinly disguised personal remarks about Sarah's intelligence and personal hygiene. "It may help if you prepare yourself appropriately for tutorials, Sarah. I've heard the application of soap does wonders for body odour."

Sarah found that she was less able to let the torrent of malice wash over her, as more than one of the lecturer's taunts found their mark. Why couldn't Ellis see that treating her like a naughty child evoked in Sarah a naughty child's response. "Shan't do anything about my behaviour to please you, "she thought, as Ellis' words stung her into a resentful rage. She adopted what her mother had told her was her most irritating expression when being told off, a kind of half smiling, heavy lidded condescension.

This of course spurred Ellis to make even more vicious remarks in a frustrated effort to evoke some kind of reaction from this student who she believed passionately was the best mind in her entire year but who had steadfastly refused to realise her potential in an appropriately grateful manner under Ellis' tutelage. What would get the girl to write something brilliant again? She'd submitted three very promising pieces of poetry in the last few months, but in between, just this sullen wastrel. She had even given up caring about her appearance.

Professor Ellis tried the one thing that had worked in the past. "Well, Miss Martin," she hissed, "it's obvious that you must be working on something of great importance to have neglected your seminar paper to such an extent, so I look forward to seeing your completed project on 28 May. That will be all for today."

There was a collective indrawn breath from the other students. The date mentioned was a full two weeks before they had to hand in their work. Sarah swallowed and blinked as she took in the implications of Ellis' words. The back of her eyes stung with unshed tears of frustration and a deep sense of the unfairness of her treatment. But she would never show that bitch Ellis any weakness. She smiled lazily, drawing it out, "No problem," she replied, looking down and gathering her things, but not before she'd seen a satisfactory tightening at the edges of the lecturer's lips.

She managed to exit the room, then had to lean against the wall to take in oxygen. The only other girl in the group, a sloe eyed Asian woman known to everyone as Lisa because they couldn't deal with her given name, came up to Sarah to ask if she was alright. "That was a bit steep, what she did," she added.

Sarah managed a weak grin. "Don't worry, I'll manage somehow," she lied. Her words sounded unconvincing even to herself, but Lisa took them at face value and made her escape. Disaster was contagious after all. Sarah braced her shoulders and checked the money in her purse. She was going to need two cheese scones from the snack bar this morning rather than one. Wearily she retraced her steps to Derwent, unconscious of her tutor watching from the window of her study.

Sarah   Now

Excuse

It had been getting rather more difficult to keep taking the poems from Suzanne's desk over the previous few weeks. Because we hadn't been getting on so well for some time, she'd started locking her desk drawers and then hiding the key in different places amongst her things. It had taken me some time to work out the four or five locations which she rotated the key amongst. She had also taken to coming back in unannounced, or at times when she'd agreed she would not be there. Both of us felt let down by the other I guess.

I was disappointed in her adherence to a relationship with Dick that I considered demeaning to her. "How come you are still going out with that creep?" I burst out one day. No reply. Just a stunned silence and a slammed door. The worst of it was I knew why she stuck it out, but of course I could never own up to why. "By the way, I fancy him too," would not have gone down well.

My dependence on stealing her work to survive on my course was gnawing away at my self confidence. I felt that at any minute she would find out and I'd be exposed for the fraud that I was. All of this made me stiff and unresponsive when she was around, so Suzanne felt let down that I had challenged her view of me as her best friend, refusing to conform to the scenes she had reserved for me, and I kept saying the wrong lines.

"Sarah, what on earth is the matter with you?"

"Nothing," became our normal exchange. Having been so close, our falling out was all the more severe.

Ellis had put me between the proverbial rock and the hard place. The more she pushed me, and the harder I tried to write for myself, the more impossible it became, the words retreating out of earshot, over my inner horizon. Even conversation became more difficult, I started forgetting the words for things in everyday speech too. "Are you going to town in your lift?" I once asked some surprised and puzzled classmate, hoping they would save me the bus fare. Well, you get in a lift and go somewhere, as well as into a car. Some vital synaptic link was obviously shorting out.

Prose was no problem. I managed to squeeze out the sentences required to scrape passes in my other modules, and I did eventually buckle down and start spending more time in the library among the book stacks than in the snack bar on its ground floor. I'd done my research and I'd managed to cobble together a skeleton framework to showcase my supposedly brilliant creative poetry. All that was lacking was the damned poetry. I needed some time to sort through the work in Suzanne's drawer to find some that would fit the themes of what I was trying to argue.

I was desperate, the project was due in the next day. There was no possibility of an extension, even though I could probably have taken it through the Student Grievance procedure if I'd been thinking clearly. Ellis' demand that I submit two weeks before everyone else was clearly discriminatory and even in those days I would have been sure to win my case. I had some misplaced sense of outrage, that, "I'll show you, you won't defeat me, oh no". I'd backed myself into a corner and could feel the walls pressing against my shoulder blades. That's the only excuse I can offer for how it all turned out.

Sarah   May 1979

Discovery

Sarah tiptoed up to the door of the room she shared with Suzanne. She didn't know if Suzanne had planned to spend the night with Dick. In any case, she wanted to be in and out of there as fast as possible. Mary from the room next door was already up and making coffee in what passed for the shared kitchen. Really it was just like a wide corridor with a shelf for a Baby Belling and a water heater on the wall which took ages to boil water. Sarah scrabbled in her bag for her elusive keys. Neither her brain nor her fingers seemed to be working this morning.

Yawning, Mary acknowledged her fumbling. "Heavy night then, Sarah?" she said.

"A bit," Sarah acknowledged ruefully, trying to remember the name of the woman she had spent the night with in Wentworth. Alicia? Brenda? No, that was last week. Oh, yes, she'd got it. "Josie's a bit athletic."

In fact, most of her tiredness was due to the fact that the beds in Wentworth were not only narrow singles designed to discourage students from sharing them, but were also constructed in some cunning way so that if either body veered too close to the edge they tipped over suddenly, sending all occupants sliding to the floor in a very unromantic fashion. Once this had happened it was very difficult to right the bed without wedging one of more of you under the desk. She had spent most of the night trying to avoid this scenario, with a resultant lack of sleep.

Mary on the other hand, looked tired but glowing. She swept past Sarah to the bathroom in her brilliant purple silk kimono. She was an imposing woman, over six feet tall, and broad with it, masses of black hair which she had clearly not inherited from her father, some balding singer with a sixties folk group still doing the rounds.

Sarah found her keys at last, and deliberately lined up the room key with the keyhole. As she managed to connect the two, the door to Mary's room opened again, and a short man, wrapped only in a hand towel, scuttled out towards the toilets at the other end of the corridor. Sarah paused in the act of turning the key. Wasn't that Bernard, the geek of the year? She dimly remembered he'd tried to chat her up once, and Jules had had to firmly move him aside when he persisted in refusing to take no for an answer. She was surprised to see him, he was normally in the chemistry lab across the road in Alcuin by this time.

Before she could open her door, more noises from the next room were followed by the emergence of Stefano, the "Italian stallion", as he was known around the college, similarly attired in a towel and looking like he'd had a shower already, rivulets of sweat running down his hairy torso. Unlike Bernard, Stefano paused in the doorway of the room, to check whether he had an audience, then, assured of Sarah's attention, smirked and winked at her before swaggering off towards the showers. Mary sailed back into the kitchen, collected up the three mugs of steaming black coffee and with a brilliant smile vanished back into her room and closed the door.

Sarah blinked. Not only had she never seen this amount of traffic in the corridor this early in the morning, but she was having to readjust her picture of Mary as a straightlaced, celibate goody-goody who was a leading member of the God Squad, or the Young Christians as they called themselves. One of them had even fainted in the kitchen when they came for a meeting in Mary's room that time she and Suzanne, at the beginning of the year when they were still talking to each other, were preparing a fish supper which involved gutting the fish in the sink. As neither of them had ever done it before it had been a hilarious and messy process. The sight of fish blood and entrails all over the place, along with the smell, had been too much for one of the participants on her way to the prayer circle and she'd keeled over, narrowly avoiding smacking her head on the edge of the formica work top.

She and Suzanne had entertained Jules and Dick later with a recitation of events, together with an action replay. "Blood up to my elbows!" crowed Suzanne, as Sarah had sunk gracefully to the floor. The evening, fuelled by cheap wine, finished off with her and Jules stumbling back to Jules' room, where Jules had done a hilarious impersonation of a salmon fighting its way back upstream wrapped in her sheet before the amount of noise they'd been making caused her neighbours in the shared house to bang on the walls and they had to be quiet and swim in each others' juices. This led to more noise and more wall banging.

The joy of remembering that evening was quickly replaced by an ache at all she had lost in the last six months. Sarah opened the door. The curtains were not drawn—a good sign, probably meant that Suzanne had not slept here last night. Sarah nudged the door shut with her heel and walked over to her wardrobe, sorting through shirts and jeans till she found a clean one of each, then rooting through her chest of drawers for clean underwear.

Her fingers brushed a pile of papers, stuffed underneath some tee-shirts. Drawing one out, she saw that it was one of Suzanne's poems. She must have forgotten to put them back after sorting out the ones she needed for her project, the project which was due in today and which sat, neatly completed and snug, in her bag. The hours in the library before her assignation with Josie had paid off, and now she would be out of Ellis' clutches for ever. She pushed it back with the others, she'd sort that out later. Lastly she picked up shower gel and a towel. Hopefully the two men had finished using the facilities and were now back in Mary's room. Just as well she hadn't been here last night, it would have been noisy.

As she turned to go back out of the room, she noticed Suzanne's red leather ankle boot, sticking out from the edge of her bed on the other side of the room, underneath the window. A glimpse of the day when Suzanne had bought them in the market in York flashed up from her memory. All at once, her eyes took in the rest of Suzanne's body lying motionless and fully dressed on the bed, one arm outstretched with the fingers drooping stiffly towards the floor, where the contents of Suzanne's ubiquitous shoulder bag lay scattered, the bag itself upended on the carpet. She took a half step towards her, hoping that she could just be asleep, but also registering that there was no breath moving in and out of Suzanne's chest.

Another hesitant step, then something snapped. She dropped what she was holding, ran to Suzanne, with one touch she confirmed her suspicion. The flesh was cold and hard, like wood. Without a pause she ran from the room, slamming the door open, running next door to Mary, hammering on her door, shouting, screaming, "Help, I need help, it's Suzanne! Mary, open up, please."

Which, long seconds later, Mary did, rewrapping herself in her kimono, her frown of annoyance melting as she saw the look on Sarah's face.

"Bernard, Stefano, see what's the matter," she instructed the two men lounging on her bed as she pulled Sarah inside and sat her on a large squashy armchair covered in a plaid rug, which was surprisingly comfortable. Mary further upset Sarah's image of her by pouring a large measure of brandy from a bottle of Remy Martin she plucked from the bookshelves into a mug decorated with two pigs copulating and the legend, 'Making Bacon'.

Sarah automatically took a gulp of the dark brown liquid and realised too late that she was going to be sick, so that when the men returned Mary was holding her head over the sink as she retched and gagged. Whatever look passed between them, Sarah couldn't see, but Mary swiftly issued new instructions.

"Bernard, go to the porter's lodge and get them to call for an ambulance. Stefano, go wake up the Dean. And boys, get your trousers on first!" Sarah gratefully let Mary assume control, allowed herself to be laid on Mary's bed, covered with the plaid rug from the chair, while Mary wiped her forehead with a cool flannel.

"Drink this, "she was instructed, this time a glass of clear, cold water. She felt her eyelids drooping, weighed down by the aftermath of the rush of adrenalin at finding the body, as well as the lack of sleep and the strain of being constantly on guard against discovery of her plagiarism over the past months. She was aware of Mary moving around the room, of a ray of sunlight slanting in, catching the swirling dance of dust in its tracks. Some voices, mostly male, Mary's amongst them, footsteps back and forth along the corridor. Somehow it all seemed very far away, it didn't matter, she didn't have to worry. She let sleep take her down into the softness of Mary's quilt.

Suzanne   May 1979

BIRTHS, MARRIAGES, DEATHS
DEATHS

Mercer, Suzanne. Beloved daughter of Joan and Gordon, May 27th 1979. Deeply missed.

LOCAL GIRL DIES

Local girl, Suzanne Mercer, 21, has died at York University, where she had won a place to study biochemisty. Suzanne had suffered from asthma since she was a child, although this did not stop her taking a full part in the activities at Saltash Upper School. She died of a chronic attack last week.

Tragically, Suzanne's inhaler, which could have prevented her death, was found underneath her bed. Although she shared a room, her roommate, Sarah Martin, was out for the evening, and did not discover Suzanne's body until the morning. "Normally, the two girls are inseparable and are always together," said college dean Peter Barnaby. "It was just awful bad luck that on the one night that Suzanne misplaced her inhaler and had an attack, her friend was not there to help her."

Suzanne's parents, Joan and Gordon Mercer who live in Burraton, were too upset to comment. The Mercers moved to Saltash twenty years ago, before Mr Mercer's retirement from the Royal Navy dockyard in Devonport.

Sarah 1979–1980

Transition

Sarah passed Professor Ellis' class and the rest of the year, due in part to the mitigating circumstances of finding Suzanne's body which were argued by her personal tutor at the exam board. Her parents commiserated and were surprised and delighted when she took up their offer of coming back to Cumbria for the summer to recuperate. She took a temporary job in Barrow-in-Furness at the local education authority's office so that there would be no danger of meeting any of her acquaintances from school. She even managed to pick up with Paul, a local boy-made-good who had returned to Grange from his time abroad in the merchant navy with a substantial amount of money in the bank, plus a sports car and a motor launch on Lake Windermere. His mother still lived in the town and Sarah was invited round for dinner to be viewed as possible wife material.

She could see a gleam of hope in her parents' eyes that she might marry and settle down nearby. Whilst it had been their ambition that at least one of their children should go to university, they had no conception of what difference that might make to someone's life. They were upset that she no longer seemed to accept the Daily Telegraph's view as a true reflection of the world. They couldn't understand what anyone would actually do with an English degree except maybe teach, and were puzzled by Sarah's emphatic refusal to consider it as a career.

"Maybe a doctor's receptionist?" her mother ventured one day at the breakfast table.

"Do you need to finish your degree now you've got a job here?" her colleagues at the office asked her.

"Why don't you get married?" her Dad suggested.

"Who to?" Sarah replied.

To their collective disappointment, she returned to York in September to complete her degree. Eventually, Paul stopped writing to her and she heard from her mother that he'd married a reformed Kirsty. She wished them both well. She made sure she took no more creative writing options and slogged through her final year, scraping a lower second class honours degree.

She and Dick finally consummated all those years of underground lust, so that instead of coming home after graduation she moved in with him in his back to back terrace in Leeds, becoming the first of her siblings to live with a partner rather than getting married. Her parents took it surprisingly well, she thought, probably because Dick was something respectable by this time.

"A college lecturer," murmured her mother, approvingly. Sarah submitted to the waves of inertia which had been pulling at her since Suzanne's death. She let the undertow take her beneath the surface. She drifted between temporary clerical work, working at the check out of the local supermarket and behind the bar in the Shoulder of Mutton. She refused to try for any job that might actually tax her brain, as though thinking might open up that Pandora's box of thoughts which had remained firmly clamped shut since that pivotal night.

Sarah   1979–1980

Metamorphosis

The changes began subtly. It started with Sarah noticing a few stray red hairs in her brush one morning. She rationalised it by assuming that Suzanne must have borrowed her brush at some time, because it was clear from her reflection in the mirror above the sink that her hair was still most definitely blonde, although the dark roots were showing through. She decided there and then to grow out the colour, went and had dark streaks put through the gold so that she didn't look too much like a shaving brush as the dark gradually took over. Then, a few months later, more red hairs, a tinge of auburn about the brown which had never been there before.

Some things just seemed to be coincidental. Sarah finally succumbed to the campus malaise and bought a copy of Rumours by Fleetwood Mac. Not only that, but their previous album too. Maybe it had been the years of listening to Suzanne play it over and over again that had worn her down, but she found to her surprise that she liked it.

The most worrying thing was that the nightmares about Suzanne's fatal asthma attack started to transfer to daylight hours. Sarah felt short of breath, knew she was looking for something but couldn't find it, back in the room they had once shared, feeling a vice grip her throat, harder and harder. The first time she went into the bar in Derwent she thought it was just the amount of cigarette smoke that caused her to cough uncontrollably, a dry hacking that meant she had to leave after only one pint.

She was playing squash the following week when she felt giddy in the middle of a rally, missed her shot, felt her chest tighten, had to stop to catch her breath, leaning against the smooth cool walls of the court.

Then she had an attack in Ellis' final seminar at the end of exam week, where the group had gathered to receive feedback on their final projects. None of them expected to do well, they had all by now accepted that getting through the module would be a matter of survival rather than any hope for good grades. As Professor Ellis picked up Sarah's project from the file, she felt the room start to close in, lights danced before her eyes, heaving gasps broke out from her chest, Sarah could feel her throat begin to close up, her nose and mouth fighting desperately to admit oxygen to her body. In slow motion, she saw all the heads in the room turn so that all four pairs of eyes were directed at her. The sounds of their breathing seemed far too loud, especially as they were so far away. Edges of grey appeared around the picture as she slowly slid to the floor, noticing with detachment that the carpet, which she had never really seen before now, was a deep mauve, with a short cropped pile. As suddenly as it started it was all over, before the others could rise from their seats or get to her, her breath returned, the darkness receded, she raised herself up on hands that were not even shaking.

"It wasn't that bad," remarked Ellis, dryly. "In fact, Sarah, I was just about to say that this is the best piece of work you've turned in throughout the whole course. Some of the poetry was a bit uneven, but on the whole, excellent. If only you'd spell checked it and given more thought to the presentation, linked your themes to the subject matter of the poems, it would have been worth a first. As it is, I've given you a high upper second."

Sarah manoeuvred herself back onto her chair, aware that it was now the rest of the students in the room who were breathless. No one had ever heard Ellis praise anything that any of them had written before. Sarah sat blankly through the rest of the tutorial, collected her work from Ellis without looking at her, thankful to have escaped from the torture of her oppression at last. She didn't see Ellis reach out a hand to try and detain her, intending to offer her congratulations and an enquiry as to whether she might consider writing up the piece for publication in a literary journal the professor edited.

Things quietened down over the summer, although Sarah unconsciously stopped going to places or taking part in things that might set off another attack. Her parents welcomed what they thought was a more normal lifestyle, working at the Council and going out with Paul, although they also worried that she was perhaps a little too quiet.

When she returned to York in September the attacks came back. She had to give up playing squash in favour of slow and steady jogging round the paths on campus and the surrounding plain around Heslington and up to Fulford. That had to stop too when the weather turned cold and her lungs ached with the freezing morning air. She still found it impossible to sit in the college bar, and that started to extend to all the other bars on campus, as well as the Charles XII in Heslington and the Spreadeagle in town, regular haunts when Sarah and Suzanne used to indulge in bar crawls throughout their friendship.

Finally, she consulted the doctor at the medical centre, who took her blood, made her breathe into tubes and pronounced that, "There's nothing physically wrong with you," laying stress on the "physically". He continued, "If it helps you should consider treating your symptoms with an asthma inhaler".

Sarah looked at the contraption the doctor held out to her. She had to stop herself from flinching as she took it, she had not seen one of these since Suzanne had used one to quell an attack a few weeks before her death. They'd been having an argument on one of the rare occasions when they were both in their shared room, something about the washing up.

She did have one or two attacks throughout the winter, but then nothing for about six months and she thought that she'd got over whatever it was that was causing her to react in this way. When she moved in with Dick, it all blew up again. They had to replace all the pillows with non-feather ones, even the cushions on his old sofa were suspect. In the end, she had to carry an inhaler with her wherever she went, just in case. The attacks didn't go away until she got pregnant.

Dick 1977–1980

Fidelity

The funny thing is, it was always Sarah I fancied more than Suzanne, right from the first. But then Sam told me, "She's a dyke." When I saw her with Jules, I thought he was right. I'd been a bit dubious, because I knew he fancied her and probably wanted a clear field for himself. Still, Suzanne had got her claws into me by then and it was flattering, I have to admit. No man is going to turn down something when it's offered on a plate. She made it so obvious. I would have been a fool to refuse, or at least I would have been, in my thinking at the time. Twenty year old men are not known for their ability to think with their brains rather than their pricks, nor many older ones either.

Suzanne was not really my type at all. Gorgeous of course, with those big green eyes, but a bit too frail and clingy for my liking. The problem was she always seemed to be around, she always seemed to assume that we were a long term item. So the relationship just kind of limped on from week to week.

I'd told Suzanne I had a girlfriend at home in Sheffield, Janet. We'd been going out together since sixth form and she was my first great love, the first girl I ever slept with and I supposed I'd always assumed that we would get married some day. The women at university didn't mean anything and I never told Janet about them. Suzanne seemed to interpret it that I was just waiting for the right time to tell Janet that it was all over between her and me, but in reality it was Janet who dumped me for some guy on her psychology course. Then I was so angry and hurt that I did a really daft thing. I burnt my bridges with Janet by telling her not just about Suzanne but about all the others too, ever since I'd been at York. So when she broke up with this other guy, and I called to ask if we could get back together, she just laughed at me.

I wasn't faithful to Suzanne either. There was even a time when I picked up someone in the bar at college while Suzanne was there, but she was so gullible she seemed to believe the most outrageous excuses. The worst one was when I said I'd been so drunk after a party that I'd passed out and woken up under a tree in the grounds of Heslington Hall. In fact, I'd got off with some woman in Langwith and spent the night in her room and I was so shagged out the next day we didn't surface until lunch time. If I'd been out in town and hadn't managed to score, I knew I could always go round to Suzanne's room at 3am and she would let me in.

I can't believe, looking back, that I was such a callous bastard. I hope that I would have told her eventually that we couldn't carry on. I tried to justify it to myself that I kept on lying because I knew if I told her the truth about me she would have been devastated. I did try once or twice to suggest that we have a trial separation, or not see so much of each other, but she never took the hint. I would have had to be brutally honest in order to get through to her that I was basically a shit and she should have nothing more to do with me.

I still feel guilty that the first emotion I had when hearing that she'd died was one of relief that I wouldn't have to deal with breaking up with her. I suppose, if she hadn't died, Suzanne might have got her wish, we would have just drifted along into marriage and children. How weak that sounds. Do men often do something because they are too scared to stand up and say, "I'm not happy in this relationship, I want more"? Yet I didn't learn, I did the same thing with Sarah later. It's still hard to admit that I never loved Suzanne, even though she was funny and feisty and knew what she wanted. I suppose I just kept hoping that she would see for herself that she was worth much more.

It was tougher to deceive her once she had moved into that shared room with Sarah. She went on about how, "It'll be cheaper for both of us," and that, "the room is about four times the size of a single. Anyway, Sarah and me are best mates and we can share food and cooking." The real killer was, "Both of us probably won't be using own rooms much anyway, so it's crazy to pay for two when one will do." I knew what she meant, Suzanne would expect to be staying in my room more, which was the last thing I wanted. She went ahead anyway and I went along with it, but it became more and more complicated to have other flings and in the end I just got too lazy to keep on lying to her.

So I became faithful by default, and we settled into a kind of mock domesticity, undemanding and unexciting. I got into the habit of having Suzanne in my bed most nights during the week, even having dinner altogether every Saturday night with Sarah and her latest squeeze.

I know it was hard for Sarah not to feel guilty when we got together after Suzanne died. I couldn't tell her that I'd never loved Suzanne in the way that both she and Sarah seemed to assume I had, that I was upset of course and sorry that Suzanne had died so young, but not devastated at the loss of the love of my life. After all, she already knew that I was a lying dickhead who'd been cheating on Suzanne from the day we'd met. At the beginning there was a charade on my part, playing the part of the grieving lover, and it was natural that Sarah and I should spend so much time together, because we'd supposedly we'd loved Suzanne the most and so we knew how the other felt.

I'd got myself into another impossible situation. I'd wanted Sarah from the start, but I couldn't let her know that because she was Suzanne's best friend. Then when Suzanne died, I had to keep going along with the picture she had of me that I was devoted to Suzanne's memory, so I thought, because if I hadn't I would have revealed myself to be the lying shit that I was. Eventually I found out that even Suzanne had known about my rutting behaviour all along, so I need never have bothered keeping up the charade.

We wasted almost a year, in a kind of highly charged emotional limbo, when every time I was with her I had to physically restrain myself from just taking her beautiful head in my hands and kissing her forehead and her eyelids and her lips, tracing the line of her neck with my tongue. The wanting was unbearable, and yet I couldn't stay away from her. Amazingly for me, I didn't want any other women, although I had plenty of offers of consolation for my supposedly broken heart. Sarah even tried to persuade me to sleep with some of them, dammit. I couldn't give faithfulness to Suzanne when she was alive, ironically she only achieved that by her death. Which only convinced Sarah that I was finally guilty about the way I had treated her.

It was a relief that Sarah had seemed to have given up sleeping around too, so I didn't have to listen to tales of her sexual exploits with others. She'd split up with Jules some time before Suzanne's death, and gone through a real wild child period, picking up women and men in bars and discos and parties in town and on campus. After Suzanne died, she just gave up on all of that, thank goodness. Yet I knew she wasn't happy, and of course my fantasy was that she just needed to find the right man, and if only that man could be me. It was incredible that that was how it turned out to be.

There were times when I looked at Sarah, her head bent over a book or nursing the baby, and I felt a warmth well up from my gut and wash right over me. It was so right, I couldn't imagine it being any other way, with any other person. Still can't, even now. If only it hadn't been born out of such a tragedy.

Sarah and Dick   May 1980

Consummation

The first night Sarah and Dick slept together began like so many others. After Suzanne's death they had started to go around together, as though by talking about their experience of her they could somehow bring her back. Their conversation at first was full of "Do you remember when she...?"

"One time when Suzanne and I..." Sarah found it surprising that after only a few weeks they had both exhausted their store of memories, as though neither of them had really known Suzanne at all.

It was difficult to feel sad all of the time. The first time they went to a fringe mime show at the Arts Centre on Walmgate and actually laughed, she felt guilty afterwards, as though by continuing with her life she was negating Suzanne's. She of course had the additional guilt of feeling responsible for Suzanne's death, something which replayed itself in her head again and again, both sleeping and waking. The dreams where she felt herself suffocating as she watched Suzanne struggling for breath, her chest heaving with effort, her hands clawing at the sheets and reaching for Sarah, when she woke to find herself drenched with sweat and tangled in her own bedclothes, were the reason she stopped sleeping with anyone. She'd picked up a woman in Derwent bar once, and a man at the Vanbrugh bop, but she never stayed the night or invited them back to her place. In the end, she found herself incapable of even going through the motions of flirting, she didn't want to be burdened with any deeper intimacy.

She avoided Jules, so that Jules would never be tempted to offer her the consolation she so desperately needed. A short while after Suzanne's death, Jules had come to Sarah's room. "I heard, I wanted to say how sorry I am," she said, hesitating at the threshold as Sarah resolutely blocked the doorway, not asking her in, not giving in to the screeching yearning of her body to take a step back and let Jules enfold her in her unbearably comforting embrace.

"Thought you'd come and try your luck again, did you," Sarah growled, her throat tight. Jules looked as though she had been slapped. She said nothing, reached her hand out as though to touch Sarah. Sarah flinched as if she had been stung by a wasp. She wouldn't look at Jules, so the other woman just turned and walked away down the corridor. Sarah watched her retreating back, then closed the door and wept silently, feeling all the hurt and loneliness wash up over her like a tidal wave, blowing her way through a whole box of tissues as the snot and tears threatened to suffocate her.

The college had moved her out of the room she had shared with Suzanne, so it was back to a single room, although not as poky as the corridor width cubicle she had occupied in her first year. This one was square, with a window the full length of one wall giving a view down onto the college, the lake and the water filled courtyard with fountains. She rescued a battered cane armchair from a skip in Heslington, so she could sit and watch the sky and the reflections of the clouds and the drooping willows in the water, her mind in neutral. Her work assignments were neatly piled on the desk, and working was a way of keeping the waking nightmares at bay. Her tutors had given her long extensions on all of her course work, but she found no problem in handing them in on time. How ironic that Suzanne's death had finally made her get organised. If only she had been like this before. After that thought she would be back in that waking nightmare again, hearing the rasping of Suzanne's dying breath, smelling the sickly sweet sweat of panic, feeling her body freeze into numbness.

Sometimes it all seemed so impossible, she could not believe that it had happened. It did not stop her continuing to plagiarise Suzanne's work after her death. It was like something out of a novel or a film, not real life at all.

She made it to the end of the year. Luckily there were no exams at the end of the second year, although the pain would only be put off until the next summer's finals. Jules graduated, and sent Sarah a card with her degree result—an Upper Second—along with the date of her graduation ceremony in July, an unspoken invitation. Sarah knew she wouldn't go, and she knew Jules would know that too, but she was stunned by the depth of love it showed, that Jules was prepared to keep on letting her know that she was there for Sarah whenever she was needed. Sarah kept the card under her pillow, and when the nights were long she stroked it so that the writing became blurred and illegible.

Term started in October with Sarah's bank account unusually in credit. Working for the summer and not travelling, having minimal living expenses at home, had restored her to financial health.

Not so Dick, who had celebrated scraping an upper second class honours degree by taking off around Europe by rail. His excuse was that it was the last time he'd be able to take off that amount of time and also travel on a student ticket. He'd come back with wild travelling tales.

"We had to sleep on the platform in Prague because we missed our connection to Budapest. It turned out all right because the guard who came to turf us out of the waiting room in the morning had a brother who lives in York, would you believe, and he invited us back to his house for breakfast."

He'd worked in a bar in Barcelona for a week to raise money for his journey home. "It was on the Playa Real, this wonderful old square near the Ramblas. Huge palm trees, wonderful arched windows. It wasn't until I'd been there a couple of days that I found out it was the centre of the Barcelona drug dealing scene."

On his return he found that all the graduate openings had been filled with more diligent students who had given up their last summer of freedom. "I don't feel ready to work either," he told Sarah. So he retreated back into academia and managed to get a research post in Leeds, science graduates being thin on the ground that year, and even managing to talk his local authority into giving him a grant to pursue a PhD.

"Perpetual student," scoffed Sarah, but it did give them the opportunity to continue their easy comradeship. Whilst Dick was still violently overdrawn, the fact that he had an income persuaded his bank manager to give him a loan so that he could buy a car—a beat up old MG Midget with a soft top that didn't quite fit. Luckily the heater worked. He would turn up two or three times a week, and he and Sarah would go to the cinema, get standby tickets at the Theatre Royal, or just go to the pub.

Sarah found being celibate, although not her choice originally, rather restful. She had begun to think of herself as sexless, not needing the complications of physical relationships. So she was surprised by the resurfacing of that old passion and chemistry the night they managed to get tickets to the opera in Leeds. She was an opera virgin; he was a committed fan.

"Why not come over to Leeds for a change?" Dick suggested. She caught the train after her lectures had finished, it was hardly a scenic route through the grey and untidy back of the industrial city. She couldn't imagine wanting to live here, she thought, not after the old stone and quiet history of York.

She'd packed light, a clean pair of knickers and a toothbrush, a rugby shirt for tomorrow, dressing up her jeans for the evening with a silk shirt and pearls, wearing her favourite blue suede boots as always. She couldn't imagine what she would do when they eventually wore out, they'd been resoled and re-heeled constantly, but the suede was starting to show bald patches on the toes and heels now.

It was a short walk from the station to the bus stop, but the chill wind cut through her jeans, making her wrap her familiar leather flying jacket more tightly around her. Even though it was lined with sheepskin, she shivered. The wind managed to blow right down the neck of the jacket, causing an icy blade to trace her spine. With a shock she realised that it was nearly a year to the day since Suzanne had died. The bus came almost immediately, its interior was warm and moist with the smell of packed animals, but the chill stayed with her. Gazing out the window at the grey streets and crowded pavements, she hardly noticed as the bus wound its way out along the Chapeltown Road, the city centre giving way to brick terraces and sari shops. She nearly missed her stop, jumping to her feet as the bus was about to move off again, smiling a weak apology at the driver who shook his head wearily.

Dick answered the door at her knock, wiping his hands on a tea towel. The lounge on his little back to back terrace had no hallway to buffer it, so it was fortunate that the house was south facing. It didn't make much difference today though.

"You look frozen," said Dick, drawing her inside and shutting the door. He lit the gas fire and placed Sarah in front of it, giving her a welcoming hug. She could feel the backs of her legs starting to burn through the denim, but the deep freeze inside her refused to budge. "I've cooked chilli," Dick said, drawing the cork from a bottle of Merlot, "we can eat as soon as you like."

"Right away, please," Sarah replied, hoping that the spicy food would chase away the coldness.

They ate balancing plates on their knees, a bowl of salad and a plateful of garlic bread between them on the floor. Sarah guzzled the red wine gratefully, feeling the alcohol do its work and numb those parts she didn't want to think about.

"What's this opera about then?" she quizzed him.

"Surprise," grinned Dick, munching on some garlic bread.

"Not too much wailing, is there?"

"No, hardly any at all. Basically, two blokes fancy the same woman."

Ouch. A reversal of her and Suzanne then. "Has it got a happy ending?"

"Oh come on, it's opera," he laughed.

By the time they got to the theatre, having managed to squeeze Dick's car into the only free street parking place left along Briggate, she felt relaxed and eager to sample the unknown delights of the Pearl Fishers.

She was surprised to find how much of the music was familiar to her, the result of filching by advertising executives, subliminally inserting bits of the opera into their adverts for cars and airlines. Although the production was sung in English, only a few of the words were decipherable, and she let the music submerge her, succumbing to the harmonies. The duet between the male singers early in the first act almost made her weep, she closed her eyes and rested her head on Dick's shoulder as the melody soared.

As they came out of the theatre into the chill night air, she slid her arm through his, eyes shining, and leaned to give him a kiss on the cheek in gratitude for persuading her to experiment with opera. Or at least, she had intended it to be a kiss on the cheek, but he turned his head towards her at the last minute and their lips met briefly. She pulled back, but not straight away, the touch of his cool, dry lips feeling strangely natural, as though they had done this many times before. "Thanks, that was great," she said, to hide her embarrassment, then blushed at the thought that he would misunderstand what she meant.

Dick didn't reply, just smiled, and they walked arm in arm in companionable silence back to his car. Uncharacteristically, he opened the passenger door for her first, saying, "Your chariot awaits, madam."

She slid into the worn leather interior while he walked around to the driver's side, feeling an almost forgotten but familiar warmth in her groin, her body languid but her mind racing. As they drove back to Dick's house, Annie Lennox played on the tape deck.

"Love is a stranger in an open car," she sang. If only Dick had been a stranger, Sarah thought. Surely they could not change from friends to lovers after all this time, there was too much between them and it would destroy the friendship that she had come to regard as a stable foundation. Even as she tried to convince herself that there had been nothing in that split second of lip contact, marshalling the logical arguments as to why nothing would or could happen, determining to resist even if Dick should make a move to take up the brief promise of that moment, her body was preparing itself for passion.

It was a relief and a disappointment when Dick simply opened another bottle of wine and put Fleetwood Mac on the stereo. Not Rumours, but their previous album, her favourite. She settled into the deep red velvet cushions of his old sofa, slipping her shoes off and drawing her feet up. Dick came to sit next to her and she leaned against him as he put his arm around her shoulders, so that she fitted snugly into his armpit. Dick's fingertips traced the line of her waist through her shirt, the fire hissed as it warmed the room, the wine ran into all the corners of her brain and switched off her whirling thoughts. Sarah closed her eyes and was dimly aware of Dick taking the wine glass gently from her hand and placing it on the floor.

"I've been afraid of changing, 'cos I built my life around you," sang Stevie Nicks. "But time makes you bolder, even children get older, and I'm getting older too." Sarah felt she could be singing those words herself.

Her shirt had got bunched up and Dick was stroking her skin now, his fingers making all the fine hairs stand up. Her lips parted, they felt dry so she licked them. Her breathing slowed and deepened, she was having difficulty doing anything but experience the intense waves of pleasure that his fingertips created on her skin. She felt him bend to kiss the top of her head, and this time it was Sarah who turned her head, deliberately seeking his mouth with her own. For a split second Dick was still, then she felt his lips respond and the contact deepened into a slow, lengthy kiss. Sarah moaned as all the years of suppressed longing emerged in the moment.

Dick lifted her shirt over her head and spread his hands to cup her breasts in his palms. Then he was fumbling with her jeans and she was naked beneath him, feeling the soft worn velvet against her back as he bent his head to take her nipple in his mouth. She felt his hot tongue teasing her erect as his hands slid down over her hips to feel if she was ready for him. His fingers explored the warm wet cave, tantalisingly tracing around her clitoris, making her shudder and moan. He drew back, undressing as he looked down at her. She felt vulnerable under his inspection. Just when she felt he would enter her, at last, he paused, with his hard penis resting against the moist opening. She couldn't wait, she spread her legs and reached out to grasp his buttocks and pull him into her. As she felt him fill her up, the warmth in her groin spread to her chest, tears pricked at the corners of her eyes. She clasped him to her desperately, biting his neck, moving against him in primal abandon.

All too soon it was over. Dick groaned and shuddered. He opened his eyes to see Sarah's questioning look, gasped an apology, "Sorry, couldn't help it," laughed, collapsed on top of her, apologised again. He managed to roll sideways so that he didn't crush her and they lay side by side, still joined, Sarah nestled against his broad hairy chest.

"My god, after all that time, thirty seconds of passion," she laughed. Then they were both laughing, at the ridiculousness of all those years of passion spent in a few moments. Somewhere inside her Sarah felt something open, a tension released, there was a feeling of homecoming.

Sarah — Now

Seduction

When I look at Dick, after all these years, I can still remember the electric charge from his fingers stroking my skin for the first time. It all seems so inevitable now, although at the time it didn't feel like it was planned, it just arose out of the situation. The whole evening felt so sharp, the luscious music, the cold outside, the warmth of the wine. I'd always thought that it was me in control, that I would have to be the one who made the first move because I'd been so brazen with all my relationships. So when Dick started to seduce me I was disorientated, I couldn't work out what was going on, couldn't quite believe it. And I was overwhelmed by how much I wanted him still, and by how much I wanted him to take control, to take me, as though I was the archetype of all those passive heroines in slushy romances that I'd scorned as an independent feminist.

My rational mind fought it and I was out of there the next morning without a backward glance, determined it was a one off, even toying with the idea of never seeing Dick again. Of course I did, and it was the same as before, we were easy in each other's company, the years of friendship had not gone away. We slept together again, and again, and eventually I even came. Never having done so before with a man I was taken by surprise that it was possible.

Somehow I managed to finish my degree, and even scrape an Lower Second, even though I wasn't getting much sleep—Dick saw to that. I can't imagine how he managed to hold onto his research post either, we seemed to be always in bed or travelling back and forth from York to Leeds. So when term finished it seemed natural to move to Leeds, that grey town I'd never liked, full of grimy Victorian office blocks stuck alongside modern acreages of plate glass, scarred with the worst of '60s planning, huge intersections and uninspiring tower blocks, just until I decided what I wanted to do with my life. Then suddenly it was autumn, and my Dad was diagnosed with cancer, and he died the following spring. It never seemed the right time to make a decision, so I never made one, it got made for me.

Dick   Now

Seduction

I planned that evening. I'd wanted Sarah for so long. Opera was the only thing that was going on in Leeds that we couldn't see in York, so it was the only thing I could suggest to get her to come and stay over at my house. Her college room wasn't really conducive to seduction, too many memories of student life and paper thin walls where you could hear the couple in the next room having sex. I remembered a night when I'd stayed with Suzanne in the old room, when we'd heard a woman crying and moaning—we'd thought she might be being attacked. I'd even climbed onto the roof of the walkway outside the first floor window, ready to intervene, before I realised that it was just a particularly noisy orgasm performance. Suzanne and I had to stuff the sheets in our mouths to stop from laughing out loud. I didn't want to provide that kind of entertainment for Sarah's neighbours.

I'd spoken to another research student at work who knew about such things as to what he would recommend for a first timer. But I didn't want to go in blind, I wanted to make sure I wouldn't make a fool of myself, as I'd told Sarah I was an opera fan, that I went all the time, that she should try it out with me. So I'd been to the opera earlier in the week just to check it out.

The night we went together, even the weather was helpful, a sudden cold snap, so lots of excuses for hugs. I worked hard to create the right atmosphere. I chose the wine, the food, the music. The opera was successful, Sarah loved it, she even kissed me on the way out. I didn't want to rush her though, didn't want to blow it, kept my cool till we got home, more wine, snuggling up on the sofa. At one point I thought I'd misjudged it, she seemed to be falling asleep, her mouth fell open, her body was heavy against me. I took her wine glass in case it spilled, not that it would have made much impression on the paisley carpet I'd inherited with the house.

That woke her and I knew it was now or never, so I made my move. Her skin was so smooth, she was so languid and compliant after all the wine, although I thought at one moment she was going to panic and want me to stop. But then she opened up and pulled me inside her. I can still remember the overwhelming embrace of her cunt, silky wet velvet, it can still make me hard just to think about it. So I did blow it, all those years and then sensory overload, I couldn't stop myself, just felt it roller coaster up from the base of my prick, up to the top of my head, down to my toes. I felt so stupid, Sarah lying there beneath me, looking at me with those big wide questioning blue eyes. Thank God she thought it was funny.

Even though she left in the morning before I was awake, slipping out of the house to catch the early bus back to the station, so that I woke to her smell on empty sheets, I knew she'd be back. It felt so right, like we'd always been lovers. I couldn't get enough of her, I spent all my spare time driving over to York, or picking her up from the station. One time we were so desperate for each other we barely made it inside the house before tearing our clothes off and making love right there on the sofa like the first time. We had the most lusty, graphic phone conversations, I'd get hard just hearing her say, "Hello, Dick." Another evening I stopped the car in a tiny side lane on the way to the pub we were going to, outside York in some village on the Ouse, and had her on the still warm bonnet of the MG. We'd just managed to get our clothes back on when the police arrived. It turned out the lane was the driveway to some big house and somebody had thought we might be planning to burgle it.

The first time she came, it was electric, she was so moist and soft when I entered her afterwards. I felt pretty pleased with myself when she told me it was the first time it had happened for her with a man. When she finished her degree, I asked, "Do you want to move in with me, just while you decide what you want to do, nothing heavy, no pressure". She fell for it.

Sarah   1967

Parents

I always loved the water when I was a child, just like my daughter Zanne does. We always used to go on holiday to the seaside, north Wales or the east coast. The water was freezing but clear, I loved to swim with my head under the waves, eyes wide open and aching with salt, looking at the sand and pebbles on the sea bottom. We used to stay on the beach for as long as possible, I don't suppose that there was as much to do with kids then as there is now.

My dad liked swimming too, and I used to feel a special connection with him because of that. My mother never went in the water at all that I can remember, she would just sit in her swimming costume, if it was warm enough, on one of the folding chairs that my dad had carried from the boot of the car. She would always insist that we ate our picnic at noon, then, "You must have at least an hour's rest before you go back in the water, or else you'll get cramp", just like Suzanne's mother's advice to her. I sometimes wonder where mothers get these snippets of information from, and when will it be my turn to acquire some? Maybe Zanne will have the same feeling about things I've said one day.

We had one holiday in Cornwall, which is why I warmed to Suzanne when she said she'd come from there. We stayed in a little guest house in Fowey. I was about eight, and Debs and Noah were off with their own friends. Debs was youth hostelling round Windermere, Noah had earned enough at his part time job for a package to Ibiza. I had a little room above the front door, with a huge sash window which looked out across the river to Polruan. It was a real treat, normally we'd stay in a caravan. We'd come all that way because the Whites, who were friends of my parents from Grange, had moved back to Cornwall where they had both been born and bought the guest house. Mrs White was plump, blonde and short. She had soft roly poly arms and always wore a pink cotton housecoat with a variety of flowered aprons. She always called me "my lover" in that wonderful Cornish burr.

Normally a fussy eater, I had bacon and eggs every morning. I ate practically everything she cooked, including vegetables. My mother, who'd been fond of complaining that my eating habits were sending her round the bend was caught between being pleased that I was finally enjoying my food and being jealous of the fact that it was Margi White's cooking that had performed this miraculous transformation.

"My God, Sarah, you've eaten all your peas," she exclaimed.

"Well, at that age, they're always eating, aren't they," beamed Mrs White. My mother grimaced. She'd never found it so.

I loved it in Cornwall. It was hot and sunny, we were only ten minutes walk from a small rocky beach, whose cliffs were topped by a ruined castle. The air was so bright, but soft, without the bite that it had in Cumbria. I used to wake every morning before anyone else in the house was stirring and kneel by my open window, elbows on the sill, watching the fishing boats go out and the town slowly come to life, feeling the sun warming up the day. Sometimes we would go into the town and visit the small aquarium, or take the passenger ferry across to Polruan, but the beach was my favourite.

"Can we go to the castle? Can we go swimming?" I'd keep up a barrage of questions until my wish was granted.

My mother always kept to a strict lunch schedule, wherever we were. At twelve noon, out would come Mrs White's carefully packed sandwiches, normally luncheon meat or cheese, with hard boiled eggs and hard crisp tomatoes that spurted seeds over the sand when I bit into them. There was always fruit for afterwards and a flask of tea, with a Tupperware tumbler of orange squash for me. Then I had to have an hour's dry play before I could get back in the water.

One day, having bored of building yet another sandcastle which would be erased by the incoming tide, and spurning my father's offer of a game of beach cricket, I wandered off towards the rocky pools that lined the cove. It was hot, the sun high in the bleached blue sky, but my mother had equipped me with a floppy brimmed sun hat and a coating of sun cream, although there were no fears os skin cancer then.

I started off by poking at some of the closed up anemones that had been left behind by the sea, then got distracted by a translucent shrimp in a small seaweed lined puddle. There were crabs too, and even a tiny fish. The tide was out so I drifted around the headland to the pebbly beach round the corner. There was a thin rim of sand, and I found a washed up jellyfish baking, its blue veins visible through its milky body, tentacles smashed and squashed into the sand. Further on there were seabirds nesting, wheeling around and swooping into the cliffs. There was a smooth wall of rock with just enough hand and footholds to be climbable.

For once, the post lunch hour flew by, and more besides. At some point I turned and noticed that the sand had disappeared and that the sea was lapping at the rocks around which I'd walked to get here from the cove. I was the only one left on that bit of beach, so I started back, having to scramble over the rocks as the water had deepened to a green swirl, and I had had it drummed into me that I was not to swim until my mother consulted her watch and gave me permission when the requisite amount of time had passed.

As I came round the headland, I could hear my dad calling me, "Sarah, where are you?" Then I could see him, at the far side of the cove, his head weaving about from side to side like the seagulls looking for fish.

I jumped down onto the sand, ran to him, calling out, "Dad, dad! I found a jellyfish," full of my adventures and the sights I'd seen. He turned and came towards me, I was so excited I didn't see the raised hand before he hit me, the blow striking my shoulder and making my bones ring, hard enough to knock me to the ground.

He was shouting, "Where the hell have you been? Your mother's going frantic! You could have been drowned!" I sat on the sand, I cried with hurt and puzzlement. How could he do this to me? I hadn't done anything wrong. I didn't see beneath the anger to the love, every parent's worst fear. Then he half dragged me back to my mother, and added to my confusion by buying me the largest ice cream of the holiday, with a chocolate flake as well.

I didn't understand the mix of emotions that flood you when you notice that your child is suddenly, inexplicably, not where they are supposed to be until the first time that Zanne gave me the slip in Mothercare when I was buying her a pair of shoes. One minute she was standing next to me, I looked down to write the cheque and when I looked up a few seconds later, she was gone. I felt cold, breathless, my eyes and ears pricking with adrenalin as I raced wildly round the shop, calling her name.

I rushed up to the security guard at the till, "Have you seen a little girl, pink top, blue leggings?" I shouted at him. He got onto his walkie-talkie, the whole shop swung into action, doors closed, staff moving in formation down the aisles. Of course, she had just gone to look at the train set that they had laid out, and was happily pushing the engines around the track. The feeling of panic transformed through relief into anger in a split second. A memory of that day on the beach caught me just in time as I grabbed her, my hands tight claws on her arms, turning the shake and slap into a hug as I buried my face in her hair.

"Mummy, get off me," she said, exasperated, "look, they've got trains. Can I have one?" She didn't see the joke when I laughed.

Even when the children are away from me, even now that they are grown and more than capable of taking care of themselves, now I'm just an embarrassing fuss pot, I am aware that they are somewhere in the world. Once you have children it is never the same as before, you are always conscious of their existence somewhere in your being, even if you bury it under work or play.

It's sad that I can't tell my dad that I finally understand why he hit me that day, that I'm sorry that I wasted years when that was the most vivid memory of my childhood with him, rather than walking up hills together or digging in the garden or making pretend cement or learning to swim. Although I can still feel the pain of that slap, and feel the burn on my sun drenched skin where the red imprint of his hand appeared, the rest of that week is a blur. We never went back to Cornwall again. It became a kind of golden mythical memory for me, ending in that inexplicable outburst.

Sarah   August 1980

Cancer

The first stirrings of dis-ease about her father began about a month after Sarah had moved in with Dick. Her mother mentioned that he had been losing weight and was losing his appetite, which she initially welcomed as the loss of his pot belly.

Sarah had always experienced her father as remarkably fit, being able to out-walk the rest of his family and most of the younger parents of her friends at school. He had once made her mother a cup of tea, which he had taken to her in bed, left the house to walk two miles to the nearby hill top golf course, played nine holes, then walked home in time to make the breakfast. He liked to swim in the sea whenever he could and had even plunged in on Christmas Day when they had been on holiday in Scarborough. When he retired he had immediately set up his own business doing gardening for what he called "the old biddies" in the village, many of them younger than himself. He had continued to maintain the house and garden, including painting the woodwork on the upstairs windows using a rickety extendable ladder propped at an unlikely angle, constantly building and rebuilding fences.

Watching her father mix concrete for yet another round of garden constructions had been an early childhood memory for Sarah, as it had been for her siblings. Apparently, her mother regularly trotted out at family gatherings, "Deborah filled his gumboots with liquid concrete one lunchtime when she was five". The other regular anecdote was Sarah's own penning of a poem describing the day her father spilt paint all over her bedroom floor whilst redecorating. "He knocked over the paint remover as well," added Margaret. This had also been included in the poem. The thought of him being ill didn't occur to her.

It wasn't until it got to the stage of him going for "tests" that she registered that this might be serious. Her father denied that anything was wrong—always a bad sign. She could hear the fear in her mother's voice as she told Sarah, "The doctor's sent him for more tests, and they want to do X-rays and maybe a biopsy. His red cell count is down." They made him take a barium meal so they could track the damage in his body.

"Polyps," was her father's first self-diagnosis. Sarah began to worry then. That was what they had told Suzie's father. Suzie had worked in the bar at the pub in her summer before university, and her father had died six months later from cancer of the pancreas. She didn't even know what polyps were, some kind of vague term for growths where there weren't supposed to be any. In the end they finally told her father the news that it was cancer of the stomach, but that it had spread into his liver, making it inoperable. No one would tell them what that meant in terms of time, or whether there were any other treatments.

Her father remained upbeat and belligerent. He had talked to a neighbour who was into food supplements and vitamins and had agreed with him a strict regimen of vitamin C and other tablets. He had always been fussy about his food and the novelty soon wore off, no matter how much Sarah encouraged him to stick with it. Slowly she could hear the tiredness creeping into his voice.

"I don't think I need to take them every day, you know," he'd say. "Chris always was an old fuss pot. And they give me stomach ache." She still didn't really comprehend, or want to admit, that this might be fatal.

When she went to stay at Christmas she was shocked by how thin he had become, and how little he could eat. "Aren't you going to marry that fellow, I'd like to see you settled," he asked her.

"No, we don't want to get married," she'd said. "We're happy the way we are, we don't need to have a piece of paper. It's not like it was in your day, Dad, lots of people just live together." How pompous her words sounded to her when it was too late.

Over the next few months her mother would ring to update her on how he was deteriorating. When her father came on the phone he was full of denial.

"I've had another blood transfusion and Chris has found something in a magazine I'm going to try, raw food or some such.". Although he had short remissions after trying one thing or another, nothing lasted very long. Sarah supported him through all the experiments. She didn't want to think that her father might be dying, so she chose to believe him rather than the warning tones of her mother.

"He's really changed, you'd be shocked to see him," her mother told her, to no avail. After his death she regretted not spending more time with him, it wasn't as if she had anything else that she had to do that couldn't have been altered or postponed. She could have rearranged her shifts at the pub or the supermarket without much trouble. Lethargy overtook her, dragging her further down into the pit of unfeeling which she had wallowed in since Suzanne's death. Dick encouraged her to go and visit more often, but she resisted him, too.

The truth was that she was afraid. She didn't want to admit the truth of her father's illness because that would make it real. If he died, a part of her would be lost forever. He had always been there, she didn't want to look at what void his death might create in her picture of the world. She delayed going until a few days before his death, and was horrified to see the living skeleton he had become. The cancer had grown, he could eat little, and anything that he did he vomited back up, along with a black, sticky tar that her mother told her was digested blood. His body was consuming itself.

Her brother and sister came too, so that the family was all together for the first time in years. Her father tried to keep all their spirits up, like he had always done. "My God, they've lost the patient!" he joked when Debs and Margaret made a botch of trying to get him out of his pyjama top and lost his thin arms in the sleeves." His efforts at humour tired him.

Sarah could see that he was afraid too, he didn't want to think about what was happening. Her parents had never gone to church, so she was surprised that the vicar came to visit regularly and that her father accepted and welcomed him in his own way. "Oh, is it you again, vicar? Well, I'm not dead yet so you might as well come in." It was a shock to discover later that he had agreed the hymns for his funeral, whilst he was putting on a brave front for his family.

The night before he died, her sister suggested that they take turns to sit with her father during the night, to relieve their mother who had nursed him since the onset of the illness. Sarah sat with him in the evening. "I've got something to tell you all," her father said, "but it can wait until tomorrow." She was often to wonder what it was, and whether she should have pressed him then. Instead, her mother took the first night shift, and Deborah sat through until morning. Jeffrey never did reveal what it was he had wanted to talk about.

The next day it was clear that he had got much worse. His breathing was laboured. Noah was with their father that morning, so Sarah and Deborah went for a walk along the lane they had known since childhood. The sun shone brilliantly in an azure sky. Spring was well underway, daffodils waving in yellow clumps in the hedgerows. Lambs squawked for their mothers, the sharp wind blew through Sarah's hair, making her ears burn with cold. "It doesn't seem possible that this is all still going on, does it?" remarked Debs as they walked away from the house where her father was struggling for every breath.

"Shouldn't there be a thunderstorm or something?" agreed Sarah, torn between relief at being outside and guilt for enjoying the feeling of breath in her lungs. The unspoken thought, would their father still be alive when they returned, hung between them like lead in the clear air.

As they got back to the house, they heard Noah call out suddenly, "Mum! You'd better come!" Sill in their gloves and coats, the women rushed to their father's bed. He was breathing slowly and painfully, his chest barely rising.

Sarah's mother clasped his hand tightly, his eyelids flickered as his eyes started to go upwards into his head. Her mother sobbed, and her father seemed to make an enormous effort to pull himself back from the brink. His breathing became deeper, after a few seconds he opened his eyes.

"What are you all doing here?" he asked sharply, seeing them all leaning over him. "I'm not dead yet you know." Sarah realised she had been holding her breath, and let it out in a long sigh. "I need a wash, Margaret," her father said, looking at his wife.

Sarah's mother wiped her eyes with the back of her hand. "Could you help me, Sarah?" she asked. Sarah nodded, dumbly. She didn't want to, but she helped her mother remove her father's sweat and urine soaked pyjama bottoms and brought the hot water in a bowl. She tried not to stare at her father's shrunken legs and genitals, but she realised that this was the first time she had seen him naked, and probably the last. Her father grimaced to hide his embarrassment as her mother washed and cleaned him and changed the sheet with practised movements. Her father managed to roll slightly from side to side, Sarah lifting him under his armpits so that they could remove one sheet and slide the clean one underneath him. He was so light, but so thin it was difficult to keep hold of him. Then it was done.

"Get Noah to call the doctor," her father said, closing his eyes in exhaustion.

The doctor came quickly. It was Doctor Fennemore, the same doctor that Sarah had seen when she had gone on the pill in her teens, asking him not to tell her parents. She thought that he probably knew a lot about all of them. As he went into her father's room and closed the door, she heard her father's voice saying wearily, "Let me die. I just want to die. I'm so tired."

After ten minutes the doctor came out. "I've given him something to help him sleep," he told Sarah's mother. "He's very weak." He didn't have to say, "It won't be long now". Her mother nodded, her shoulders sagged, she looked defeated. "Have you been getting any sleep yourself?" Doctor Fennemore asked. Her mother shook her head. The doctor took a small brown bottle out of his bag. "Take one if you need it," he said, pressing them into her mother's hand. She looked at the bottle as if she had already forgotten what it was for, but closed her fingers around it anyway.

Sarah looked through the open door of the bedroom. Her father was asleep, what was left of his wispy grey hair was spread on the pillow. His breath was laboured and rasping, like a saw on wood. It continued like that for another three hours, getting progressively softer and with longer gaps between breaths. The family tried to distract themselves with the usual things, cups of tea, lunch, daytime television. It was her sister who first realised that the noise that they had been listening to with such concentration, that had underlined all their futile attempts to ignore it, had finally ceased. "Listen!" she said. They looked at each other, then went into the room where the body lay, still looking like he was sleeping.

Sarah's mother reached out and stroked the cooling head, automatically tidying the wisps of hair behind his ears. Sarah realised that both her mother and sister were crying silently, and was dismayed to find that she felt nothing. She hugged the other women, but she felt like an observer rather than a participant in their grief. She was the only one who saw her brother reach over and slip her father's watch from his wrist and put it into his own pocket. He looked up and saw her staring at him. He put his finger to his lips and winked at her. Some dimly remembered reaction of childhood conspiracy prevented her from speaking out, but she never spoke to him again after the funeral, nor asked him to her wedding. She did eventually tell Deborah what he had done, but she could never tell her mother. Deborah did that, years later.

She called Dick to tell him. "Dad died."

"Oh no, I'm so sorry," his voice sounded so far away.

"Well, we knew it was going to happen," Sarah admitted for the first time. "I'm coming home tomorrow. The funeral's next week so we can come back for that. If you want to come with me, that is," she finished lamely.

"Sarah, of course I will. Is there anything else I can do?"

"Could you ring the pub and the shop and tell them, so I can get time off?"

"No problem. Give my love to everyone there."

She didn't go back to work regularly at either place in the end. On the train back to Leeds she used her Walkman to shut off from the chatter of the other people in the carriage, but she watched them eating and drinking and squabbling and shouting at their children. She stared out at the passing countryside, hills and rivers still bathed in spring sunshine, and tried to make sense of that fact that life was going on exactly the same as if nothing momentous had happened the day before. She waited for the realisation that her father had died to break through the wall of insulation she had constructed.

It finally happened at his funeral. The vicar had hardly started to speak when she felt the tears running down her cheeks. She let them flow, not attempting to wipe her face, letting them come. When it got to the hymn, "For Those in Peril on the Sea", the flow became a torrent, she couldn't sing, she knew it was one of her father's favourites. She loved the tune, she could feel each of the harmonies pierce her. Dick held her as she swayed and wept throughout the entire service.

Then the family followed in convoy behind the hearse as they drove to the crematorium. Sarah was shocked that her mother had chosen to do this, she'd imagined some kind of traditional gathering at the graveside, gazing at the coffin that now rode ahead of them. There would have been earth to throw and some kind of permanent memorial to visit. The crematorium was white and angular, and although the staff did their best to recognise what the families who came here were going through, it felt like what it was, an incinerator for animal remains.

After a few words from the vicar, the coffin rolled into the oven, the curtains closed.

Sarah gazed at the Garden of Remembrance outside, a bleak paved area with a few tubs of crocus and primroses, the wall lined with concrete plaques. She was grateful that her mother had decided not to commemorate her father with one of these stone notices, that she'd already said, "I'm going to scatter his ashes on the golf course at the top of the fell. He was always up there."

Deborah stayed with her mother for another week. Sarah and Dick drove back to Leeds straight after the cremation. Sarah buried her face in Dick's chest that night and wept some more. She began to wonder whether she would ever stop. All the months of holding back her feelings meant that she felt everything much more sharply than ever now. After a couple of weeks she could listen to the radio without crying at every song that reminded her of her father or Suzanne, or something that she had done with one of them. It took her months before she could watch *Casualty* without sobbing as soon as the opening scenes started to set up those people who would die or get injured in the next forty minutes.

She'd confessed to Dick that she loved him just a week after the funeral, the first time they'd made love since her father had died. At first she'd found it difficult to respond to Dick stroking her skin, but then it seemed like she needed to have him desperately, wildly. Not denying her father's death, but affirming that she was still alive. They lay together afterwards, and she said, "I love you, you know".

"Yes," he said, as if he'd known all along.

"Dick, will you always love me?" she asked, foolishly. What had possessed her, the words had just slipped out. His arms tightened around her. She held her breath.

"Sarah, you know I will," he sighed into her hair. She'd never entertained the thought of Dick leaving her before. It had seemed like his love for her was immutable. Now, after his confirmation of that, Sarah began to fear for the first time that she would lose him.

Dick   1958–1968

Childhood

Dick grew up in a huge Victorian house on the edge of a small town in Cheshire. I was a bit taken aback when he showed it to me, it was far bigger than what I had expected. Of course, his parents had to have a large house with six kids, plus they had his father's mother living with them for some years before she died. Dick was the fourth child, the eldest of the younger group. His older siblings varied in age from five to fifteen years older, and formed their own kind of sub-group, not really having much to do with the younger ones, Dick and his sisters Ruth and Jennifer. I never really got a sense of why Donald and Irene had so many children, I mean they weren't Catholic or anything. Irene told me horror stories.

"I mean, it took me all my time to do the washing and cooking. We didn't have automatic washing machines and refrigerators then," she confided. I couldn't imagine it, it had been hard enough to deal with my two with most modern labour saving devices. We didn't get our own washing machine until after I'd had Zanne and realised how punitive it was trailing up the road to the laundromat every two days with piles of babygros.

His parents always seemed enviably laid back about the whole process. Donald related a story about how he and Irene had once been sitting in the living room of their three-storied house at the end of the day, chatting, having a cup of tea. "We were having a new roof put on and the roofers had put up a complex system of scaffolding to get access to the top. Lucy, Jane and Jack came down the stairs from their bedrooms and went out of the front door into the garden. Half an hour later, Lucy, Jack and Jane came down the stairs and out of the front door into the garden." This happened twice more before Donald started to feel a creeping sense of *déjà vu*. "I realised that I'd not seen the children go into the house, so where were they coming from?"

"They were climbing up the outside of the house on the scaffolding, and walking along four feet of guttering to get to one of the attic windows," laughed Irene. "They thought it was so much fun they had to do it again and again!" Both of them seemed to regard this incident with amused pride in their children's accomplishments. Irene told me that, "Jack could probably climb before he could walk. He got to the top of the old elm when he was four. I only know because I was upstairs in my bedroom looking out of the window and saw his face in amongst the leaves!"

Dick inherited his siblings' love of heights and foolhardy pursuits. "When he was seven months old, I left him alone in the bathroom in the middle of changing his nappy to go and get something from my room," said Irene. "He was on the vanity unit next to the sink, I didn't think anything could happen." Already a strong crawler, and freed from the inhibiting mass of terry cloth nappy, Dick had apparently flipped over and moved towards the sound of a branch tapping against the open window. "Luckily Jack happened to come in to use the toilet and saw Dick disappearing out onto the window ledge and managed to grab him by the ankle." I couldn't believe that all her children had made it to adulthood.

Having a large house meant that squabbles between the children had to be dealt with amongst themselves, often they were simply just out of earshot of any adult intervention. It also meant that when the elder group discovered pop music and converted one of the basement rooms into a teenage hang-out, that their parents could largely ignore the noise and benefit from knowing that their children were not out drifting around the streets of Crawsham. The younger crew were discouraged from entering the den of course, but were allowed to watch from the doorway as local youth gyrated to the Beatles and the Who.

I envy Dick his comparatively free and peaceful childhood. I enjoy his family's visits to our house more than I enjoy visits from my own. They are not overlaid with the same need to prove myself that I feel when my mother or sister are around, plus Dick's family just gets on and mucks in. His position as middle child of a larger group also seems to have left him with less need to live up to his parents' expectations than I had, another domino that had such disastrous results.

Sarah and Dick   Summer 1982

Wedding

It was a perfect day for it. The sun rose early, burning off the mist on the back garden to reveal a bright hot morning. They were staying in her sister's house but Sarah had still woken up snuggled against Dick's belly as usual, with his arms wrapped lightly around her breasts and his face tucked into the back of her neck. She wriggled round to face him and he stirred. "Last chance to back out," she told him.

"Mmmm?" he replied.

"If you want to escape you had better go now, or Nigel will be after you with a shotgun if you try to make a break for it later," she continued.

Dick smiled in his half sleeping state. "Would you like to run away with me and get married today?" he asked. "I know this really nice place in Bath we could go, the registry office is booked, how about it?"

"Oh. Alright then," Sarah agreed, mock grudgingly. "But only if you make me a cup of tea. Now."

Dick rolled out of bed and fumbled around for his dressing gown. "Yes, my queen," he said. "Your wish is my command."

"Glad we're starting as we mean to go on then," Sarah said smugly.

After he'd closed the door she drew the sheets up to her chin and luxuriated in the wide clean bed, spreading her feet and hands out into the four corners, like a starfish, enjoying the anticipation of being served. Being brought a cup of tea in bed was one of the things that Dick had soon discovered was really important to the success of their relationship. Maybe that was why she had always resisted her attraction to Jules, who was like a log in the mornings and had never succeeded in fulfilling this essential role.

It was probably due to the fact that her Dad had always done this, right from when she had been about seven and started to drink tea, right up until she left home. He'd even continued to do it when she'd gone home to visit, meaning she'd had to be careful to not embarrass him by sleeping in the nude as she did at college. It was one of the things that signalled his absence more sharply than anything else when she went to visit her mother.

She was going to marry Dick today. She reached over for her book and rotated her shoulders into the pile of pillows to a perfect angle. She could indulge in five minutes reading before Dick came back with the tea. Marrying Dick today! Butterflies performed a swift foxtrot in her stomach.

After tea they did some pre-breakfast moiling in the bed, before emerging pink and breathless from the shower to enjoy creamy scrambled eggs and buck's fizz. "Thought we'd better start the day off right," said Sarah's brother in law, Nigel, as he eased the cork out of another bottle.

"Just as well none of us is driving to the registry office," said Deborah.

The flowers and caterer arrived whilst Sarah was upstairs getting dressed. By the time she came down the stairs in her floor length cream silk shift, embroidered on the front with a spray of cream lilies, her bouquet was waiting for her. The roses and freesias in her bouquet and the matching posy for Deborah matched the spray of yellow and cream icing sugar flowers on the single tiered cake on the sideboard The side of salmon lay on the wide oak table in the cool open dining space of the converted barn, surrounded by salads and breads.

Dick was already dressed, and he turned and smiled to see her. "You look gorgeous," he said, stepping forwards to kiss her lightly on the lips.

"You look pretty hunky yourself," she replied, and he did. His skin was lightly tanned from working in the garden in Leeds and the week they'd spent walking in the Lake District where they'd decided to get married, only six weeks ago. His hair was shorter now, dark curls against his scalp and neck, but his eyes still had the power to melt her. He stood straight and tall under her measuring gaze, in his new linen suit and yellow silk tie. The man she was about to marry.

"The cars are here," Nigel announced, sticking his head round the front door. "Bride's party please," he grinned.

"See you there," Sarah said to Dick, putting on her cream straw hat and picking up her flowers. She climbed into the Bentley with her mother and sister. Her mother squeezed her hand.

"Nervous?"

"No, not really," said Sarah, although those butterflies were at it again, careering around like a grand prix. "But could we have the window open?"

Standing facing him in the registry office, she repeated the words the registrar provided, words that she was more than familiar with through countless renditions in films, books and plays, "I call upon these persons here present."

She didn't feel the overwhelming embarrassment she'd anticipated to be so exposed in front of her family and friends. Instead, although she was fully aware of everyone standing behind them, witnessing their declarations, she was only conscious of Dick's eyes, looking straight at her without any filter. She could see her own reflection there, she wanted to dive in and immerse herself in him. Time stretched and contracted at the same time. It was over all too quickly, but when they were saying their vows she had felt as though every syllable dropped into the waiting space like a crystal.

They had the reception in the garden of Deborah and Nigel's house. Only a few friends and immediate family, but then Dick had so much family they'd managed to fill up the room at the registry office. It was the first time she had met them. His mother, Irene, was small and compact, a white-haired matriarch who obviously made the rules in her relationship. Yet she was relaxed with her children, six in all. Sarah could see why Dick was so capable about the house, and why he could listen to women so well. He'd had plenty of practice, with two older and two younger sisters, as well as a role model in his older brother. Jack was just as charming as Dick, and had the same twinkle in his eye as their father, Donald.

His sisters, the two older ones with shadowy, eclipsed husbands, were a blur of noise and colour. It was to take her a few years to be able to tell them apart with confidence. Lucy, Jane, Ruth and Jennifer all looked like slightly different moulds of their mother, the same basic face and body shape with different accessories, dark or blonde hair, blue or hazel eyes.

Every so often she would catch a glimpse of her own family amongst them, her sister and her brother-in-law playing the hosts whilst their children, ten year old Beth and seven year old Simon, organised their cousins by this marriage, Dick's nephews and nieces and hers too now, into games of croquet and cricket at the far end of the paddock behind the house.

Once she had done the rounds of both their families, Sarah was content to lounge in the shade of the old willow, eat cake and sip champagne. She felt drowsy from all the alcohol and more than a little dizzy. The friends they'd invited were really only Dick's. She couldn't have invited her two closest women friends, she didn't know where Jules was and Suzanne, of course, was dead, or this event would never have taken place. A slight movement at the corner of her eye made her look round. A cold shiver ran down her back and made the hairs on her bare arms stand erect. For a split second she'd thought she'd seen Suzanne slipping through the people mingling on the lawn, dressed in her ankle length Laura Ashley chintz. But no, of course that could not be.

The friends they knew in Leeds were through Dick's work, and a couple of them had come with their wives, both of them fitting the stereotype of science lecturers. Daniel Beckett had a long dark beard and wild hair above a broad, bald forehead, and Patrick O'Neill looked like an older version of Roger Daltry, with masses of grey blond curls loosely tied in a red bandana. Their wives were thin and nondescript, as though they had been coloured with the same khaki watercolour wash, merely serving as appreciative backdrops to their husbands' eccentricity.

She hadn't been able to find a job to interest her yet, so she had no corresponding workmates. She'd tried without much enthusiasm or success to get herself into the Yorkshire Post's graduate training scheme for journalists, with a vague idea that at least it would involve some kind of writing and so an English degree might come in handy. She'd managed to get an interview for a researcher post at Yorkshire television but had been let down by her absence of knowledge about the news programme she would have been working on. Too many soap operas, she admitted. So she'd drifted from one temporary job to another, typing and secretarial work, a brief and unhappy phase as a doctor's receptionist, without telling her mother that the reality was nothing like Margaret's fantasy, and still working at the supermarket and bar from time to time. Now she had found a job as a library assistant, and settled into it like sediment drifting down to the bottom of a fast flowing river, more from convenience and lack of resistance than from any ambition to do it from choice. It paid better than the bar and the shop, she got to sit and read books for a large part of the day as the library was hardly ever dealing with more than ten people at a time. It was only five minutes walk up the road so she could walk home for lunch and the hours were nine to four with the occasional Saturday morning on rota.

She and Dick still lived in his two bedroomed back to back terrace in Chapel Allerton in which they had first consummated their relationship and had used for wild nights of passion when she was still finishing her degree at York. He was lucky to have bought it at a reasonable price when he had first moved to Leeds to take up his research post. It had been decorated in plain, muted creams and whites by its previous owners just before one of them had got a job in the south. Dick had been free to make his own mark on the plain walls and spread bright, deep rugs on the stripped pine floorboards.

"You can paint it different colours if you want," he'd offered.

"No, there isn't anything that I want to change," she'd replied. She was content to live in his space. That way it felt like she didn't have to take responsibility for it. The kitchen was a tiny space carved out of the living room and half suspended over the steps to the cellar, which were accessible through the larder. The bathroom was nightmarishly cold in the winter, and she'd often risked a fatal encounter with a small electric bar fire positioned just inside the doorway so that she could bear to get out of a cooling bath.

They'd been living together amicably for two years. Although she could describe her aimless experiences with jobs as drifting, she and Dick did not drift, they sailed together like the crew of a racing yacht. They fitted together in such a seamless way she couldn't believe they had ever not been together. It was effortless to be with each other, talking or silent.

She looked at him now, telling a story to Daniel, lots of gestures and smiles, probably about their ascent of Helvellyn and how he'd proposed at the summit.

Hill walking was something she'd rediscovered with Dick. As a young child, she'd been keen to follow her parents to the top of the fells, full of energy, chattering all the way. When she reached teenage, walking was one of the things which she abandoned because her parents liked it. It had been a surprise and a delight to find that she revelled in the feel of the wind, drinking in the views as they revealed themselves in different guises the higher they went. Otherwise a creature made for central heating and hot baths, she found that she even enjoyed the experience of walking in rain and hail, the grey and bracken landscape of the Yorkshire Dales made dim and blurred by the weather. Of course, ending the day with one of those hot baths, snuggling in their quilt on a battered second hand sofa in front of the gas fire watching some ancient black and white film on the television was made all the sweeter by the effort it had taken to get there. Dick laughingly accused her of being a born again Calvinist, "You enjoy comfort so much more if you've had to suffer to earn it!"

What had made him propose, she wondered, and why had she accepted? They'd been doing fine before without any talk of marriage, even though her mother had hinted at it just before her Dad had died. "It would make him so happy, to see you settled," she'd said. But Sarah had been gently firm, she'd told her father she didn't believe in marriage, things were different these days. Now they had gone and done it anyway, and her Dad had not been there to give her away. Not that anyone had given her away, that not being part of the format in a registry office. She missed him, with a sharp bolt of need that she had not felt for a couple of months. She wished he could know that she'd been a dutiful daughter and done what she was supposed to, find a man to take his place. Why couldn't they have done it last year?

That would have meant she would have missed that mad scramble up the edge of Helvellyn, where they had lost the path within sight of the top and found themselves on a treacherous mixture of slippery scrub and muddy shale, with a lake winking below them in the grey light, held in the mountain's horseshoe embrace. One slip and a thousand feet straight down with no hope of stopping. Biting back the rising panic that she knew would make it impossible for her to function she'd somehow got herself up those last few yards, following Dick's fell boots till they emerged over the lip of the mountain to a blast of icy wind and blaze of sudden sunshine breaking through the clouds. They'd fallen together, laughing with relief and thankful to be there at all, and Dick had stumbled over a spine of millstone grit. He'd gone down on one knee, grasping her round the waist to steady himself. She'd jokingly asked, "Are you about to propose then?"

She had been rendered speechless when he'd said, "yes, and Sarah, my darling, my love, my queen, will you marry me?" The breathlessness she felt then made her sway dangerously, so that he had to hold her tightly to stop her toppling over the edge they had just defeated. She could hear a buzzing in her ears over the noise of the shrieking Lakeland wind, and tiny black dots threatened to obscure her vision.

She'd gasped, "yes," from her gut, without thinking, then burst into tears, which were dragged across her face by the wind, making red wet tracks. So the resultant picture, recorded by Dick at arm's length with a disposable camera he'd hidden in his windcheater pocket, showed a triumphant Dick and a blurry eyed, windswept Sarah with a distant view of purple hills behind them. They'd stumbled to the windbreak to eat their sandwiches and chocolate, fighting off the persistent sheep who kept trying to raid their pockets. Then he'd pulled out a box, with the single diamond that she wore next to her wedding ring now. She was outraged at his planning and presumption.

"How could you have been so devious? And what made you so certain I would agree?"

He'd laughed and called her Contrary Mary. "Well, you did say yes, didn't you? You're always telling me that you like surprises and weren't you worrying about the romance in our relationship fading only last week?" She'd had to agree, and accepted the ring more gracefully.

The next day passed in a whirl of phone calls. They'd thought of doing it straight away, with passing strangers as witnesses, but abandoned that idea for a small gathering of those they felt closest to. Sarah's sister had volunteered her house for the reception venue, Dick had secured the only available slot at the registry office in Bath for the day they wanted. Sarah had tried on every dress in Monsoon before deciding on the one she was wearing, picking up the hat as an after thought when she was on her way out. Flowers, food, cake and cars had all been sourced and booked locally by her sister as a magnificent wedding present.

Sarah's mother had been delighted for an excuse to buy a new hat to celebrate her youngest child's wedding, and voiced what Sarah herself was thinking, "If only your Dad could have been here."

Sarah came to with a start to find she'd been sleeping underneath the tree and the afternoon was drawing to a close. Everyone was starting to put their jackets back on, which they'd abandoned in the earlier heat or to play croquet or cricket. The sun was beginning to sink behind the gable of the barn. Dick was looking over at her and grinning, and as he caught her eye, raised his glass and his eyebrows in a silent promise of a continuation of their pre-breakfast activities. Sarah felt a moist warmth between her legs. He could still do that with just a look. She smiled and nodded her acceptance of his invitation, then rose and stretched, and brushing the grass from her dress she returned to the party. She refilled her empty champagne glass, wishing she could shake off that nervous fluttering in her stomach, but hell, it wasn't every day you got married, she thought.

The queasy feeling didn't go away, though. Within a week Sarah discovered that she was pregnant. She'd put the fact that her period was late down to the stress and excitement of getting married, rather than the night that had followed Dick's proposal. Both of them had climbed into the bath in their hotel to nurse their aching limbs with lavender oil and a smuggled bottle of champagne from the local off licence, putting the overflow severely to the test. Dizzy with heat, alcohol and emotion, they'd collapsed onto the bed to make Zanne.

Sarah   Now

Children

There were times, sleeping next to Zanne when she was young, lying awake in the night after a feed when she was curled into my armpit, her milky breath soft against my skin, that I just couldn't believe that I could be so happy. Not actively happy either, but a deep-lying feeling of rightness, a feeling of being part of the whole universe.

When I was eighteen I hadn't wanted children at all, I'd been vehement when assumptions had been made by family and friends about what my eventual path, as a woman, would naturally be. "But I don't like children," I'd said, when the truth was that I was afraid of them. They'd known it, like dogs they sniffed me out. Toddlers regarded me with a suspicious, serious faced stare, resisting all my efforts to charm and amuse. They weren't fooled.

"He's never normally like this," their mothers would say. And babies were worse.

"Oh, Sarah will be OK with her." My mother would volunteer me for babysitting her neighbours' children because after all what were teenagers useful for if not to relieve their parents' friends of the obligation of looking after their own younger offspring? She assumed rightly that I would appreciate the extra cash, but I always felt that somehow the price I paid for it was too high.

They would be peacefully sleeping when I'd arrive, but as soon as their parents had left for some interminably long two or three hours, no matter how quietly I tiptoed around, as soon as I had made myself a cup of tea and was gingerly lowering myself onto the sofa to watch some vital part of a TV serial, then the wails would start. They knew an interloper was in their house, someone who could only hold them stiffly with the fear that I might drop them and their heads would come off. No matter how many times this happened, I would always have the feeling that my expectation of a quiet evening watching television for money had been taken away from me, when I had no basis to expect anything of the kind. So resentment was added to my feelings of frustration and fear, as I helplessly watched my tea cooling to an oily frigidity.

"It'll be different with your own," they smoothed condescendingly, nodding in that superior, we've been there, done that, we know best way. Then, infuriatingly, all the old wives, including my mother, were proved horribly right when Zanne arrived, not even a planned baby. Because it was different. I couldn't believe it, she was so perfect. I know mothers always say that, but she was. Still is, for that matter, even though throughout her teenage she took to addressing me in the same tones as she would if she was looking at some rather unpleasant dog turd she found on her shoe.

Even the sleepless nights were a delight, though in the daytime I would pay for my nocturnal pleasure with heavy lidded inability to remember how to make a cup of tea. I used to watch her for hours, beside me in the bed, her smooth cheek lying against my skin, smelling that vanilla smell that babies' heads always have, her hands often thrown up above her head, open and vulnerable, full of confidence that I was there to deflect all the dangers that the world might have in store for her.

Dick, the man I had lusted after from that first day at university despite all my other adventures and affairs, was lying back to back with me in our wide married bed, a bed I had no right to be in. Watching Zanne, even the ghost of the other who should have been in my place couldn't trouble me, my mind was completely taken up with watching that ever so slight movement of her chest, up and down.

In the daytime that ghost would sometimes intrude with crashing effectiveness, striking me down with the thought that so much happiness would have to be paid for, particularly because it had been bought at the price of another's life. "What goes around, comes around" and "You reap what you sow", would echo in my head in the middle of preparing stewed apple or folding Zanne's army of baby-grows. The thought would be accompanied with a scalp tightening, then a constriction in my gut, a deep, deep coldness travelling around my blood stream from my heart to my head. What would it be, what would be the price?

Even calling my precious after her, which was Dick's idea, a cruel irony that I could not explain to him, could not propitiate her. Suzanne, he maintained, had brought us together. Not by choice, I knew.

Later, Martin morphed Suzanne into Zanne in his baby talk, which became Zany, her teenage nickname amongst her friends. That relieved me of calling her by the name of my friend and rival.

Yet looking at that downy head in the early morning darkness, feeling her breath on my skin, I knew that whatever the price, it would be worth it. If the other had been in my place then this perfection would never have existed, and she was so clearly meant to be. She had been such a determined foetus that she had survived the drunken night of her conception and a week of walking and scrambling in the Lakes including a plunge into an icy tarn on the fells above Derwentwater, all before I knew I was pregnant.

She had resisted all my attempts to deny her existence in the two weeks after I'd looked with horror at that tell tale line on the pregnancy test which told me that the result was positive, the two weeks when I'd felt that an abortion was the only option because it was too soon, we'd only just got married. I'd waited those two weeks before I told Dick, not because I was fearful that he would reject me and his child, but because I was afraid that he would do exactly what he did do, smile that wonderful smile, wrap his arms round me and lift me high in the air with a whoop of pure and unfake-able delight.

I'd been scared that, at the moment of having everything that I had dreamed of and planned and plotted for, that I would find that I didn't want it after all. That would have been unbearable, to have done what I did for a handful of dust.

Dick   1980–1983

Proposal

When Sarah and I were just seeing each other at weekends when she was still at York, finishing her degree, the times we were together were always exciting. She was warm in bed, but there was always a coolness, a reserve that felt like she was keeping something of herself separate. I found it arousing, trying to find the key that would unlock that secret compartment, but she never gave anything away. I loved her, and told her so, more than any other woman I'd been with. She never let go and told me that she loved me too, and on the nights when I was alone in my little house in Leeds I'd lie awake and feel hurt and frustrated and insecure.

When we met, the smell of her skin and her delight at seeing me, the way we fell into easy conversation and then into passionate sex meant that the weekend would pass in a blaze of sensation. Eating, drinking, fucking, having breakfast in bed and tonguing up the crumbs off each other afterwards. We'd rouse ourselves to go to a film or to the theatre, share a bag of chips on the way home, licking the salt and vinegar from each other's faces and fingers. On Sundays we might go to an art gallery, or walk along the river in York or the canal in Leeds, probably ending up at a pub for lunch, talking, always talking.

She told me about her family. "Christmas is always stressful," she warned.

"We're quite boringly happy," I said.

"Are you all still talking to each other on Boxing Day?" she asked.

"Yeah. Why not?" I was puzzled.

"I don't think we've ever had a Christmas when that happened," she mused. "Someone is always sulking. Often it's me. I'm the youngest, so I'm at the bottom of the food chain as far as my family is concerned, even though my Dad likes to play the hen-pecked husband. He once threatened to buy a goldfish so that there would be someone lower than him."

"Don't your family like each other?"

"Oh, yes, we're very close."

"I wouldn't say we were close, but we manage to talk to each other without sulking every Christmas."

When she finished her degree and I asked, "Would you like to move in with me?" I wanted to force the issue.

"Yes, of course," she said, as though it was taken for granted.

I convinced myself that it meant something that she agreed, that she did care for me after all, instead of, as I suspected, that she just didn't know what else to do with her life. She was still the same. Warm, friendly, but always that secret part of herself locked away. I hid my frustration in my work, I was living with Sarah, I loved her, but I couldn't stand it that she didn't want to commit to me. What a joke! The philanderer caught in his own net.

I started to resent the fact that she didn't really seem to want to do anything, just drifted along in dead end jobs, watching daytime soaps when she wasn't on a shift at the pub or the supermarket. I stayed later than I needed to at work, with the result that my research started to pay off, slowly. I got some extra teaching, my PhD started to come together, it looked as though I had everything I wanted.

I wasn't happy. After a year I'd plucked up the courage and decided that I was going to have to ask her to move out. Then her father got ill, and that sent me into a tailspin of guilt and gave me another excuse just to keep on settling for second best. It really showed the cracks though. I wanted to be there for her, but if anything she became more distant and distracted than before. I felt like I was drowning in candy floss, as though Sarah's apathy had infected me too. The only time I felt like I could breathe was away from the house, at work.

Then the dam broke. It was sad that it took her father's death for her to finally tell me that she loved me. Afterwards I couldn't remember why I had been so wound up by the fact that she hadn't told me before, because our lives went on much the same. We were living in the same house, I was doing the same job. She seemed to have settled at the library. Even though I felt that she could have done the job standing on her head, she seemed to enjoy it.

I still wasn't satisfied. It was one of those times when you desperately want something, for years, and you finally get it, to find that you have built it up to such a degree that it feels like an anticlimax. We still talked like we always had, the sex was as brilliant as ever, but now when I told her, "I love you," she would always reply.

"I love you too." It started to feel like a routine. Now I felt like I was suffocating in the ordinariness of it all. Why wasn't it as exciting as it had been at the beginning? I suppose that the thrill of the chase was gone, now I knew I had her, she was no longer a mystery, she was conquered. I'd won the contest, now I was starting to itch for the next challenge.

Barbara appeared right on cue. I'd never taught final year undergraduates before, but another lecturer was off on long term sick leave and we all had to pick up bits of his teaching. They seemed so young and yet so knowledgeable. They were scary and they were fun. They reminded me of how it had been when I was a student, not so long ago after all.

I made the mistake of wanting them to like me, to be their pal, I started meeting them at lunchtimes or after work at the student pubs. Sarah didn't question me, I'd always had pretty irregular hours. That made it possible for me to get drawn in by Barbara. She was beautiful, she had rich auburn hair and hazel eyes. In some ways she reminded me of Suzanne, but she was more substantial whereas Suzanne had always been a bit fey. There were only two women in the group, and the other was the archetypal blue stocking, dowdy and plain. Barbara would sit at the front in seminars, she always had something interesting and challenging to say.

In fact, it was her that suggested one day, "Isn't it possible that the high level of phosphorus in this sample could relate to the diet of people who live in the area," which got me interested in researching that area. A couple of times I did wonder if she fancied me and enjoyed the fantasy, but always dismissed it as wishful thinking.

One evening when Sarah was working a shift at the pub as a favour to the landlord because one of the regular bar staff had gone sick, I went out with Barbara and some of the boys from the group. This time I stayed longer than usual, the boys left, it was just the two of us. I'd just got another round in, we were sitting close together because the pub was crowded and noisy, we could hardly hear each other. Barbara leaned over so that I could speak into her ear, I caught her perfume, sharp and lemony with the musk of her skin underneath. I was distracted by her scent, she moved her head so that my lips brushed her ear and then her hair. She felt so good, her skin was warm and velvety, her hair was smooth and clean.

She rubbed her leg against my thigh, then I felt her hand reaching round underneath the table to cup my balls through my trousers. I knew I should tell her to stop, but I realised that I didn't want her to, I wanted to take her right there and then. She turned to face me.

"Shall we go?" she asked. I nodded, I couldn't speak, and followed her outside the pub. I pulled her into the alleyway and pushed her hard against the wall, kissed her hungrily, I wanted to suck in all her youth and vitality. She wasn't wearing a bra beneath her shirt and my fingers soon found her breast. I started to fumble with the waistband of her jeans, I didn't think of anything but being inside her.

She pushed me away. "Not here, Romeo," she laughed, grabbed my hand and led me to her flat. We coupled in the hall, I couldn't wait to get to the bedroom, but it was over too quickly.

"I'd better have a shower," I said. Barbara smiled and led me into the bathroom, got in with me, made me hard, licked and stroked me until I almost came, then finally we made it to her bed and I got sweaty and sticky all over again.

I finally remembered to look at my watch, realised that Sarah would be back soon, made an undignified exit still tucking in my shirt. I sat on the bus home, not quite believing what had just happened, I almost missed my stop.

It didn't stop there. I don't know if Barbara told any of her classmates. I didn't think of the consequences, I didn't think of Sarah, I didn't think about my job. It went on for the rest of the year. At first, Barbara didn't talk about what would happen after she graduated, but then she started to ask me, "Do you love me? Why don't you leave your wife and move in with me?"

"Not the right time," I mumbled, trying to sound non-committal. She came back to it again and again.

"Is it the right time now, Dick? Why don't you tell her?"

I came home to find Sarah on the phone. "It's one of your students," she said, handing me the receiver.

"Don't worry, lover," said Barbara. "I didn't tell her about us. This time." I felt as though I'd been drenched with iced water.

It became clear what she was after. Her grades were good, but they weren't good enough to get her a first, which was what she wanted. At first I refused, outraged at what she suggested, but in the end I gave in. I let her know what the exam questions would be. I second-marked her dissertation and persuaded the other marker to up it a grade. I argued her case at the exam board. I didn't see her again until the graduation ceremony. She blew me a kiss across the hall. I felt sick.

I went straight out to the jeweller's and bought a diamond engagement ring. Sarah and I had planned to go away to the Lake District after the end of term. When we got to the top of Helvellyn I asked her to marry me. About a month after the ceremony, she told me she was pregnant with Suzanne. Everything was normal and ordinary once again, thank God.

Sarah   Now

Justification

Sometimes I wonder what the point of it all is. I mean, why am I writing this? Is it just some kind of self justification? Or is it to see if there really is any meaning to what happened? And who is going to read this, after all? I can't let Dick read it, it would be too risky after all these years to let him know just what kind of person he married. Would my children really appreciate having their world view turned completely upside down? It must be just for me.

It's hard to do things just for yourself, don't you think? I mean, even though I was so determined to be a rebel, to get away and recreate myself, for myself, I just ended up being really conventional. I haven't, and I'm never going to, set the world alight. When I was a child I had this fire in my belly, I wanted to make a difference, be famous for something, I didn't know what.

Maybe it was to do with that little old lady, I can't even remember her face, I must have only been about four. She was talking to my mother, we were in a street, there were shops. I was bored, I can remember that, tugging at my mother's hand, I wanted to go to the library, or the park, anywhere. In the end, she did that thing that adults do to children, she asked me my age, I mean how predictable! Children must get so fed up with every adult asking them that.

I was out with Zanne once, she was about the same age, Martin was in a pushchair. Same scenario, little old busybody, pretending to be nice, "And how old are you, dear?" she asked her.

"I'm four and a half," said Zanne. "How old are you?" Embarrassed smiles all round.

"Ooh, older than you can count to, dear."

"I can count to sixty. Are you older than that? That's really old, isn't it? Old people die don't they?" Zanne gave the old woman one of her intent, finding out things looks. She just wanted to know. It was all I could do to stop myself letting out one of those barking laughs that got me into trouble so many times at school. Instead I smiled indulgently.

"Precocious little thing, isn't she," said the old biddy, retreating. She had those old woman stockings on, opaque flesh coloured, wrinkled at the ankles, a plaid skirt that came down to mid calf and a camel hair coat, even though it was summer. Please God, let me never wear camel when I'm old.

"What does precocious mean, mummy?" Zanne asked me.

"It means you're very clever" I answered her. "How does she know that?" asked my inquisitive daughter.

"Because you told her that you can count up to sixty. That's clever for someone who is four and a half years old."

The other interfering old bag, she followed up the age question to me with, "And what do you want to be when you grow up then?" She was obviously expecting me to say something like, be a nurse, or a teacher.

I replied, "The first woman prime minister." I was just as precocious as my daughter—where does she get it from! But children rarely get the better of adults, and it was comparatively easy for her to get her own back.

After asking me about my brothers and sisters and finding out that they were fifteen and ten years older than me, she could pronounce with authority, "So you were a little mistake, then?"

Just a few words. But after that, I was never sure whether I had been a wanted child. I mean, my parents seemed to care for me in all the usual ways. I got Christmas presents, they fed me and bought me clothes. I used to have daydreams that I had been adopted, that was why I was born so long after my siblings, that I was really a princess and someday my real parents would come to claim me. After a while I gave up on that one though.

Maybe that was why I was so keen to prove that I was worthwhile, that I hadn't been a mistake after all, that I was better than Debs and Noah. It could have been why I wanted to go to university, because neither of them had wanted to and it would be my chance to do something better than them, to fulfil my parents' fantasy about sending at least one of their children there. I suppose that was why it was so awful when I thought I might get chucked out, because that would confirm what the old witch had said, that I was just a mistake, that I had no reason to exist at all apart from some unplanned pairing of sperm and egg due to a broken condom or an extra glass of wine.

Not of course that I could ever imagine my parents actually doing anything like having sex. That's not unusual, I know. There was incontrovertible physical evidence that they had done it at least three times.

One day I was poking around in the cellar, where I kept all my candle-making stuff. That makes it sound more technical than it was. What I had was some old white candles, a few nightlights, an old tin which I used to melt the wax in, some birthday cake candles to add colour, a few old yoghurt pots to use as moulds and some string to make wicks from. I used to mash up the white candles, put some of the little candles in to make the wax some kind of faint pink or green, then pour it into the yoghurt pots, having first suspended a bit of string over it, tied to a bit of twig from the garden so the wick hung down into the wax. I could make striped ones by letting the wax solidify, then melting some more and adding a different colour to it. My things were in the far part of the cellar, after the part where Dad had his workbench and kept tools and screwdrivers and drills, with bits of old wood, "just in case" they came in handy. I wanted some newspaper to put some finished candles on, I'd squeezed them out of their moulds, I saw some paper peeking out from underneath some boxes under the bench.

When I pulled the paper out, it was a magazine with pictures of naked women in it. I studied it quite closely. I couldn't quite work out what it was at first, or why it was there. I was fascinated by their shapes and colours. They had breasts, some of them huge, and hair in places I didn't. They were sitting in a variety of poses which looked really uncomfortable, yet they were all smiling at the camera, pushing their chests forward, spreading their legs, touching themselves in that place which I had already discovered brought a pleasant warm feeling. Looking at the pictures gave me something of the same sensation.

I started to wonder whether that was why Dad had them. Yet, if they were hidden in the basement, that meant that probably there was something not quite right about them, you weren't supposed to like them or want to look at them, I guessed. After a while, I put them back. I never said anything about them to Mum or Dad, but the next time I went down in the cellar they weren't there. It was not unreasonable that Dad would have been interested in the unclothed female form. I still could not connect that to actually doing something physical about it with my mother. After my sister left home they moved into separate, single beds, and a few years later, into separate bedrooms, because of my father's snoring, Mum said.

After Suzanne died, I didn't want to be famous anymore. I just wanted to get through, at first just from day to day, then gradually from week to week, and eventually I could handle whole months at a time. It was as much as I could do to concentrate on my course work, so that everything else that happened, going back home, going out with Paul, working at the council offices, finishing my degree, all occurred without me doing anything, even getting together with Dick and moving in with him.

When Dad got cancer there was no brain space to think of anything else. Events after he died all tumbled together. Getting married, getting pregnant, having Zanne and then Martin. By that time being famous seemed to be unimportant. So the fact that I am famous now is a strange irony, and that it is all because of Suzanne's work completes the circle.

When I sit here in our wonderful house, bought with the money I won for Suzanne's poem about her and Dick, I look out at the garden and my mind goes into neutral. It's always the same images that come up, those times when I decided to do one thing instead of another, that led to the next fork in the path, and so on, right up to the garden I'm looking at and the house I'm sitting in. I read a book by Richard Bach, called *One*. Somehow he and his wife got to experience all these different lives, the what ifs and if onlys, for instance, if he'd never spoken to her in the lift when they first met, if he'd not agreed when she wanted him to make a commitment. He got to see how the life he had was the best one that he could have made.

I'm not sure that I feel the same way. It would have been better if Suzanne was still alive, if the poems had never been published under my name, if Dick and I were still living in the back-to-back and getting by. There's always the problem that if Suzanne hadn't died would Dick and I have got together? Do we really always do the best that we can with the knowledge we have at the time?

I'm not so sure. Sometimes my best doesn't look so great.

Sarah September 1988

School

Sarah stirred and realised that Zanne must have got into bed next to her at some time during the night. The small body was curled into her armpit, her fine blonde hair spilling over Sarah's arm. Sarah snuffled her nose into the curve of the child's neck, enjoying the warm sweet smell of her skin.

"Mu-umm, stop it," Zanne complained sleepily.

"Sorry, sweetie," Sarah apologised and eased her arm out from underneath the child's head. She glanced at the clock, It was 7.30am already. She registered that Dick was not lying beside her and that a cooling cup of tea stood on the bedside table. He must have let her sleep in. Today of all days!

She swung her legs out of bed and padded through to the bathroom and had a rudimentary wash. "Zanny, sweetie, wake up, you've got to get dressed, it's your first day at school," she said, making no impression on the sleeping child. She hurriedly pulled on tights and rifled through her wardrobe to find a shirt that wasn't too badly crumpled and she could wear without ironing and tucked it into her plain black skirt.

She sketched some make-up onto to her face, reflecting not for the first time that she still followed the same make-up routine, on the rare occasions when she used it, as she had done when she was at school and had picked up pointers from *Jackie* magazine, so that it was about fifteen years out of date. Calling to Zanne again, she rushed through to the child's bedroom and gathered her new school uniform, checking briefly by sticking her head round the door that Martin was not in his room and praying that that meant that Dick had got him up and dressed. She could hear the faint sounds of Radio 4 in the kitchen downstairs.

She persuaded Zanne into her clothes, trying to excite her by repeating, "Your first day at school, wow! What a big, grown up girl you are!" Eventually she got through to her about the momentous nature of the occasion, but this only served to make Zanne start jumping up and down on the bed as Sarah tried to capture her feet in the new white ankle socks and insert her arms into the navy blue cardigan. "Zanny, stop. Go and show daddy and tell him what you want for breakfast," she said, gritting her teeth to stop the rising wave of panic from breaking over them both. "Late, going to be late!" sang her inner voices.

At last it was done, Zanne ran downstairs, shouting "Dad, dad, I'm going to school today!" as Sarah checked her face and clothes in the mirror to see if she'd got even more crumpled in the melee.

Dick, bless him, was helping Martin spoon Weetabix into his mouth without getting too much of it onto his clothes. Zanne's breakfast of toast and jam and juice was laid out on the table, although the child herself was jumping around like a frog, shouting "School today! School today!" Sarah grabbed a bowl of corn-flakes and some orange juice, putting the kettle on for a fresh cup of tea.

"Zanne, sit down and eat your breakfast or you won't be able to go to school," she threatened emptily. Of course Zanne was going to school, otherwise she couldn't go to work, she wouldn't get paid and then the whole precarious pack of cards fell down.

Dick finished helping Martin with his breakfast, cleared the table and started the washing up. Sarah realised that they hadn't yet spoken to each other that morning, but then any pleasantries and social chat between them got submerged under child care arrangements. She ran through the day in her head. Dick was dropping Martin off at the childminders, Sarah taking Zanne, as the school was just opposite the library. Angela, mother of one of Zanne's new classmates, would pick up Zanne and take her home to her house, where Sarah would pick her up at 3pm.

Dick was now wondering aloud, "I'm not sure that I can get to the childminders at five in time to pick Martin up. I think the Dean might call a meeting today to discuss possible staff redundancies." Sarah felt the end of her day extend into more rushing from place to place, getting children in and out of coats, getting them back to the house just slightly too late for it to be in comfortable time to make tea before they started to get cranky and tired.

"But it won't affect you in any case, will it," she protested. "Why do you have to go?"

"I don't know, I'll have to see. I'll ring you when I know what I'm doing," Dick was stuffing his briefcase with papers and marked assignments.

"But when will you know?" Sarah felt her voice start to whine, her carefully constructed day crumbling into uncertainty.

"I don't know, I'll call you. Bye." He kissed her briefly on the cheek, then bent to hug his daughter. "Bye, Suzanne, have a great day at school!" He held her tight, his dark head next to her fair one. Sarah realised that Dick was the only one who called Suzanne by her full name. Then he was gone in a whirl of jackets and gloves and hats for him and Martin, leaving Sarah to chivvy Zanne into cleaning her teeth, check her school bag and put their own coats on to make the short walk uphill to the school on Chapeltown Road.

Zanne's class was in the back playground, children were tearing around shrieking as parents stood about, no longer the centre of their child's world but merely an attendant clutching the school bag and PE kit, occasionally catching each other's eyes and grimacing in shared experience of the morning panic of getting their children ready for the first day at school.

Where had it all gone, thought Sarah, that passion and excitement, not being able to keep their hands off each other, necking over breakfast, always a full on tongue swizzler of a kiss before Dick left for work? Was this what she had come to, a dowdy mother in the playground, feeling more love for her children than her husband? A bloody librarian to boot. Working to pay the bills, not even able to afford a holiday.

The teacher came out into the playground, ringing a hand bell, just like Sarah's own first day at school. The children were tamed into lines and trooped inside behind their respective class teachers. Zanne, focused on the day ahead, didn't look back to see Sarah's forlorn wave.

As she walked up the road towards the library, Sarah found a string of images crowding into her head, starting with her own first school days, through her teens, to her hopes in going to university, meeting Dick for the first time, and of course Suzanne, that other Suzanne, always her, lying stiff on her bed. Was this what it had all been for?

Sarah shook her head to get rid of the pictures but instead they swirled around like snowflakes in a plastic dome. Somehow the image of the poems she had taken got stuck, it wouldn't flush away. It occurred to her that they had got her out of one mess, they could get her out of this one. The thought took root, no matter how she weakly tried to resist it. She'd seen an advert in *Woman's Own* for their poetry competition, there was a prize of £500. What if she won it? At least they could take that holiday, get away, have some time together, the four of them. She could tell Dick she'd got some kind of bonus at work maybe, or some premium bond had come up.

She bought some stamps on her way back from work and posted her entry to the competition, using one of Suzanne's poems, on the way to pick up Martin from the childminder, bribing Zanne with sweets so she would walk without throwing a tantrum. As she slipped it into the box she caught a quiver in the air, a bend in the cosmos. Another domino fell.

Sarah   Now

Pregnancy

It amazes me, looking at my children, that I gave birth to both of them. There's Zanne, my bright and shining golden daughter, who draws everyone to her with her bright blue eyes and open nature. She was a wonderfully calm baby, belying the turmoil I had gone through with my sudden pregnancy, having to carry a pocketful of dried apricots and soft white bread rolls around to stave off the constant nausea.

"Morning sickness?" I would bark, "I'd be OK if it was morning sickness. This is twenty-four-hour-a-day sickness."

Then of course there were those unaware, insensitive, puzzled enquiries after my health, "But shouldn't you have stopped all that by now?" as the sudden breaking off of conversation to run for a toilet continued into the fourth month and beyond, right up until I was in labour, dammit. They managed to make it sound like I was doing it on purpose.

"Yes, silly me," I felt like saying, "I'd better stop it now then hadn't I?"

I fought my pregnancy all the way along with Zanne. I hadn't wanted to be pregnant and I didn't feel ready. Dick and I had only just got married, even though we had been together for over two years, and I wanted to enjoy that. I also hated all those knowing looks that told me that they knew the real reason why we'd decided to get married in such a rush then, when it hadn't been the reason at all. The icing on the cake was that my mother approved of us at last, and went round preening that her youngest offspring was to make her a grandmother for the third time. It was unbearable.

There were moments when I reconciled myself to the fact that I was going to be a mother, but only moments. As soon as I realised I was feeling happy and accepting, something would always leap in to make me feel disgruntled and resentful of the baby growing inside me, without any effort of conscious will on my part.

"Now I'm going to be stuck at that damned library for another eighteen months," I moaned to Dick. I was just within the time to claim maternity leave but would have to return to work for three months afterwards.

"You never told me you wanted to leave," he said, glancing up from his paper to watch as I paced back and forward across the living room, not easy in such a small house.

"That's not the point," I whined. As it turned out I was only back a year before I left to take maternity leave with Martin, then back again when he was seven months old.

"What about all that travelling we were going to do? We probably never will now," I muttered gloomily.

"Sarah, we've never even got around to discussing where it was we want to go, or when, or even saved up the deposit for the tickets." Dick attempted to rationalise me out of my bad mood.

"Now we're going to be stuck in some godawful resort on the Costas or in the Canaries, with loads of other couples with squalling brats. We'll never be able to go out because we won't be able to find or afford babysitters. We're going to have to convert the study into a nursery. We'll probably never have sex ever again," I wailed, my list of complaints getting longer the more I thought about it.

"That's ridiculous," Dick replied, returning to his newspaper. "We've got the evidence of several families of our acquaintance, including our own, that sex is possible after you've had one child."

"Well, just in case, maybe we'd better make up for it now. After all, we don't have to worry about contraception," I reasoned, suddenly horny, whipping his paper out of his hands and starting to unbutton his shirt.

"See, always a silver lining," he gasped, reaching around to pull me onto his lap.

When I was about seven months pregnant with Zanne, I woke at 4am to go to the loo. This had been my habit since the very early weeks, much sooner than it should have been according to everyone who of course knew far more about my pregnancy than me. It finally hit me that I was going to have a baby soon. I'd been musing on the fact that while I was wakeful and wandering round the house that there were other people, normal people, in Leeds that were asleep at that moment.

"Only another six weeks of this to go," I'd thought gratefully, then realised the absurdity of the thought, because after that there would be another small organism in the house that would think it was normal to be awake in the middle of the night.

Two weeks later, the enormity of what we had managed to create so thoughtlessly was brought home when I saw a woman walking along not with a pushchair but with a boy of about ten. Pregnancy led to a baby, and then that baby was going to be around for ever. Aargh!

The labour was long and painful. Near to the end of the twenty-four-hour long marathon I announced, "I've had enough, I want to go home, I'll come back tomorrow and start again but now I'm bored and that's it, thanks."

The midwife, who'd obviously seen it all before, informed me "Well, if you expended the same amount of energy in pushing the baby downwards and less in spouting hot air through your mouth, then we might all get home in time to watch the next episode of *Eastenders*".

That did the trick. Out she came, with a mass of dark curls and little black button eyes that regarded all around her calmly, as if to say, "Ah, there you are, at last", as if it had been me that had been dawdling, not her.

She was a wonderful baby, she slept through the night after only six weeks, as long as she shared our bed. In her own cot she was restless and fretful, so we gave in to her then like so many times as she got older. She had an air of expectation that everything would come to her without effort, that all would be provided, and of course it was. She knew exactly who to dimple at for maximum effect. Her father was under her tiny thumb virtually from the moment he cut the cord. She walked early and talked late, but made up for the latter by packing in all those words she'd been longing to say for the previous months. She sailed her own course, with a fair following wind, through nursery and school. Her teenage years were the usual battle, as she fought every step of the way to convince us that she knew best. She'll probably graduate with a first class degree. Unlike my own wrestling with the system, Zanne has charmed the lecturers as well as her contemporaries, to judge by the number of adoring swains she has brought back with her for weekends, and the bill for her mobile phone.

Martin was different from the start. He was a restless foetus, in fact at one ante-natal examination the midwife had difficulty measuring him because he wouldn't keep still and ended up splayed out like a starfish, stretching the boundaries even then. I, on the other hand, remained relaxed throughout. I slept long, dreamless sleeps. The birth was quick, he was impatient to be out. Martin didn't want to sleep and he wanted company in his wakefulness. I don't think he slept through the night until he was about ten. The day that he learnt to operate the video recorder independently when he was three was a momentous occasion in our house, when Dick and I looked at each other and blearily realised we'd slept in and were both late for work.

Rather than Zanne's navy-blue-eyed blondeness, Martin took his dark hair from his father' side, and his blue eyes were so pale as to be slate grey in most lights. As he grew he continued to be restless, walking before eight months, climbing a month later, making it to the top of Zanne's bunk beds before he was a year old. He was never that interested in words, he was content to make do with the few that satisfied his basic needs for food, warmth, and more food. In contrast to his sister's torrent of communication, he has always managed to get by with the minimum of words, choosing subjects at school which allowed him to work silently, like maths and computing.

Yet once he is on the football pitch he is a meteor, trailing sparks from his studs, never seeming to taunt the other players with his skill, a superb team player so that he is always popular. He has never made as much noise about what he wants as Suzanne, he has just quietly gone and got himself where he wants to be. He agreed to complete his A levels, but is immovably adamant that he will leave school to play for any professional club when they decide to sign him.

Both my children know who they are, they've never had to hide or to run away to be someone else, like I did. They would never have made the same dreadful mistake that I did, although I'm sure they've got plenty of their own to make. But then, what do I know? I expect my mother never thought she'd given birth to a murderess.

Sarah   March 2000

Local Woman Wins Poetry Prize

Cumbrian-born Sarah Challenger (nee Martin) has won the first ever Pepper Weinstock Prize for Poetry, worth £50,000. Her poem, *Breathe*, was "a tour de force of language, a deep insight into the nature of inter-dependency," said the chair of the judges, poet laureate David Morgan.

"I'm surprised and honoured," said mother of two Sarah, 41, who attended Ulverston Victoria High before gaining a place at York University to study English. Her latest collection of poems, *Blank Space*, has been on the best sellers list for four weeks.

Her mother, Margaret, stills lives in Cumbria, in Grange over Sands. "I always knew she'd do well," she said. "I'm so proud of her."

"Sarah was an excellent student and always got excellent results in English," said her old headmistress, Samantha White (retired).

Sarah is married to renowned biochemist Dr Richard Challenger, whom she met at university, and has two children, Suzanne, 16, and Martin, 14.

Sarah   Now

Winning

Winning that damn poetry prize three years ago was the last straw. I didn't know what to do with the money at first, I didn't want to spend it. Then Dick found this house in Roundhay that we live in now, so I get to live with my guilt every day. What a burden. Occasionally I get twinges of nostalgia for his back-to-back, cramped though it was, even though we were always scrimping to make ends meet.

Winning made me look at my life and see what a load of lies it's been based on. I denied my attraction to Dick, I went off with Jules to avoid Sam, I lied to Jules when I said I didn't love her. I used Suzanne's work as my own so that Professor Ellis wouldn't throw me off the course and I'd have to go home to my parents with my tail between my legs.

The only true things in my life are my children. They are not fake, nor are my feelings for them. Does it make it another lie if they don't really know what their mother is capable of? When Suzanne was young I was so afraid that something would happen to her, that she would be harmed because of my past actions.

When Martin came along the ghost who'd followed me around since the first Suzanne died got buried under nappies and playgroups and all the mind numbing drudgery of cooking and cleaning and washing, endless washing. The only light relief was talking to other mothers at school coffee mornings and playgroups, when we could have the small luxury of some adult conversation, even if it was often only "Did you see last night's *Eastenders*?"

What a respite from discussions of all the different engines in Thomas the Tank Engine stories. I hated them, sanctimonious group of whingers for the most part, and totally misogynist. Why do children like them? All of the women knew we only had our children in common, so that when a child left to go to a different nursery or school, contact withered despite all our promises to keep in touch.

There were some bright moments, when I connected with someone else who had a child the same age as one of mine. Angela's daughter, Emily, was in the same class as Zanne. We had similar wants. A quiet place, some child-free time. Trips to the Turkish baths in Harrogate on Sunday mornings became a regular outing. We gave ourselves a gift of care, all too rare. Normally we were lavishing care on children and husbands. We had to form an alliance to remind us that we could actually treat ourselves.

"Do you ever read a book?" she would ask me.

"Heard of it. Thing with pages?" I'd query. We would reminisce on all those pre-child activities. "Remember swimming?"

"You mean, as in, up and down the pool, not just hanging about freezing in the shallow end with somebody wearing armbands?" she replied.

Sometimes I went to the Turkish Baths alone, allowing myself the treat of not talking to anyone else for an hour, just lying in the heat and feeling it get right into my bones. Leaping into the icy plunge pool and coming out feeling alive all over. Afterwards I'd trudge up to Betty's Tea Rooms to indulge in hot chocolate and cheese scones. It was the same one as I had found refuge in that summer before Suzanne's death. No longer a student, I could even just about afford their amazing Yorkshire rarebit once in a while, sizzling in its steel dish, browned on top with crispy bacon artistically draped on the cheese. Bliss!

The world of mutual babysitting and sleepovers opened up when the kids got old enough, even the occasional free night when I managed to arrange for both of them to stay with their friends at the same time. Emily was a regular sleepover partner for Zanne, so that Angela and her husband Jack got to play at being a couple again too. Martin was more difficult to place, but occasionally the childminder would do an over night for us. Although it was great to be just the two of us to catch up and remember why we were together in the first place, the house always felt quiet and empty until they came home again. Often we'd find that all we talked about were the kids anyway.

"Do you think Martin is ever going to speak in whole sentences?" I'd worry.

"What? Like me?" Dick would joke.

"You do most of your thinking below the waist anyway," I'd tease him.

"Funny you should mention that. I've been having a few interesting thoughts recently," he smiled, pulling me towards him.

Those years of struggling to make ends meet on Dick's salary as a lecturer also obscured the power of that ghost. I came across that wedge of papers in the cellar where I'd hidden them, when I was looking for the stabilisers to Suzanne's old bike so I could fit them to Martin's. It was easy to give in to thoughts of using them to enrich our lives. I started by sending them to poetry magazines and newspapers, at first to pay for a holiday, then whenever one of the kids needed new shoes or a winter coat. It got to be more frequent, not even needing a special purchase to allow me to justify the deception. I always signed them "SM", just to keep alive the illusion that I wasn't really taking credit where it was not due.

Greed was my downfall of course. There was a call for poems on Radio 4. If I hadn't sent them, Cynthia would never have heard them and rung me up, wanting to be my agent. She wouldn't give up either. She kept ringing, and writing. "Please answer my calls, Mrs Challenger," she would plead on the answerphone. She even managed to get a publisher interested and sent me a suggested figure for royalties on a first volume. I was a bit stunned by the figure she suggested, not that it was overly large or anything, just £500. The problem was that Dick and I had just decided yet again that we couldn't go on holiday that year, we couldn't afford it. He found the letter in the kitchen letter rack where I'd stuffed it the day before, to avoid having to deal with it.

He was amazed, but also pleased and proud of me.

"I hadn't realised that you've been keeping us afloat with your writing. Why didn't you tell me? Why don't you accept the book offer? Don't you want your work to appear in print?" he asked.

"Well, of course I do," I admitted, but how was he to know that it wasn't my work. None of it. The writer's block that had hit in my second year with such devastating consequences, the ripples spreading out affecting all those lives, had never lifted. I'd regarded it as my penance. I'd forgotten that once I graduated I'd promised myself that I would never seek to gain anything from using Suzanne's work again, and even though I'd broken that promise again and again, publishing a book seemed like taking it too far. Yet because I couldn't tell him the real reason for my reluctance to agree to Cynthia's offer, all my excuses sounded weak. So of course it ended up with me agreeing to go ahead.

My first book came out thirteen years ago. I'd hoped that would be the last of it, but of course it was just the start. There have been two more since then. The last one, *Blank Space*, managed to get onto the poetry best seller list somehow. That meant interviews with the local press, on local TV and radio. Even an appearance on the South Bank show with Melvyn Bragg. "Any excuse to get another Cumbrian on the show," he told me.

The same questions over and over again. I was forced to retell my life story so many times it started to feel like a novel, with a very unlikely plot.

"Where do you get your inspiration from?"

"Who was the most important person in your literary life?"

"Who influenced your writing the most?" I couldn't own up to the truth. Who was that woman who had gone to university in 1977 with such high hopes and a foolish plan to reinvent herself? What had I done with my life since I left?

"I'm was just a housewife and librarian," I'd reply weakly. I could tell all the interviewers thought I'd wasted my degree by getting married to my university boyfriend, had two kids and never worked at anything much.

"So where is all this amazing poetry coming from?" one asked me. A box in the cellar, that's where, sang the silent reply in my head.

I suppose Dick might have started to get jealous from all the attention I was getting, even though it had been him who had pushed me into it in the first place. Luckily, at about the same time as the first book came out, he had an article published in a journal about some research he'd done on phosphates in soil and how they illustrated what kind of things people had used to eat. He'd been working with the people at the York Archeological Trust. This prompted some big pharmaceutical company to sponsor more research, and he was appointed to lead the team. I guess that the publicity I was getting around the books helped, as it was always mentioned that I was married to him and what he was doing.

So now here we are, twenty-five years on from my first theft of Suzanne's work to fulfil an assignment that I probably could have completed on my own if I'd just sat down and thought about what I was doing, rather than sleeping around in an effort to deny my feelings for Jules and my commitment phobia. We live in large detached Victorian house near Roundhay Park. My daughter got herself a place at Oxford, she's going into her second year now. Martin goes to Allerton Grange, just down the road. It's not a brilliant school, but it suits him. He's even condescended to take A levels in computing, maths and technology. He just wants to play football and he's even got himself spotted by some scouts for Northampton so he's going for a trial soon.

Everything looks fair but it's all founded on darkness, like Snow White's beautiful apple that's glossy and red on the outside but rotten at the core. My penance is that I have to bear it all alone, I'm the only one who knows the truth. I've paid the price after all.

Sarah and Dick   July 2000

The Prize

The prize-giving was held in the Brewery in the City. A strange place for a literary event, Sarah thought, as she and Dick travelled to London in a stretch limousine, courtesy of the prize sponsors. She found it hard to hang onto her private outrage that she had been put in the position of accepting a cheque for £50,000 for Suzanne's poems, watching the spectacle of Dick enjoying the ride.

"This is what it's all about, isn't it?" he said, slouching in his chair, which was more like an armchair than a car seat. They were drinking chilled champagne from the fridge and watching television, Dick channel-hopping with the remote control. Sarah smiled and watched the motorway slip by outside the tinted windows.

"Better not get too used to it," she warned.

"Why not? I could cope with being a kept man," he smirked.

The event was better than she had anticipated. Her agent, Cynthia, was there, of course, along with Ann Marie, the publisher's publicity woman, who wanted Sarah to submit to a round of media interviews.

"We've got *Channel 4*, the *Guardian* and possibly the *TLS*," she gushed.

"Only if I can do them from Leeds," said Sarah, hoping this would put her off. She hadn't realised that in the era of ISDN and remote TV feeds, that she could participate in nationwide television from the BBC studios in Woodhouse Lane, or Yorkshire TV in Kirkstall. Radio was the same. The literary magazines would be satisfied with a phone call. At least she didn't have to cope with much right then. There were a few photographers there from the nationals, but winning a prize for poetry was hardly front page news.

Dick had insisted, "Let's splash out on some new clothes for the occasion."

"But I don't even have the cheque yet," she protested. "And why waste all that money when we'll probably never get to wear them again anyway?" But there he was in his new tux, and she had to admit he did look delicious. She rarely saw him in formal clothes. For work he dressed in old cord trousers, gone baggy at the knee, brushed cotton plaid shirts and loose V necked sweaters. At the weekends it was much the same, although he swapped the cords for ancient denims. They rarely went out, so they never had an excuse to dress up. Whilst the income from her books had meant that they could take holidays abroad and live reasonably well, this payment would make all the difference.

Dick had already started to get estate agents' details and there was a wonderful house in Roundhay that he had dragged her round at the weekend.

"We could use the money for a bigger deposit so we could afford the mortgage," he said. "It makes it easier now that I've got Principal Lecturer." He had succeeded in the last promotion round due to the fact that his latest research proposal was about to bring a load of cash into his department.

"Can't we get a smaller house that we could afford just on your salary," Sarah had argued. "Zanne will be off to university soon, and Martin will probably leave home too." She knew she was fighting a losing battle, and seen the way his eyes had lit up as he had walked round the house. After years of getting by, he wanted to live richly, to the limit of their resources. She would give in.

She let herself enjoy looking at her husband. He seemed at ease, as though he wore a dinner suit all the time. It was a change to be able to see the lines of his body under his clothes, and he'd chosen a well fitting and flattering cut that emphasised the lines of his trim bottom. She licked her lips, just as Dick turned and caught her expression. He grinned and raised his eyebrows, signalling that he fully intended to enjoy the king size bed in the hotel the publisher had put them up in. As always, Sarah felt her body moisten in anticipation.

She caught a glimpse of herself in the floor length mirrored glass as they went through to the reception. Dick had insisted on coming with her to buy her dress.

"Left to your own devices you'll just wimp out and go for something on the reduced rail at Marks & Spencers," he suspected, rightly. Instead they had spent a delirious afternoon trying on evening dresses in a variety of department stores before he pronounced, "It's got to be this one." It was a floor length blue velvet with a plunging neckline from the designer shop in the Cornmarket. He had made the right choice, the dress skimmed her curves and was kind to her thickening waist. It brought out the deep blue of her eyes and emphasised the length of her neck. She wasn't the slim streaked blonde who had gone to university but Sarah thought that she looked pretty good for a woman, over forty, who had had two children.

The event was informal and relaxed, and the presentation happened at the beginning of the evening after a minimum of speeches. Sarah said a brief, "Thank you," to her agent and publisher, and to Dick and the family for supporting her. She didn't mention Suzanne Mercer, whose work was published in the slim volumes that she signed for those who wanted to buy them. She didn't even wince as the chair of the judging panel read out the winning poem, *Breathe*. She looked at Dick when it was read, wondering if he realised that it was Suzanne's words that were being read.

Later, Dick made good on his earlier promise. Despite the quantity of champagne he had drunk, he made love to her slowly and deliberately, pressing all the buttons he knew so well. He stroked her back with his fingertips, making all the hairs on her body stand erect, teasing her by running his hands around the sides of her breasts and groin until she was moist and ready. Then he spread her legs and placed his hot mouth deliberately in her bush, flicking her clitoris with his tongue. Sarah gasped as he reached up and squeezed one of her nipples between his finger and thumb, massaging her breast with the palm of his hand, causing a lightening bolt of heat to shoot through her body.

She couldn't tell any longer what he was doing to her, or where, or with what. There was only pure sensation, filling her up, making it difficult to breathe. Somewhere far away she could hear someone moaning, a deep animal sound deep in the throat. Her fists clenched, all her muscles tightening. She was riding the crest now, on and on, close to breaking but never quite falling, until at last the orgasm crashed over her in a shower of sparks that flashed beneath her eyelids.

Dick slipped into her as the aftershocks rippled through her body, prolonging the sensation, she reached out and clasped him to her, drawing him deeper and deeper in, right into her molten core. She was desperate, abandoned, she twined her fingers deep in his hair, raised her head to bite his chest. She could feel his breath on her cheek, quickening as the sensation moved up his prick till at last he was spent too, and they lay together, a tangle of limbs on the wide bed.

"My God, Mrs Challenger," he murmured when he had recovered his breath enough to talk," you are an amazing fuck." Sarah smiled and let sleep take her under.

She dreamed of Suzanne, a mixed up kaleidoscope of images of their friendship. Meeting on the first day got jumbled up with Suzanne propositioning her in the bar at Goodricke, only this time they kissed. She could taste the wine on Suzanne's tongue. She realised that Dick and Jules were watching them from the corner, his hand in Jules' shirt. Then they were all at the prize reception and she was taking the cheque when Suzanne started screaming, "Thief! Thief!" Her face was close up, Sarah could see her reflection in her wild eyes, saw her own hands reach out, circle Suzanne's neck and start to squeeze. But although the light in her eyes dimmed and her body slumped to the floor, still Sarah could hear her voice, shouting out, "You stole them all! They're mine." When she looked around the brightly lit room no one else seemed to have noticed.

She woke with a start, the room was dark, she couldn't remember where she was, who was the sleeping body next to her. Slowly the nightmare slipped away from her and she could feel the cotton sheet against her skin, hear the familiar rhythm of Dick's breathing. Her heart was racing, her head ached and her throat was dry, but this was no hangover. She lay next to Dick and watched the numbers on the digital clock next to the bed change minute by minute, but she didn't want to sleep. At last, just as dawn was beginning to lighten the sky behind the thick brocade curtains, she fell into deep dreamless sleep that was broken by the acid tones of the morning DJ on *Radio One* as the alarm went off.

Sarah   Now

Sex

There was always something new when I had sex with Dick. Food featured highly in our adventures. One time, shortly before I moved in with him, I had gone over to Leeds. It was a warm June, the sash windows of the lounge were open, a soft breeze moved the air. We had unfolded the old sofa bed onto the sanded wooden floor and were lying on it, wrapped together like tulip leaves, watching some old Fred Astaire film, probably a video. Dick knew that I had a weakness for the old black and white dance movies, which had the advantage of having no real plot to speak of so that anything you missed in the middle could be easily surmised. And of course Ginger's dresses were always to die for.

It was quite domestic really, apart from the fact that Dick began to stroke the band of skin he liked, just above the waistband of my jeans. And of course that just turned me to jelly, quivering. Then we started to undress each other, slowly, button by button, piece by piece. Shirts, jeans, underwear, peeled off and discarded. We didn't speak, there was no need. The soundtrack from the movie played in the background. All my senses became focused on the touch of Dick's fingers, of his mouth on my skin, the texture of him against the palm of my hand. Everything started to melt. But then, he wasn't there. I started to surface. What was going on? He was back just as suddenly, with fruit. A mango, ready peeled. I realised later that whilst many things with Dick seemed spontaneous, he had planned ahead.

He took a bite, but didn't swallow. Instead he bent his mouth to my breast, taking the nipple in with the soft flesh of the fruit, I could feel the juice run down my chest into my navel, sticky and warm. Then his mouth was on mine, feeding me. I took the mango into my mouth and swallowed, feeling it slide silkily, while Dick followed its progress with small, wet kisses down my throat to the hollow of my neck.

The mango was so ripe he was able to gouge a handful and press it onto my belly, spreading it like butter, then licking it up. At the same time he was oiling me with mango juice, moving his hands up over my breasts, around my rib cage and down, down to my thighs, up the inside of my legs, pushing his fingers inside me. Everything was wet and sticky and lush. Then he licked me all the way from my clitoris to my lips, sliding his prick inside me. We were slick with fruit, the sweet smell of the mango mingling with sweat and sex. I felt like all my senses were overloaded, smell, taste, touch. I could tell he was just about to come.

I lay back, expecting the rush as he filled me, but he stopped moving, drew back so that he was kneeling up on his haunches, still inside me so that I was spread wide before him. Slowly, deliberately, he licked his fingers and made them even wetter, then reached down and started to stroke me so that I came in just a few minutes, writhing against him to make the sensations last longer. As the excitement died, he started to move again, so that the feelings came back even stronger, as he stimulated all the nerve endings inside my cunt. I felt the stirrings of another orgasm building, I couldn't believe it, this had never happened to me before. I was lost in our gruntings and gaspings, every muscle in my belly and thighs tightening, taut as a bow string until I could feel Dick start to come inside me and then we went over the edge together. We lay together, exhausted, unable to speak, inarticulate, my eyes were wide open remembering the intensity.

As we started to untangle ourselves, we realised that the heat had melted the sugar in the juice and we were stuck together like Velcro, so that peeling apart was a slow and mildly painful process. I was amazed to find that I had left fingernail weals on Dick's buttocks and back as I had fought to pull him even deeper into me, and that I had a huge bruise on my neck where he had sucked and bitten me. We stumbled and crawled up the steep stairs to the bathroom, where we managed to persuade the ancient plumbing to part with enough water for a reasonably hot shower, which of course involved more mutual stroking and rubbing with shampoo and shower gel, but we were both incapable of taking it further.

It was then we began to discover the questionable wisdom of using mango as a sex aid—we were picking the strands of fruit out of our pubic hair for days afterwards. I even found some ground and mashed into the floorboards a few weeks later. So we could never quite bring ourselves to do it again, although "eating a mango" became a kind of secret password for having sex, and could be slipped into the conversation at any moment, causing my toes to curl and my thighs to squeeze together at the mere mention.

After that we tried body painting with Smarties, licking and swirling the colours, writing our names on each other. Then there was the toffee yoghurt, cold from the fridge, supplemented with maple syrup and that canned whipped cream that feels like dandelion puffs on the tongue. That was a particularly sticky and hilarious mixture, as we unwisely added a moulting feather boa to the mix, so we looked like plucked chickens and again had the problem of disposing of the aftermath. The feathers blocked the plug hole of the bath and had to be scooped out with my eyebrow tweezers.

Strawberries and champagne were more successful. The berries could be mashed onto the skin without the enduring problems we had with the mango, and champagne could be licked up from all orifices. Ice cream was a bit touch and go, as I over enthusiastically slapped a slab of maple butter walnut onto Dick's chest which threatened to cool the temperature of everything else too.

The wildness and frequency diminished after Suzanne was born. We were often both too exhausted to even go through the motions of the missionary position until Martin was over a year old. We had laid the foundations well and things soon picked up again, although never to the level of that first year. There was nothing to beat that magic moment as we got into bed together at the end of the day and laid our bodies alongside each other, skin to skin, fitting neatly into position, my head on Dick's chest, my shoulder nestled under his armpit, his arms wrapped around me and holding me close. In the morning, we'd wake up and gravitate towards each other in the warm bed like heat-seeking limpets. I am constantly amazed by the combination of hot, primal passion and everyday companionship that we have. How could Suzanne have ever thought that he was hers?

Dick 2000

Knowledge

I've known for years what Sarah did. I was going to use that old lie, I can't remember exactly when I found out, but of course I know when to the day.

She talks in her sleep, you see. Most of the time I sleep through it, but sometimes she has especially energetic dreams, thrashing about, struggling to swim across the sheet, throwing the quilt around like tossing a lifebelt in a storm.

It was a week after we went to London for the award. She had got the cheque in the post the day before. We drank yet another bottle of champagne to celebrate after we had paid it into our bank account. No more money worries for us.

I couldn't understand why she was so reluctant to think about buying a bigger house, we had lived in that rabbit hutch for far too long. Martin was starting to develop a hunchback as his bedroom was in the other dormer room under the eaves and his ceiling sloped across half of it. Suzanne's room was overflowing with the detritus of teenage womanhood, and she never seemed able to fit all of her clothes in the wardrobe. The bathroom, well, even Sarah couldn't pretend that was adequate. We'd installed a wall heater, but in the winter it didn't make much of a dent on the chill in there. You could just about stand to get out of the bath as long as you could leap into the two foot square area on the floor where you could actually feel any benefit from its activity, but soon the backs of your legs would start to burn. The kitchen was cute when I first moved in, but I was a bachelor then. It was ridiculous, there had to be constant washing up and putting away to free up any work space at all as most food preparation had to be done on the draining board.

I'd seen the details of the house in Roundhay three weeks before we knew that Sarah had won the prize. The picture in the estate agent's window just down from the bus stop caught my eye as I walked home one evening. It had that imposing Victorian front to it, but what made me stop was it looked like the house was slightly lopsided, like it was smirking somehow. There were some kind of designs in the brick, so that there was a mouth to the right of the front door, which sort of looked like a nose, and over the window on the first floor were two asymmetrical lines like eyebrows, one raised higher than the other. As well as that, a winding garden path led up through a dense thicket of forsythia and orange blossom, bracketed by beech hedges. For the second time in my life, I fell in love. Or rather the intense desire that I experienced, the need, the wanting to possess this place was more like lust. My mouth watered. For a moment I stared at it, my finger tips just touching the plate glass of the window. I went in and asked for the details.

I was surprised that it was less than I thought it would be, but it had been empty for nearly a year. The last inhabitant, an old lady, had gone into a nursing home and then died there. Whilst she had been away the garden had been allowed to run riot, and when we eventually did get around to viewing it, there was a light layer of dust over everything inside. The bathroom and kitchen needed modernising too, but she'd installed central heating and double glazing. The words tinkled musically in my ears as I read them. No more cowering in a tepid bath followed by the risk of third degree burns on my calves.

I had a suspicion that Sarah would throw cold water on my plan, so I carried the photocopied sheets around in my briefcase for over a week. Back and forth to work they went, like some secret love letters to an admirer. It was almost like being unfaithful, but far less stressful and messy. Before I told Sarah I went to see the bank manager to ask about a possible mortgage, and found out that whilst I could certainly get a mortgage on my new improved Principal Lecturer salary, we had nothing like what was needed for a deposit. I didn't throw the details away, I hoped that something would turn up to make my dream come true.

The next thing, Sarah found out she had won the poetry prize. £50,000! It couldn't have been better. Enough for a larger deposit which would reduce the amount of mortgage, sprucing up the kitchen and bathroom, a few new bits of furniture and the odd bit of decorating. Maybe some left over for a decent holiday, just the two of us. I even skipped round the living room when she told me, whooping and yelling "Yes! Yes!", and swinging her up in the air.

She didn't seem that excited by the news, muttered something about, "I don't deserve it, there must be better poets around."

"Nonsense!" I cried. "And even if that is true, why should it matter? They've given you the prize!" Without understanding the signs of her resistance, I plunged right in and told her about the house right away. "It's perfect!" I enthused, "You'll love it."

We viewed the house three times before the prize giving. Each time I fell more in love with it, each time Sarah found more things to pick holes in. We got a survey done, negotiated the price down a bit more because of what that revealed about the lack of damp courses and the need for a new roof. We had estimates for the essential work in the kitchen and bathroom, plus decorating the main bedroom and the lounge, which had a neat little alcove-type room off it which would be ideal for Sarah to have as a study. I could see that even she felt the pull of the jungle like garden in the back. "Fifty feet of rainforest," was how she described it.

By the time we went to the prize giving, we were at the make or break point, where we were either going to leap in and buy the damn thing or retire hurt. We had a great time in London, I hoped that at last Sarah had got used to the trappings of semi-fame. However, during the same time period it seemed that her nightmares got worse and more frequent. I would often wake to find her absent, then discover her asleep wrapped in her old towelling dressing gown on the sofa downstairs.

A week after we got back, I was woken by Sarah yelling and crying in her sleep. At first I couldn't work out what she was saying, apart from, "I'm sorry, Suzanne, I'm sorry." I thought for a moment she was talking to our daughter, but then she made some references to assignments and a lecturer called Ellis, so I realised with a pin prick of unease that brought me fully awake that she was talking to her long dead friend, my ex-girlfriend. She was really unhappy, I wondered whether I should wake her up, pull her out of it, but a confused remembrance of not being supposed to wake up sleep-walkers prevented me. She seemed to be so engrossed in what was going on in her unconscious, I was scared to catapult her out into the waking world.

I listened as she spilled the whole story. I couldn't believe it at first, maybe my ears weren't working properly. Then, I felt a rising chill from my intestines to my throat as I realised that it was all true. How could this woman that I had loved and lived with for so many years have done such a thing, and then continued to benefit from her crime by submitting Suzanne's poetry as her own? The Sarah I thought I knew didn't seem capable of such cold-blooded and planned deceit. She'd lived with this for years, all through the years of our marriage and having children. Things fell into place. At last I understood why she didn't want to spend the money.

This time it was my turn to get up and occupy the downstairs sofa in the early hours, my brain crowded with the images called up by Sarah's words, my eyes sightlessly watching the dawn come up over the town I'd lived in for so long. This morning it looked very different, as though in the night all the edges on the terraces had been honed to flinty sharpness, the road polished with silver. People walking by to catch the bus to start the early shift in the centre's shops and supermarkets looked like cut out cartoons, distinct from the background of tile and stone.

I ran all the possible courses of action in my head. Leaving Sarah was the first one I considered. Yet however I looked at it, whatever she had done, we had been together too long for me to face the prospect of starting out again on my own with any enthusiasm. What about the kids? How could I explain to them? Then there was the house. I wanted it so badly. I couldn't get it without Sarah's prize money. The worm of an idea grew into a serpent, slithering seductively amongst my thoughts. Could I be just as cold-blooded, just as calculating as my wife?

I made her a cup of tea and took it up to her in bed. Now, although she didn't know it, I had the upper hand. "Let's play truant," I suggested. "I'll ring in sick, you're not on rota at the library today. We could go for a walk round the lake, have lunch in the White House. Let's settle this house question once and for all. At the end of today, if you still don't want to do it, we'll forget it, no further questions. What do you think?" She gazed at me over the lip of the mug, sipping the hot tea. She was probably amazed that I had been able to string so many sentences together at that hour in the morning.

"Okay," she agreed. And that was that. I played my major card at the edge of Roundhay Park lake, pressed my advantage over beer and sandwiches and then we drove straight to the estate agents and the bank and signed all the papers. The house was mine at last.

Sarah and Dick   August 2000

Agreement

They parked on the street next to the entrance to the park. The high iron gates were strung between two pillars of Yorkshire limestone, crowned by lions. Sarah was grateful for Dick's offer of a truce. She had found it tough to resist that pleading look in his eyes every time he took her to his dream house and hoped that she would say "Yes, let's buy it!"

She couldn't tell him what it was that was making her resist. The bottom line was that she felt that she didn't deserve the Prize, which meant that she shouldn't spend the prize money. Her problem was that the person who did deserve the prize was dead. She didn't even know where Suzanne's parents lived, so she couldn't contact them and make some futile gesture of recompense. That would involve explaining why she felt compelled to make it. She was stuck in a circle of ill-defined promptings of guilt and fear.

It was a bright late summer morning, the sun making occasional appearances between high scudding cumuli, a brisk breeze slapping the water of the lake into wavelets. Sarah settled comfortably into her place, tucked under Dick's arm, her arm around his waist. As they walked across the dam she reflected that she had lived in Leeds for almost twenty years now, a place she had once sworn that she would never inhabit. "Times change," she thought.

"How's your new job?" she asked Dick, wanting to steer any conversation into a neutral area.

"Well, my teaching will decrease because they have to give me more time for my research. I'm supposed to participate in what they call, 'the strategic direction of the Department' though. More boring meetings I suppose."

"I thought it was what you wanted to do, though?"

"Yes, it is. I'm getting tired of teaching the same stuff to inattentive eighteen year olds," he said. "And I've never set a paper that I wasn't bored with after I've marked five of them. I keep hoping that I'm going to read something enlightening, or at least interesting, but I'm constantly disappointed!"

"How do you think our daughter is coping with her mock GCSE's," he queried her in turn. "I've not seen her for ages, she always seems to be closeted in her bedroom, playing awful music."

Sarah smiled. They were an old married couple for sure now, she thought. "Isn't that what our parents said about the music we played?" she said. "I'm sure she's fine. It's just that she speaks to me in that awful, snotty tone of voice, then I lose it, she slams the door and off she goes into her bolt hole. But the teachers all seem pleased with her."

They meandered through the wood alongside the lake, round the loop at the marshy end and by some unspoken agreement took the right fork up the hill to the bandstand. As they climbed, Sarah could see the grey roofs of the city start to come into view. The wind picked up, so that at the top they were able to lean into it and still not fall. She remembered the windswept mountain top where Dick had proposed, seventeen years ago. We've come a long way from there, she thought.

"Well, I'm worried about those friends she hangs out with up by the park in the Meadows," Dick went on. "Who knows what they are doing? Could be drugs or anything." Sarah pursed her lips.

"I can't imagine not trusting Zanne to do the right thing, but I suppose it's possible that she could get drawn into experimenting by Cathy and Jude. They're her two favourite friends at the moment."

"Is Jude the one with the pierced tongue?"

"Yes, I find myself staring at that silver stud like a mouse watching a cobra every time I try to have a conversation with her."

"Me too. It clicks against her teeth, doesn't it?" Dick grimaced.

"Thankfully I don't have to talk to Jude that often, they're at that age where it's painful to attempt to converse with adults," Sarah sighed. Both of Zanne's friends had left school at the end of the year, having achieved D's in a raft of GCSE's. They now worked in Sarah's old place of employment, the supermarket, although it had moved to larger premises just next to the pub.

"That's part of the reason I think we should move," Dick was saying. He stopped, put his hands on her shoulders and turned her to face him. Looking directly into her eyes he continued, "Don't you think you owe it to Suzanne to use this money?"

Sarah caught her breath in the instant before she remembered that Dick used Suzanne's full name. How could she have thought he was talking about her dead friend Suzanne, that he knew that she was the true author of the poem that had given them this thorny problem to resolve? She shook her head. "I don't know, I'll think about it," she prevaricated.

They returned to the road where they had left the car, and continued to the White House. The pub was dark and cosy, its rosewood panelling complemented by the buttoned leather sofas. They ordered sandwiches and lager, and settled onto the end of the deep cushioned Chesterfield. Sarah felt the house pressing on her. She could feel a weight of unease as she waited for Dick to raise the subject again. He was bound to make another pitch for it, he had said this was make or break time.

"Even if you think that the judges made the wrong decision, that they gave the prize to the wrong poem or the wrong poet, I just think you've got an opportunity to do something really good with this money," he prodded her.

Sarah knew in that instant that he was right. However she had come by this, whatever deep secret she had to keep to maintain the façade of the housewife poet that was her public image, she did owe it to Suzanne to spend the money well. She could make something good from her bad actions, lying and cheating, benefiting from her friend's death.

"Okay, you win," she sighed, feeling the heaviness drop away from her, casting herself onto the stream and letting it carry her away.

They signed the papers that afternoon and six weeks later they moved into the house on David Avenue.

Sarah   January 2001

Petra

Despite herself, Sarah found that she was excited about their trip to Sinai and Petra. As the date for their departure got nearer she found that her misgivings about spending the last of the prize money on a jaunt to the Middle East on their own got more and more submerged under her anticipation of the sights they would see.

They'd picked the tour from a brochure in the local travel agents. Eastern Promise ran all kinds of exotic trips to unusual parts of the world, combining the thrill of being in a less travelled location with the comfort of tour guides and concrete travel itineraries and reservations in top class hotels. It seemed like an acceptable compromise between Dick's desire to go backpacking totally on their own and her need to feel secure. She also wanted to make the best of the time they had together rather than, as she put it, "Schlepping around half the time trying to find a place to stay that isn't full of nocturnal night life—animal and insect!"

They arrived at Heathrow to join the party and found that they were the youngest couple in the group of twenty. Sarah bit her lip to stop herself laughing at Dick's lip-curling look of dismay at the sight of the people they would be travelling with. "My God, a load of wrinklies," he muttered under his breath to her. "We probably won't be able to get on the plane for all their zimmer frames."

"That's hardly accurate," she corrected him. "They are all moving independently without artificial aids."

"But for how long?" he queried. Of course, as they got to know the rest of the group they found that appearances were deceptive. Most of them were veterans of Eastern Promise, and Dick's eyebrows raised as he listened to the tales of where they had been before. One couple, Belinda and Terry from Eastbourne, had been up and down the Nile several times, taking in not only the main tourist hotspots of the Pyramids and Abu Simbel but also travelling to far flung oases in the Western Desert.

"We spent ten days climbing the foothills of the Atlas mountains in Morocco, but that was a bit too basic for our taste," said Terry.

"Yes, I'm a bit too old to cope with squatting toilets now," confided Belinda. "We're going to see Ephesus in Turkey next year." Terry was a retired builder,

Belinda was an avid reader of travel books, and they had set out to visit all the sites she had read about.

"I'm just along for the ride," confessed Terry, although they found out later that due to his time in Montgomery's desert rats in the last war he was fluent in Arabic and was a very useful person to have around when haggling in the marketplace.

Being the youngest meant that they became adopted as surrogate children by the others, who would give them tips on the best buys to look out for, how to avoid the attentions of the hawkers around all the sites the visited, as well as what was an appropriate amount of baksheesh. "You need to stock up with ball point pens and chewing gum," advised Charles, a writer on a photography magazine whose hobby was archaeology. "The kids out there love them." His wife, Bertice, agreed.

"You can get some fantastic silver and lapis jewelry," she told Sarah.

Their flight was called and they settled in for the six hour journey to Sharm-el-Sheikh on the Red Sea coast. Sarah tried to work out whether she and Dick had ever flown together as a couple. Dick had had the occasional trip to Europe to deliver academic papers at various conferences, they had had a couple of family holidays in Spain, but this was probably the first time it had been just the two of them. She leaned back in her seat, thumbing through the magazine which told her what films would be showing on the seat back screen in front of her, what duty free goods she could buy, what meals would be served.

Half an hour after they left the ground, she accepted a complimentary glass of sparkling wine from the stewardess. "Enjoy it while you can," advised Bertice, sitting across the aisle. "Some of the hotels we are going to are dry, because they are all Muslims of course." After an indifferent lunch of chicken salad, Sarah snuggled down against Dick's shoulder to try and catch up on some sleep.

"That's probably why you can never get to sleep in a bed," he grumbled, light-heartedly. "Napping in the middle of the day." Sarah smiled and nestled against his chest as he circled her with one arm, the other holding a copy of the *Rough Guide to Egypt*. It seemed only minutes later that she was waking from a two hour sleep, with only a third of the flight left to go. Dick had fallen asleep himself, his head lolling against the headrest, his book having slipped to the floor.

She raised herself off him and amused herself by reading a book by Dorothy Dunnett, who she had discovered in the library. Not normally a reader of huge historical novels, Sarah had been intrigued to find that one of the dramatic climaxes of this particular tale, *The Unicorn Hunt*, took place at dawn at the summit of Mount Sinai, which they were to climb in two days time to see the sun rise.

They spent the next two days recovering from their journey, lounging by the hotel pool in Nuweiba. They discovered the delights of the hotel's own coral reef, a few hundred yards up the sandy beach and thirty feet offshore in the clear blue water of the Red Sea. It was Sarah's first experience with snorkelling. She almost curtailed it at the start when she was so shocked at the vista that presented itself as soon as she dipped her head beneath the surface, that she gasped involuntarily and took in a mouthful of seawater. The coral lay twenty feet below on the seabed, but because of the perspective in the clear water it seemed that she could reach out and touch it, that it was just a few inches beyond her reaching arms. Shoals of bright yellow and azure blue striped fish swam amongst the fronds of the living reef, and came up to investigate this strange pink object floating above them, weaving around her waving arms but never allowing her to touch them.

They were roused in the mid-night darkness for their trip to Mount Sinai, Dick managing to fall asleep on the bus almost immediately whilst Sarah stared at the outlines of rock and desert softened by the absence of light. After an hour they disembarked in what seemed to be a deserted car park in the middle of nowhere. It was cool, they had been warned to wear layers. Sarah wore leggings under her cheesecloth skirt for warmth and because the first part of their ascent was to be made by camel. Surly faced beasts grunted and moaned in the pre-dawn, their drivers negotiating rapidly with their tour guide about the price to take them as far up the mountain as they were able to go. The acrid smell of camel dung made Sarah gag, she found herself wishing that there wouldn't be enough animals to go round, maybe it wouldn't be so bad to climb all the way to the top? Fate intervened, another driver arrived with two more of the grumpy beasts and soon the whole party was mounted and ready to go, Sarah and Dick bringing up the rear, their camels swaying up the steep path. She found that it was simpler to let herself go with the animal's swinging stride rather than attempt to consciously ride it. She could sense Dick behind her, and hear his occasional attempts at communication with the driver, using phrases he had learnt from Terry.

The darkness on the trail was broken by the lights of the chai sellers, dispensing mint tea and cold sodas. Sarah wondered at what time they would have to have ascended the mountain themselves in order to be in position to offer their beverages to the tourists making their sleepy way up. As the trail wound higher, she was grateful that her wish to be left without a camel had not been granted. It really was a long, steep climb. They got to the camel station at the top, where all was bustle and noise, and where she gratefully climbed off the pungent beast. She remembered vaguely her father telling her some war story about when he was stationed in Egypt, taking a camel ride and being bitten by his mount. Her own beast showed no interest in taking a nibble of her flesh, settling gratefully onto its haunches with a "whumph".

"How was it?" Dick asked her.

"I think I'm saddle sore," she replied, rubbing her buttocks.

"Sure I can't do that for you?" he offered.

"Later," she laughed. "Not in front of the camels!" There was little time for conversation, their guide was already ushering them up a narrow passage in the rock. It was only 5am, dawn was an hour away, but they still had a way to go. Hundreds of steps were cut into the mountain, rough and uneven, Sarah had to concentrate on her footing and not crashing into the people in front, aware of Dick's breathing behind her. She couldn't raise her eyes from the ground. They climbed flight after flight, reaching a corner only to find more spreading ahead of them into the night.

At last they came to the summit. Again Sarah was surprised at the activity and bustle at this hour on this remote mountain top. More sellers of refreshments of course, set up beneath the walls of the small chapel and mosque. How on earth had anyone built these structures so far from anywhere? She saw several people who had obviously spent the night here, huddled together in clumps of sleeping bags and rucksacks.

As her watch hand crept towards 6am, she and Dick installed themselves on a ledge on what seemed to be the side of the mountain everyone expected something to happen. She couldn't remember how to define the points of the compass to locate the east. They leant together, not speaking, just watching the muted activity around them.

Slowly the night sky started to change to grey, then pinkish white and rose tinged with gold as the sun started to make its everyday journey over the horizon. How many times had she watched the sun rise? Sarah thought it must be dozens, at York as a result of drunken all night parties, in Leeds after persistent dreams had woken her. Yet never over such a landscape, the hills of the desert stretching out on both sides, the horizon wide and empty. The air had a different quality, citrus bright. Logically she knew it was the lack of pollution, but somehow that didn't seem enough to explain how every breath she drew here felt as though it filled every centimetre of her lungs. She looked behind them at the plain grey walls of the chapel, tinged with the glow from the dawn. Perhaps it was because it was the land of the Sunday school stories of her childhood, the birthplace of religions, so that every stone and hill was overlaid with the patina of myth and fable.

The bright rim of the sun started to edge up into the sky, turning it from pink to azure. Sarah watched the disc for as long as she could, but all too soon the heat from the far distant star had burnt off the drifts of mist. Looking down, she saw that one of the backpackers still slumbered in his sleeping bag. She nudged Dick. "Imagine climbing all this way to find that you have had slept through the main event," she grinned ruefully.

Already the groups of tourists were milling and assembling for their descent. She spotted Belinda and Terry already making purposefully for the stairs. They had arranged to meet back at the bus. Charlie and Bertice were haggling with a vendor of trinkets, Bertice overacting as she picked up first one necklace and then the other, pursing her lips and frowning before she condescended to make an offer, the trader throwing up his hands, clasping one to his heart, miming shock at how low her price was. But soon the deal was done with smiles all round and the couple departed with their booty.

They waited for the log jam to clear before slowly making their way down. This time, Sarah could afford to gaze around her at the changing views as they descended, the ranges of grey, yellow and pink rock stretched out before her. They reached the camel station and refused the offer of a beast downwards, although they could see the others in their party swaying down the track below. Sarah and Dick skipped and skittered from rock to rock, striding over the sandy track.

"What did you think, then?" Dick asked at last.

"I thought it was...," Sarah searched for the right word. "Overpowering," she settled for, although she didn't feel cowed by the experience.

"Inspirational?" he queried.

"Maybe," she muttered, unsure whether that was adequate either.

She would have been grateful for the chai sellers on the way down as the temperature rose and the rock brightened into gold, but they had packed and left, to return for tomorrow's travellers.

They reached Petra two days later, having spent a day travelling from Nuweiba by boat and bus. The high speed hydrofoil across the sea to Aqaba was swift, but they had to enjoy hours of filing through hangar-like customs sheds at both ends as they left Egypt and entered Jordan. Without explanation they were made to wait whilst stern officials examined every item of a random selection of passengers' luggage. They held up cameras and video recorders, poked at personal stereos. Then just as suddenly, several people would be ushered through without hindrance.

The hotel was cool and modern, with the straight corridors and cropped carpets common to so many of the hotel chains around the world. "We could be anywhere from Bangkok to Bognor," she said to Dick.

Dick threw himself full length on the bed. He had taken advantage of the fact that this was one of the few places on their journey where alcohol was available to over do it on wine and beer. "Well, I have to tell you that I haven't been to either of those places and I don't intend to, so we'll never know," he replied, closing his eyes.

"Dick, do not go to sleep in your clothes," she warned him, prodding him without noticeable effect. In reply, he uttered a snore. "We're getting up at the crack of dawn to go into the city," she said, exasperated, as she pulled at his shirt and started to undo the belt on his trousers.

"Lower," he said, opening one eye and giving her a grin.

"You swine," she said, laughing as he pulled her down beside him.

They prepared for their excursion into the so called lost city with high factor sun screen and making sure that they carried bottled water with them in their day packs. Charlie had advised them to purchase the white lengths of cloth from local traders, and demonstrated how to tie them simply and stylishly into an effective headdress, leaving enough over to protect the backs of their necks.

The group assembled by the gate to the city, where their guide was explaining that whilst government regulations required that they pay for a horse to take them down the narrow rock alley, they were not required to actually ride one. "It's a way of the government subsidising the horsemen," he told them. Sarah and Dick looked at the crowds of young Jordanians racing their dusty black mounts up and down the canyon, and decided to walk, as did most of their party.

As they filed down the narrow cleft in the rock the guide told stories of the biblical incidents that had occurred here. It was the place where Moses was supposed to have struck the rock with his staff to bring forth water in the desert. "The Nabateans were very accomplished," he said, "and built vast sisterns in the rocks here to store water in between rains. So it is possible that Moses could have punctured one of these with his staff." Other stories were less picturesque. "The rains were so dramatic and sudden that torrents of water could wash down the narrow valley we are walking down and sweep unlucky travellers away." The tourists cast anxious looks at the sky, searching for rain clouds. Then it was time for more mythology. "One of the hills overlooking the city is the site of Aaron's tomb," he added.

Their first sight of the city was dramatic and elusive, a slender fissure of pink and gold. They emerged from the rock alleyway into a wide natural courtyard, to be presented with a towering structure cut into the cliff, with Roman pillars flanking a high Grecian gable. Venturing inside, they found only a small empty chamber, blackened by the smoke of Bedouin who had used the ancient tomb as shelter until the government discovered that more money could be made from tourism if they were evicted into a sterile concrete town a few miles away.

Sarah gazed at the strata of red, orange, gold and white rock which formed natural murals inside the cave like tomb, the pink elements giving Petra its nickname of the Rose Red City. It was clear that the Victorian traveller who had coined the term had been taking artistic licence. It was much more than that.

They walked further on into the ruins. The guide explained, "Only the tomb structures embedded in the rock survived two major earthquakes that had razed the rest of the ancient city." A vast empty plain was surrounded by highly decorated cliffs. Signs of recent archaeological activity had raised the beginnings of an avenue of Roman pillars, standing in the middle of a jumble of blocks and rediscovered pavements.

Bertice had been right about the jewellery. Groups of women and children held out handfuls of bright necklaces and bracelets, beaten silver mounted with sprinkles of blue, green and amber. Sarah resisted being drawn, she felt diffident about approaching these people she felt had been obliged to surrender their homes and independence to rely on the charity of foreigners. Bertice and Belinda were busy making purchases however, as were several members of the group.

They passed a huge amphitheatre set into the rock. "The Nabateans were so effective at storing the water in their huge cisterns that they had enough over to flood the theatre and stage mock naval battles," the guide informed them.

"It's incredible," Dick wondered, obviously awestruck. "A two thousand year old civilisation managed to make the desert come alive. Look at it today!" The sand stretched all around. The tour was to end with a climb, to the rock building called the Treasury, although it was actually another tomb. Before that they regrouped for chai, sitting on long woven and embroidered rugs under the black awnings of the Bedouin tents set up near the start of the trail.

Donkeys were the method of transport offered to take the tourists to the top. Sarah, emboldened by her success with the camel, opted to take one, although she regretted this decision as the beast climbed higher and higher, its hooves slipping and clicking on the sharp stones of the path. Despite its hard rounded belly it was constantly on the look out for food, snatching at clumps of dried grass which grew alongside. It seemed to have a grudge against the animal in front, which it kept trying to nip on the rump, with the effect that the recipient tried to edge Sarah's mount off the path. They wound upwards through a series of sharp hairpin bends, Sarah gulping as they swung close to the edge of the ravine. She could hear the pebbles dislodged by the donkeys' hooves bouncing and clattering to the floor of the valley hundreds of feet below. With relief she relinquished her bad tempered helper at the top, stepping out onto a flat plateau of rock, with the Treasury carved into the rock of the mountain to the right.

"I think I'm getting tomb-shock," she said to Dick, who stood beside her as they gazed up at the cornices high above them.

"Me, too." They moved away to the edge of the plateau and the whole panorama of the Nile's Rift Valley spread before them, mountains reaching out and striding away into the misty distance under the brilliant sky.

At the end of the day, lying on their hotel bed after a much-anticipated cooling swim in the pool, she closed her eyes and let the images of the wonders they had seen play themselves out on the screen of her eyelids. Colours swam and merged, waves of pink and blood red, corners of rock, not blunted by acid rain, endless vista of mountains and sky.

The final day of their tour was to be a climb to the High Place of Sacrifice. "I'm not using any kind of animal to get up here!" she declared firmly. Dick and she were the only two to opt for self propulsion, so they were left behind as the rest of the party set off up the steps on their donkeys, chattering and complaining.

They stopped often to gaze at the way they had come, taking advantage of the brief islands of shade. "I can't believe I'm here," Sarah panted, looking down at the stairs descending below them."

"I'm not sure my eyes can take in any more of this," said Dick, "We're so lucky to be here."

"Yes, lucky," agreed Sarah. It was better than thinking she was responsible for her actions in getting them to this place.

The advantage of going slowly was that they arrived after everyone else had "been there, done that," and were descending to the next set of tombs and temples. They had the Place to themselves.

The first sign that they had reached the temple where it was believed that the Nabateans used to sacrifice both animals and humans to their gods was the sight of the two obelisks which commanded the edge of the mountain closest to the town below. Unlike most constructions, the Nabateans had not built these on top of the mountain, they had cut away the surrounding stone to leave them behind, literally growing out of the rock.

"They're supposed to be full of psychic power," said Dick, reading from the guidebook. "Connected by some form of ley lines to the pyramids in Giza and some ruins on Crete. Better be careful," he warned Sarah, who had frozen in the act of reaching out to touch the dark stone.

She could feel the hum, like a sleeping swarm of hornets deep inside the mountain. Her palm rested flat against a band of warmth two inches from the surface of the stone. As she wavered, swaying slightly, the top of her head hanging from the sky and her feet rooted on the rock, her skin touched what felt like a pile of crushed nettles, buzzing and stinging. "You don't have to do this, step away," warned her superstitious side. "Come on, don't be a wimp" rang the voice of her logical brain. "It's just a lump of old inanimate fossilised sand."

The obelisk towered above her, she stood in its shadow. It drew her in, gripping her hand in its embrace, she pushed through the sharp sensation and connected with hard coldness. At the same time, a flash of light exploded behind her retina, she was falling down a long tunnel, red and gold sliding past her temples. "You are guilty," she heard a voice say. "You must pay." And then she was back on the mountain top, Dick was standing next to her.

"What happened?" she asked him. "Who was here?"

"What are you talking about?" he replied. "There's just us." Sarah looked down. She was not touching the stone any more. She reached out towards it again. There was nothing, no hum, no sting, no cold. Just the feel of smooth silk. She turned away, her feet released from suction, her head once more back on her neck.

After that, the site of the sacrifices, tunnels cut into the rock to take away the rivers of blood from multiple victims, the alter for their ritual slaughter, all seemed anti-climactic. Sarah drifted to the far side of the ancient temple, looking out at the ranges of the Rift marching northwards.

"There's another way down," called Dick, pointing to the sign of a lion carved on a boulder overhanging a narrow path which disappeared downwards. They took this less travelled path, winding past empty tombs just as spectacular as those in the main part of the city. They were the only two in the landscape, until they came to a makeshift café set up next to a Romanesque opening flanked with pillars. At first it seemed deserted too, but as they trawled amongst the ever present boxes of shards of pottery which the Bedouin recovered from the city sands, an old woman appeared from behind the tent flaps at the back.

She indicated the chairs, balanced uncertainly on the uneven ground. "Coca cola?" she asked, the universal indication of cold soda. They shook their heads.

"Chai?" queried Dick, earning a quiet smile. She nodded and disappeared once more, resurfacing with two glasses of the sweet mint tea, brewed strong and dark. Dick and Sarah sat, sipping hot sugary liquid. Dick indicated several of the pieces of pottery he had prospected from the box, thin slivers of ancient porcelain. "How much?" he asked. Sarah watched as they haggled over the price, the woman adding in pieces to make the price higher, Dick subtracting them and raising his bids until they agreed on a compromise both were happy with. He paid her for the pottery and the drinks and they rose to go.

As Sarah made to move past her, the woman laid a restraining hand on her arm. Sarah was surprised, and initially thought the woman wanted to sell her something else, started to shake her head. "Free," said the woman, pressing something into her hand. Sarah looked down. She held a piece of finely made terracotta, thin as glass, the size of a Ritz cracker, delicately decorated with brushstrokes of green and ivory. At the side, however, although it was cut off by the broken edge, was the representation of the obelisk at the top of the mountain. The woman closed Sarah's fingers over the medallion. "Keep," she said. Sarah nodded, rubbing surface of the pottery with her thumb and slipping it into her pocket.

On their return to Leeds she placed it on the windowsill of her new study in the Roundhay house. "Maybe it will inspire me to write," she thought.

Sarah and Zanne   October 2002

Oxford

It was a perfect day for it. The car was already packed, stuffed to the roof with Zanne's belongings. No blue trunk would be waiting for her on her arrival though. There were two suitcases, a box of CDs, a music system, another box of books that had been listed as essential purchases, and of course various electrical goods, such as a toasted sandwich maker, kettle and hairdryer. Unlike Margaret, Sarah knew about the packets of pills and condoms tucked away in Zanne's underwear—after all, in this post AIDS world, better safe than sorry.

She had had a talk with Zanne about sex and contraception when she was barely fourteen. She never wanted her daughter to be in the same state of ignorance that she had been. She had gone with her to the family planning clinic when she was sixteen to find out which pill would be most suitable, but Zanne had not wanted to start taking them then.

"There's no real need, Mum," she'd said. "There isn't anyone I'm interested in enough to want to do that." She still hadn't found anyone, but both had agreed that it would be easier to get a prescription before she went rather than having to go through the process with a strange doctor in a strange town. Sarah couldn't have imagined that kind of conversation with her own mother. She felt that her mother would rather regard conception as rather biblical, immaculate, with no messy fluids and unattractive body parts complicating matters. Even after the physical evidence of grandchildren indicated that her daughters must have engaged in sexual activity, it was not one of the allowed topics of conversation in Margaret's house.

Sarah and Zanne were making the trip to Oxford to install her. Dick and Martin had a weekend of football planned, a visit to see Leeds United play at Elland Road, followed by watching the highlights on Match of the Day with copious quantities of beer and pizza. Dick had promised that they would remove all traces of their debauchery by the time Sarah returned.

"Even the pizza crusts down the side of the sofa cushions?" she queried, eyebrow raised.

Dick saluted. "Scout's honour, ma'am!" The women set off early, as planned, after a light breakfast of toast and tea, sliding onto the motorway before 8am. There were only a handful of cars heading south.

The autumn Saturday sun was bright, showing the Yorkshire countryside off to its best, its bracken browns and purple hills. As they drove, the landscape softened and became greener. Whilst in Leeds the leaves had turned and were beginning to fall, as they journeyed into warmer climes Sarah was surprised to see that the autumn cycle had barely begun here. How could this be, in such a small country, she wondered. It wasn't like they were crossing the Arctic Circle from Leeds to Oxford, just two hundred miles or so of motorway.

They took turns choosing the road music. Sarah stuck to her old favourites, Talking Heads, Eurythmics, the Beatles *One* album, gritting her teeth over Zanne's choices of Echobelly, Cracker and Moby, although they compromised over Sheryl Crowe and Coldplay. "What's this?" asked Zanne, digging out a CD from the bottom of the glove compartment. Sarah glanced over, and her breath caught as she realised it was that hoary old chestnut, *Rumours* by Fleetwood Mac, that had accompanied her own university days. She must have gasped involuntarily. Zanne's eyes widened with concern, "What's wrong, Mum?"

Sarah switched her attention back to the road. "Nothing, just some idiot cutting in ahead," she lied. Her brain was working away, off in its own little time warp. She knew she hadn't bought the CD, she'd only had the album on vinyl, and since they had switched to a new stereo system with no deck, it had been banished to the attic with the rest of her collection. So Dick must have bought it sometime, and been playing it in the car. But she had thought he didn't even like *Rumours*. She shook her head to stop the questions whirling around on their racetrack in her head. None of them could be answered here and now, and asking Dick would only raise more of them.

They made good time, the Volvo eating up the miles of road at a steady 80 mph despite its age, so they reached the Northampton turnoff towards Oxford by 10.30am. "Let's stop for a cuppa," she suggested and Zanne nodded her agreement. They avoided the motorway services and turned down a side road off the A34 towards a signposted village and struck gold with a small bakery with two tables for weak willed customers who found it impossible to get all the way home with their purchases. Sarah wasn't surprised. She gave in immediately to a giant cheese scone, but managed to resist the plump chocolate éclair, its filling peeking out tantalisingly through a gap in the dewy chocolate topping. Zanne, with the benefit of youthful hormones, decided on an apricot custard Danish pastry which looked as though it could satisfy a family of four. They carried their booty over to the table by the lace flounced windows along with two large mugs, tea for Sarah, coffee for Zanne. "Are you sure you can manage that?" Sarah asked her daughter, and received a blank stare in response.

"Why not?" Zanne replied, sinking her teeth into the orange and yellow confection, flakes of pastry and blobs of syrup sticking to her cheek. For a moment she looked just like an eight year old rather than an eighteen year old, with the same absorption in the cake as she had had when younger, approaching a "99" ice cream cone with determination, the chocolate flake sticking out at a dangerous angle as she licked all around it to "save it for last".

Sarah recognised the trait. She'd always saved her favourite foods till the end of the meal, mopping up the roast potatoes and gravy before tackling the chicken. Even now, she was eating the bottom of the scone first, so she could look forward to the chewy melted cheese on the top of the other half. Had she learnt nothing in all those years, in between today and her happy and satisfyingly boring childhood?

Why was she so resistant to change? It had been proved many times, over and over, that waiting for gratification didn't make it any sweeter, it just prolonged the agony of expectation. How had her parents, not Church goers themselves although her mother had been keen to send Sarah to the local church's Sunday school, managed to instil in her some kind of Protestant ethic about things that you enjoyed being bad for you? Especially as it had been a Methodist church. She wondered what unconscious phobias and beliefs she had managed to instil in her own children.

She was still waiting for Zanne to go through her teenage rebellion years. Although she had adopted the normal scornful way of addressing her parents and had refused to be seen in their company for a couple of years, there had been, to Sarah's knowledge, no similar adventures to her own with sex, alcohol and dope. As she sat across the table, finishing the last of the pastry and licking her fingers to remove the last remnants of syrup, Sarah wondered whether her daughter was really as confident and calm as she appeared, or whether it was all, like her own appearance at nineteen, just some elaborately constructed and exhaustively maintained façade. She supposed that she would find out in the next few years, as university stripped away the old skin and enabled Zanne to grow a new one.

Glancing up she noticed that they were eating beneath the legend, "Betty's Bakery—Traditional Homemade Bread and Cakes". She started to laugh. Talk about coincidence. Quite appropriate for a first day at university. She explained the joke to Zanne. "I used to go to Betty's in York for a treat at the end of every term, so I guess you should start off on the right foot!"

As they strolled back to the car, Sarah caught a reflection of the two of them in the bakery window. Zanne was tall like her father but fair like herself as a child. Sarah saw for the first time that Zanne was the taller than her. She remembered how when she had first realised this with her own mother, that Margaret had refused to admit the fact for years, maintaining in the face of physical evidence that "You're wearing shoes with heels on," or, "You must be standing on tiptoe". Then she had taken to subtly managing never to stand next to Sarah for some time, before at last gracefully conceding, when the differential became too obvious to ignore, that, "Yes, Sarah might actually be *slightly* taller".

Zanne strode out, long legs, eyes forward, looking to the future. Sarah noticed her own image seemed faded, just like the hair colour she had given up using some years ago. No longer blonde, feathers of salt and pepper framed her face. She made a mental note to get herself a haircut. Yet they looked alike, her daughter was a newly minted version of the woman next to her. The window bleached the colours out, giving them the aura of a sepia tinted Victorian portrait.

Out of the corner of her eye, Sarah suddenly caught a flash of tangerine, a wisp of strawberry blonde, but turning her head to follow it, she saw only the door of the bakery they had just left, swinging shut after the next customer. She shivered, shaking her head to get rid of the tautness at the base of her skull.

"Mum, what's up?" Zanne was frowning at her.

"Nothing, just remembering my own first day at university. And maybe someone just walked over my grave." Or someone else's grave, she thought.

They wandered along the pavement, window shopping out of habit. Sarah wondered at the variety of merchandise on offer that she would never have imagined that anyone would buy, let alone herself. "Do you think women really buy those nylon housecoats anymore?" said Zanne with disgust, gazing with horror at the garments so prominently displayed in Marge's Best Buys.

"What about those nostril hair clippers" retorted Sarah, pointing to the contraption in the window of Jason's Apothecary.

Zanne stared in disbelief, then suggested, "Shall we buy some for Dad?" Both women giggled at the thought of Dick trying to work out what the implement was for.

The rest of the journey was a bland collage of dual carriageways and high speed traffic jams, interspersed with a few roundabouts. "We're all stuck with the same crowd of cars here," Sarah remarked to Zanne. "The only difference is we are all travelling at eighty miles an hour". They drew into Oxford's crowded streets just after 1pm.

Zanne had been accepted at St Mary's College, a little further out of the centre than blue-stocking Somerville. Parking of course was nowhere to be found, so Sarah parked on double yellow lines beside the college entrance, with an 'Offloading student' hand-written note on her windscreen and hoped that the traffic wardens would be uncharacteristically kind. They weren't. Half an hour later, having been away from the car for five minutes with the last of the loads of paraphernalia, Sarah winced as she peeled the parking ticket off the window and read that her cavalier behaviour with regard to Oxford's parking restrictions had cost her £25. Still, she supposed, the city council must rely on such acts of carelessness to fill their coffers every autumn, although with the ever increasing number of restrictions on which roads you could drive on at all, let alone park, she couldn't imagine that they had a correspondingly huge bill for road maintenance.

She was still reeling from her brief immersion in the breathless atmosphere of the first day of term, with suitcases, boxes and exited new students and their nervous, hanger-on parents crowding the narrow corridors. Even though the part of the college where Zanne's room was situated was the newer, custom built section, Sarah wondered why they had still not been able to make the hallways wide enough to accommodate the traffic of people and luggage. She and Zanne jostled and were jostled by the other parents and young women. St Mary's had been a women's college, although it had recently opened its hallowed and virginal doors to the male sex and admitted that after all, in this regard at least as far as the tradition steeped colleges of Oxford would allow, times had indeed changed. Some students still arrived with trunks, she saw, which had to be wheeled, manhandled and shoved to their owner's rooms, although there were lifts now, so there wasn't the same problem with getting them up stairs and an army of Sams were no longer necessary. In any case, there were porters provided by the college.

There was the same kind of reception table, staffed by second and final year students, checking off the new arrivals, telling them where their accommodation was, reminding them about the various events lined up for Freshers' Week, starting tomorrow, including a similar round of social activities and introductions to university societies that had been the staple fare of her own initiation into college life. There was a package of information telling Zanne where to go for her first lectures, who her personal supervisor would be in the English department and what times her tutorials would be in future weeks. Sarah was glad that there was some reference to the academic activity which was supposed to have brought all these fresh faced women and men here in the first place.

Sarah had expected to feel both exhilaration and regret, and she did. It was impossible to brood on the past in the buzz of activity, or not be infected by Zanne's delight at discovering that somehow she had been allocated one of the better rooms in her block, spacious and light. "Look at that!" she squealed, appreciating the view down onto the courtyard at the centre of the college.

"My God, your own shower and toilet," said Sarah, inspecting the tiny bathroom. None of that scuttling down the corridor in the middle of the night for a pee or an illicit shower with a lover for her daughter, she thought. Zanne was already into instant home making, arranging and rearranging her belongings with each load that they brought up from the car, giving Sarah a distracted peck on the cheek as she said, "Goodbye then, I'll see you at 8pm for dinner in Browns, OK?" It was impossible to ignore the silent echoes of her own first day, so long ago and yet carried with her constantly like an invisible shadow, containing all the seeds of the events to come, making her head spin with nausea as past events overlaid current ones like an off-register print.

She had decided to treat herself to a night at the Randolph before her drive home in the morning, taking advantage of its valet parking. She imagined that the travel worn Volvo would look out of place amongst the Jaguars and BMWs which seemed to be depositing the other guests, but the doorman took her keys with no surprise or suggestion of condescension. She expected that her dinner with Zanne would be the last substantial amount of time they would spend together for the next three months. It was unlikely that Zanne would feel the need to make the trip north by train for a weekend, as it would involve either a slow and unwieldy five hour journey via Birmingham or a slightly faster but more expensive one through London.

She felt a tug at her gut at the thought. It wasn't that Zanne had never been away from her before, she had gone on holidays with her friends since she was fourteen, youth hostelling and hiking, and on school skiing trips and the obligatory language exchange trips to Germany and France. The latter had resulted in a successful pen pal relationship with a girl who lived on the outskirts of Amboise in the Loire valley, so Zanne had also been to visit her on her own a couple of times. Sarah and Dick had been away for the occasional weekend on their own, leaving Zanne and Martin in charge of the house. All of these absences had only been for a fortnight at most, and Sarah had always been grateful to get back home, or to see her daughter stepping off the train or through the arrivals corridor at the airport. Now not only would she have to live with that nameless ache that always set in two or three days after Zanne had left on one of these trips, which was only assuaged on her return, she had to face the fact that her daughter was grown, a young adult with her own path to carve. The next wrench would be experiencing the empty nest when Martin left home, and if he was successful in his bid to get accepted to the training school of some professional football team that might be sooner rather than later. After that, she'd be looking at her own mortality as she and Dick advanced into middle and old age. Soon she would no longer be able to regard herself, as she still did even now, at forty-three, as a young woman.

To stave off these morbid thoughts, she indulged herself with a cream tea in the hotel lounge, realising that she had not eaten since that cheese scone this morning in Betty's Bakery in the village she could not remember the name of, and that she was never able to find again on any subsequent journey to Oxford. "It must be like Brigadoon," she said to Dick one time when they were driving around the Northamptonshire countryside, in dire need of a cuppa. "You know, that Gene Kelly film where he finds some village in the Highlands of Scotland that exists in some parallel universe and only appears in this world for a day every hundred years or so. He manages to fall in love with some Brigadoon woman and has to decide whether to stay with her and take his chances or return to his own world and never see her again," she explained to his puzzled frown.

"What has that got to do with cheese scones?" he asked.

On this afternoon, tiny finger sandwiches of chicken and egg mayonnaise, garnished with a delicately sculpted cherry tomato in the shape of a rose on a bed of cress occupied the bottom tier of a china and chrome tower. Two small plain scones accompanied with raspberry jam and clotted cream sat on the middle plate and a miniature pair of eclairs on the top. Sarah ate the lot, sipping her tea from the gold rimmed china cup, so different from Betty's hefty mug, filling and refilling it from the matching tea pot.

Afterwards she walked down to Blackwell's bookstore to get herself a paperback to read in bed, able to recreate one of her single pleasures without the danger of waking Dick, out of habit checking out the poetry section and getting that chill of surprise, delight and unease that always occurred when she saw her own name on the shelf amongst all the other poets. Or would that be, "other *real* poets", she corrected herself. Even though it always reminded her of those days of desperation and theft, it was like a drug, an obsession, scratching an itch that would never go away, she was compelled to put herself through it again and again as some kind of expiation for spending the royalty cheques.

She still had a couple of hours before she was due to meet Zanne, so she filled in the time with a long soak in her hotel bath, emptying all of the bottles of shampoo and shower gel that had been left nestled in a soft white flannel in a wicker basket on the marble counter top into the hot running water to create a Himalaya of foam. Sarah closed her eyes and slid down into the water, enjoying the semi-weightlessness of her body as it floated, only lightly touching the sides and bottom, her ears filled with the noises of the hotel's hot water system being replenished and her own blood rushing around her circulation system. She pushed herself up, the foam making a snowy ruff around her face, which she lathered up and rinsed off with more hot water before climbing out and flopping onto her bed wrapped in the thick white towelling robe that had been hanging on the back of the bathroom door.

Maybe she hadn't got all of the foam off, because she could still feel it, in her ears and prickling her face, only now it wasn't soft, it had hardened into bramble-like thorns, which stung as she tried to move her head from side to side to avoid getting it on the bedspread. She could sense the water in the bath start to seep up from under the bed, icy now, not hot. She seemed to be lying in a puddle which was gradually getting deeper. Her mouth and nose started to fill up, she couldn't get enough air, her head felt like lead and she couldn't lift it from the rising water. She was going to drown on her hotel bed.

She could hear someone moving around in the next room, putting their things away, opening drawers and wardrobes. Beyond, she could even hear the sound of gulls and the crash of waves even though Oxford was miles from the sea. If she could only get that person's attention, she would be alright. Sarah struggled to frame the words, "Help me, please!" But no sounds would come. Her mouth was full of sand and seawater, salty now not soapy. She felt cold fear that she would never be able to get off the bed before the water rose and covered her totally.

She heard the door to her room open. "Please!" she managed at last, but her mouth was blocked with tiny pebbles. She couldn't turn her head to see who it was who had come in, although her ears were working with unforgiving clarity, registering every slow step towards her. What was the matter with them, couldn't they see she was in trouble here? Why didn't they hurry up? Then the footsteps stopped altogether, just a few feet away from her. At the same moment Sarah found she could turn her head, to see Suzanne, both Suzannes, her daughter and her lost friend, looking down at her, their faces distorted by the water that lapped over Sarah's face. She reached up to clutch a hand, but all her fingers closed on were the stack of her poetry books from Blackwell's, which came tumbling on top of her, blocking out the light and weighing her down, taking her down to the ocean depths.

Sarah sat up, gasping, drawing in oxygen, desperately trying to make up for all the breaths she had lost. She was on her bed in the Randolph, which was totally dry apart from a pool of spittle on the pillow that must have run from her mouth as she slept. The other pillow, her paperback and a glass of water which had been on the bedside table were lying on the floor, knocked off by her thrashing hand, the liquid soaking into the oriental rug. She gaped at the digital clock. She had been asleep for half an hour, it was five minutes before her rendezvous with Zanne at Brown's.

She sprang up, pulling clothes from her overnight bag, searching for her pre-bath discarded underwear. She managed to dress herself in black jeans, emerald green silk shirt that bore minimal creases, performed a basic make up, smudging eye shadow onto her lids and waving mascara at her lashes. A smear of amethyst lipstick and long golden earrings with turquoise beads and she was done, pulling on her soft leather slouch ankle boots and grabbing her bag and coat from the chair as she left. Sarah opted to dive down the stairs over waiting for the lift and sprinted up the street towards the restaurant, making it only ten minutes after the time she had arranged to meet her daughter.

Zanne was not there. Sarah sat at the bar and tried to recover her breath with a large Campari and orange juice, gulping the bitter cranberry coloured mixture as though it were fruit juice. Her pulse had almost returned to normal when Zanne arrived ten minutes later, full of apologies. "I've been invited to a party later that night. One of the girls on my corridor has an older brother at Balliol, so we are all meeting in the Lamb and Flag at 10pm before going onto his house," Zanne gabbled, the words pouring out of her. So it starts, thought Sarah, feeling the thudding of her heart in her chest slow and retreat to its normal steady pulse.

Her daughter across the restaurant table already seemed a part of the scene here, fitting in like a piece of a jigsaw puzzle, while she felt like she was outside looking in, Alice on the other side of the looking glass. They ate pasta and drank red wine. "No dessert for me, Mum," said Zanne, "I'm going to be late."

After a parting hug, Sarah watched her skitter across the wide road like a faun, then returned to her hotel room in a calmer state than the one in which she had left it, breathing in the warm night air which carried the promise of leaves turning. She read her novel in bed while sipping a Cointreau from the mini-bar, to dull her senses and fill her head with other images, but she was not revisited by her nightmare. Instead she awoke to the knock of room service with her breakfast and the Sunday paper, both of which she enjoyed in bed before packing up and retrieving her car for the long drive north.

Sarah							Now

Housework

I love cooking for Dick. I'm surprised by how much I enjoy mixing, baking, stirring. At school I was always determined I was never going to be any sort of *hausfrau*, that I was meant for higher things. I resisted taking in any of the instructions we got in Home Economics, although I quite liked messing around with the food. But domestication was definitely not my scene. My report read, "Sarah works well, until it comes to the washing up". That's still the same really.

I got into doing the cooking when I moved in with Dick so that I could avoid the clearing up. Now we have a dishwasher. I'd like to give thanks to its inventor and worship at his shrine. As soon as Suzanne and Martin were old enough, their job was to help out by drying and putting the dishes away. Most of the other housework I can cope with, mainly because I adopt a kind of version of Quentin's Crisp's advice on just not doing it. He apparently said that after two years, the amount of dirt carried into the house on people's shoes reaches an even level with the amount that gets carried out, so that it achieves equilibrium. Using that as my back up position, I hardly ever dust and get the vacuum cleaner out about once a fortnight. There have been times when it was less frequent, like just after Zanne was born. I gave up cleaning altogether for about six months. People used to ask, if she was wakeful, whether the sound of the vacuum might put her to sleep?

I used to reply that, "As she's got no idea what it sounds like, it might just scare her to death."

Washing. I hate it. The act of putting all the stuff in the machine I can handle, and just about deal with getting it out and hanging it on the line. Now we have a tumble dryer that sits next to the washer in the utility room for wet and winter days when it would be no good putting it out, because it would just freeze into petrified boards, like fossil exoskeletons with vanished inhabitants. Because I was always at home more of the time than any of the others in my family it fell to me to be the washing fairy. I am the one that empties the dirty clothes basket when it overflows onto the carpet and sorts out the piles of malingering odours into coloured and whites. I once decided not to venture into Martin's room to retrieve the piles of discarded underwear, socks thrown into corners, underpants lying in malignant heaps under sweaty football shirts, but I had to give in when the smell got too bad. Plus I began to suspect that Martin had been wearing the same pair of boxers for four days.

Dick is fairly good about emptying our clothes out and operating the washing machine, but then the remembrance that there is a load of wet clothes needing to be dealt with passes from his consciousness, so I have to be on alert in case we start growing penicillin. It's not exactly mind bending or stimulating to be concerned with such things. It was better once both children were at school, although I find myself perversely missing dealing with Suzanne's scraps of fabric that are apparently thong knickers now she is away at college. For some years I have even had the chance to read an occasional book.

Enough of housework. Cooking is entirely different. Sometimes I can spend hours just leafing through cookbooks, making lists of ingredients, planning my weekly trip down to the open air market behind Briggate, timing it so that I go late in the afternoon to take advantage of any bargains. Saturdays are the best, but I don't often get the chance to go at the weekends, that tends to be catch up time for me and Dick. There have been times when I got back with a dozen grapefruit or a five pound box of mushrooms.

"I couldn't resist, they were so ridiculously cheap," I justified myself to Dick, who was looking at my purchases with amusement. The mushroom episode led to the discovery of a recipe for mushroom soup that tasted as though I'd picked the fungi whilst skipping through dew-drenched meadows, so different from the mass-produced canned variety that I have never been able to buy it since.

Now we have a bit more money, I can experiment with more expensive ingredients, like salmon, swordfish and fresh tuna, venison, asparagus, other organic vegetables. I miss sometimes the discoveries I made by combining unlikely components into a pasta sauce or stew-like soup. Often I would only know what I was going to cook when I opened the cupboards and fridge and saw what was left, and what I had to make do with until the end of the week. There was the time I put a can of mandarins into a kind of tomato soup mixture and also added a load of left over cooked rice. Or the leftover curry from the day before to which I'd had to add cabbage, apples and raisins just to bulk it out.

In the early days of living with Dick I was a regular at the butcher's in Chapel Allerton, before it got sold and turned into a mini-freezer goods emporium. That could never really compete with the supermarkets nearby, so it soon went out of business with its packets of mass produced and frozen lumps of animals and pastry. Mr Sims, the butcher, knew me well. After a few months I gave up wearing the duffle coat which was two sizes too small for me so that the sleeves barely passed my elbows, with worn trousers or shabby skirts, so that I could look even poorer than we were and elicit his sympathy. With a grin he would produce some bones for making soup stock, or recommend the cheapest offal and any other meat on special offer as though it was the choicest cut, and I was his most favoured customer.

"Some lamb's kidney's this week? Or would you prefer rabbit?" He would affect amazement on the rare occasion that I requested bacon or steak. "Won the pools, have we?" It was fun, and I'm sorry that he wasn't there to benefit from our increased prosperity as he kept us alive through many a winter. Through Mr Sim's recommendations I learned to cook lamb's hearts with breadcrumbs and apple juice, liver with oranges, kidneys with rosemary and sage grown from our own patch of garden.

I love cooking for Dick to come home to, so that the house is full of the smells of garlic and ginger, bread and chocolate cake. Cooking fulfils my senses, taste, touch and smell are all brought into play. Bread is so satisfying to make because apart from that wonderful sensation of putting your hands into the bowl of flour and warm, sticky fermenting yeast, like the most forbidden pleasures of playing with mud when you were a child, the more you thump it around when you are kneading it, the better the finished product.

It's wonderful to take out any frustrations on the dough, and imagine it is the head of the bus driver who used to take pleasure in waiting while I ran for the bus, clearly visible in his rear view mirror, only to close the doors and drive off just as I managed to get to the stop and was reaching out to grasp the handrail. There were never many people on the buses he used to drive, probably just as well they never had a productivity scheme based on fares collected. If I did manage to catch his bus, he'd roar up to the stop at which I wanted to get off at top speed whilst I clung to the pole by the door, slamming on the brakes at the last minute to try and dislodge me onto the lap of some poor old woman who'd probably been on the bus up to the terminus and back and was too frightened to try and escape. On the one occasion I tried to circumvent this by remaining in my seat until the last minute, he had the doors open and shut in record time so that I was trapped until the next stop. Of course it was raining that day and I didn't have an umbrella and I was loaded down with vegetables from the market. I hated that man with a passion that was ridiculous and exhausting, so that waiting at the bus stop was full of tension as to whether he would be driving the route that day. Making bread was especially therapeutic when I had suffered such a bus journey, but could be just as pleasurable when I had not.

The smell of bread is wonderful too, whether it is rising or baking, and even better when I add garlic or herbs to the mix to make savoury rolls and plaits as well as honey glazed wholewheat and soda bread.

Making pastry is another thing altogether. For this, everything needs to be gentle rather than rough, cool rather than warm. I enjoy the feeling of the flour and fat against my fingertips, starting sticky and then becoming dry and sandy. It's best to put ice in the water that makes it into dough, and I prefer to mix it with my hands rather than a knife, so I have to rinse them in cold water first. Then there is the flouring and rolling, moving it round and round to make sure that it comes out evenly. Peeling it up from the surface and draping it over the dish, whatever I am making, feeling the cool silk mould itself to my hands. Trimming and cutting, decorating with off-cuts made into leaves or flowers, scalloping the edges. Then glazing with milk or egg and a sprinkle of sugar. Pastry was the only thing that my mother would allow me to cook when I was a child, my other efforts were always met with impatience at my slowness, that she could do it faster herself rather than accept my help. Leftover pastry was always available for me to fashion into little figures with currants for eyes, although they never made it as far as the oven, that not being the point of the exercise for me.

Apple pies are my favourite creation, especially in the autumn when the windfalls can be gathered from our own lawn, under the three apple trees that splatter the grass with sweet white blossom in the spring, and leaves and fruit in September and October. In the past, I would go out after dark to scrump apples from the trees in the more affluent streets of the Canadian estate, so called because all the streets were named after places in that particular corner of empire, on the other side of Harrogate Road from our crowded terraces with postage stamp gardens. I only got caught in the act once. I was reaching up to pluck a particularly tempting pippin, when I glanced towards the windows of the house that owned it. An old man stood in the unlit window, watching me silently, arms folded across his grey sweatered chest. We stood for a moment, regarding each other neutrally, although the hairs on the back of my neck were rising and starting to freeze in the sweat which had started to seep from my skin. Then he smiled, his eyes twinkling even in the dusky light from the street lamp, raised a hand in permission and farewell, and stepped back from the window into the darkness from which he had appeared. Relief made me drop the hand which had frozen a few inches below the fruit, but then I reached up and took it anyway.

Blackberries can still be found down in Gledhow Valley woods on the other side of the Canadas, lush and full, staining my hands and lips purple. I could never resist sampling them as I went, meaning that I never brought home the full amount of my harvest. Together with the stolen apples they made succulent crumbles, pies and jams. On occasion I supplemented my gathering with booty from the allotments at the top of the hill, rhubarb, gooseberries, sometimes if I was lucky carrots, potatoes and cabbage, but the cultivators seemed to operate a kind of unofficial watch patrol, and I could rarely find a time when there was no one working or walking there.

Preparing food with love is a delight to the cook and the consumer. I get to have the best of both. Today I have made a simple pasta sauce, easy to prepare, but delicious all the same and one of Dick's favourite's. It starts off simply, with the usual slicing and chopping of onions and garlic, frying them in olive oil till they are soft and golden, the garlic starting to brown and caramelise around the edges. The best onions are red, sweet and sharp, although they make my eyes water and I have to run cold water and hang my head over the kitchen sink until the stinging stops. Then tomatoes, fresh from the market, vine ripened, their skins smelling green and earthy, a pile of them sliced and chopped joining the onions in the pan. A touch of sugar, basil and two scarlet chillies, hot and spicy, sliced thinly, careful to discard the seeds that can be so excruciating in the wrong place.

Dick told me a story about a friend of his who had used chillies in the preparation of a dinner he was cooking to impress a first time date. Things progressed well, the hot food feeding the passion, they ended up in bed together. As he entered her he experienced a stab of intense pain, causing him to scream and crumple. Somehow one of the seeds had managed to get itself under his foreskin, making me wonder what exactly he was doing during the preparation of the meal whilst anticipating the events of the evening. The fledgling relationship was over before it began.

No such problems for me, though. I am always respectful of chillies. The secret of the sauce is to let it simmer for long enough to allow all the flavours to escape into the juices and meld together. Half an hour is just enough, although longer is better. I had not realised in my student days when food was a mere fuel to enable me to have enough energy to drink and screw and occasionally make it to lectures and fulfil the academic requirements of the course, that the best things take a long time to prepare. Then I was only interested in meals that took the minimum of time and effort. Anything that took longer than twenty minutes to prepare and cook never made it onto my menu.

When Dick comes home, I'll cook the pasta, bought from the Italian deli in Chapel Allerton where they make their own. Then it will be time to make the final additions to the sauce, a handful of peppery rocket, tablespoons of vodka and cream to give it bite and smoothness. While the sauce is cooking I can make the salad with lots of green leaves, cos, iceberg and romaine, red leaf lettuces. Then spring onions, avocados and slices of fresh orange, cut so that there is no pith.

If there is time, and today is one of those days when there is, I'll take a glass of cold white wine and run a bath, full of oils and foam. I love to unwind and read in the hot scented water. I used to like it even as a child, causing a log jam in the family ablutions when I discovered how to lock the door and stop unwelcome visitors interrupting me. I'd start off with the water so hot I could only get into it an inch at a time, bands of skin turning progressively to the colour of boiled lobster. I'd often have to hang my feet over the side to avoid total overheating. Sometimes I'd have to admit defeat and add a little cold water to bring it down to a breathable temperature. Then, some time later, when the water had cooled to near blood heat, I would add more hot to it, swirling it round in the tub to bring it all up to the right warmth. This could cause a rush of water out of the overflow as I took the bath to the limit of its capacity. Often I found that some engrossing story would keep me in the water until I was prune wrinkled, but I was more likely to be curtailed by the frantic banging of someone needing to use the toilet, which was in the same room and was the only one in the house. So I'd reluctantly climb out and drip into my bedroom, wrapped in one of the large towels I'd have placed on the towel rail in advance so that it would be toasty and comforting.

I don't have the same need to make the bath so unbearably hot now that we are paying for the heating of it, but I do like to prolong the ecstasy by frequent top ups. Dick bought me this wonderful contraption for Christmas last year, a deluxe bath rack. It fits over the tub, and is made of something that looks like cast iron but doesn't rust, so they must have waterproofed it somehow. As well as ornate curls and scrolls befitting what it pretends to be made of, it has really useful features, such as a book holder, including small pegs to keep your page from flipping back, a wine glass holder and a pair of spikes for candles. He paired this with a large towelling bath pillow in the form of a whale, with suckers so that it can stick to the rim of the bath and the tiles above. Before I get in, I put some music on the stereo in our bedroom, some mediaeval harmonies, or perhaps some saxophone by Jan Gabarek, Enya on occasion. Then I have a total experience—music, heat, wine, fiction and patchouli or lavender depending on my mood.

A few times Dick has come home when I've still been soaking, and has joined me in the water, bringing more wine. We catch up on the day, although I never have much news for him. We talk about our lives, how the kids are doing, the mundane conversation accompanied by washing and stroking. We managed to flood the bathroom once when this turned to vigorous lovemaking which threw water all over the floor. What little water there was left drained away when Dick knocked the plug out with his foot, causing us to have that awful down to earth feeling, as though gravity had been turned back on after a period of weightlessness, as we sank to the porcelain. Then we had to work out how to extricate ourselves whilst laughing hysterically. By the time we had worked that out, the dinner was burning, so that the smoke alarm was having a fit in the downstairs hallway. How luxurious it felt to be able to afford to order up a takeaway and have it delivered.

Life is so rich, I sometimes forget how I got to be here for days at a time. When I do remember, it feels far away, as though it happened to someone else. Yet it is always there, this life of rock built on a foundation of sand. I wish sometimes that someone else would notice and so relieve me of part of the burden of guilt, but then why should they? I am the only one who knows the whole truth of it. The longer I leave it all unsaid, the more impossible it feels to turn around this supertanker, sailing serenely across calm seas, whilst the icebergs lurk at the edges of the horizon.

Sarah   May 2003

Mirror

Sarah goes into her bedroom to get ready for bed. Automatically she starts to shed shirt, sweatpants, bra, knickers, socks, wandering around to put the used underwear and shirt in the washing basket, hanging the pants first over the back of the white wicker Lloyd Loom chair, then transferring them to the wardrobe. It's all very pedestrian. Dick is downstairs, finishing reading the paper, listening to jazz.

She catches sight of her naked body in the full length mirror inside the wardrobe door, turns sideways to check out her belly bulge, breathing in to tauten her abdominal muscles, then turns back to full frontal. She follows the lines of her torso with her fingers as they slim into her waist, then out over her hips. She looks at her breasts. Are they sagging more than they used to? They are fuller and more rounded than when she was in her twenties, when she could still go braless. Her nipples are pinky brown, in the midst of the asymmetrical circles of her aureoles. At first squashed into her skin, now they start to stand up under her scrutiny. She takes one breast in her hand, feeling the weight of flesh, absent mindedly pinching the nipple erect, feeling the smooth skin around it. Is this what Dick feels, what he sees?

She twists and turns, pinching and stroking. There is certainly more flesh on her hips and buttocks than she would like, and her belly and breasts are floppy, but she doesn't look bad for a woman who has had two children, she thinks. She doesn't have any stretch marks or tears and all the pieces seem to be in the right proportion even though they are larger all over. She stretches and flexes her foot, seeing the calf muscles tighten under the skin. She has always liked the shape of her ankles, slim and smooth, the bones making a symmetrical double pyramid just above her long, broad feet. Despite the selection of unsuitable shoes she wore when she was younger, her toes are straight, topped by varnished nails that today are the colour of vine ripened tomatoes.

They are matched by the nails on her hands, which rest at the curve of her waist, emphasising the swell of her hips. Her fingers are long and slim, no ring apart from her plain gold wedding band and that lovely, lonely diamond that Dick gave her on top of the first mountain they climbed together. They have climbed so many since then, she knows, and sometimes Dick was not even aware of what they were ascending.

She looks up to see her face, blue eyes with a touch of amber round the iris, clear whites, long dark eyelashes, tidy brows. Plucking her eyebrows is the one useless vanity she allows herself. Leg shaving she abandoned years ago. She is pale from the English winter, although she can see where her face and arms have started to colour from the spring sunshine. For the first time she notices that she no longer has freckles, the childish sign that summer was on its way. Does Zanne still get them? She must check next time she sees her.

What has she done to create all those fine lines on her forehead, around her eyes? She grimaces, smiles, frowns, sees them deepen and etch into her face. Is that the suspicion of jowls under her chin? She pushes her chin out, tightens the muscles in her neck, sees them stand out like ropes. She is getting old! She shakes her head to dislodge the thought, but it only serves to highlight the grey hairs in her dark brown hair. Her hair is still short, cut into the shape of her neck at the back, softer over her ears and brushed forward to frame her face.

She takes a step back, away from the close up. Out of ten, she thinks, what would I give this body? How happy am I with it? Probably an eight, she is surprised to find, after all those years of hiding as a podgy child, swaddling in shapeless sweatshirting as a mother. She thinks about what she wore today, baggy tee shirt and pants and resolves to treat herself to a shopping trip, throw away all those drab sacks and convert to figure hugging tops and well fitting jeans. Some new underwear too, she decides, thinking about the plain and serviceable things she has just thrown in the hamper. Something more sexy. Then a flash of searching through Suzanne's things at college sears across her brain, jumbled lace and silk, garter belt and stockings, the reason she has never worn those things for Dick.

As if her thought has conjured him up, he appears in the doorway behind her, sees her standing naked by the mirror, his eyes widen and he smiles that slow smile that always makes her weak. Without speaking he comes to her, reaches around to cup her breasts in his hands, pulling her back against him, sending his hand down to cup her bush and pull her buttocks against his groin. His tongue flicks her ear, she can hear his breath deepen as his nose and lips trace the line of her neck to the hollow of her shoulder. He bites her, softly at first, then harder, gnawing like a lion with its kill, then back to licking and tasting.

She reaches up, arms above her head to sink her fingers into his hair, greying too now, but still thick and wavy. She is already sinking into sex, her body dissolving under his touch, but she still has a moment to notice the way her breasts lift as her arms do, the flesh under her arms soft but not flabby, the sinews of her shoulders and the shape of her ribs. Dick has shed his trousers and boxers, she can feel his prick hard against the cleft of her buttocks. He has made her wet, she breathes in the smell of her cunt mingled with his sweat as he lifts her up and bends his knees to slide inside her, holding her tight with one hand as he braces them both against the mirror.

    She feels like she inhabits her body for the first time, revelling in its curves and bulges as well as the muscle and bone. At the same time, watching the couple in the mirror making love is like watching a movie, or better still, spying on someone through a keyhole. The woman is breathing deeply now, her eyes half closed, one of her hands covering the one of his that is kneading her breast, while the other is behind her back, grabbing his buttocks to lock him tight against her. The man is leaning back, thrusting long and deep, slowly, faster, then slowly again to maintain the moment. She is standing on tiptoe, as she lowers herself onto her heels he comes up to meet her, can't hold on any longer as he is totally enveloped by her. He snorts and gasps, his eyes turn up in his head as he feels the sensation start in his prick and spread throughout his body, clutching her tightly to stay standing. He nuzzles his head against her back, breathing in her smell and the smell of their sex. Her arousal, just starting to build, falters and fades, she shivers as she feels the sweat cool on her skin. She is caught, pinned to him while he drains every drop of excitement, until he resurfaces enough for them to stumble to the bed, still joined, where they fall upon it and he wraps the quilt and his arms about her. Safe in her cocoon, she falls asleep, his breath on her neck.

Suzanne   27 May 1979

Diary

I'm really worried about Sarah. She is going downhill, she doesn't even wash much anymore. I don't know how to get through to her. I've just looked back through this diary and I feel ashamed that I could have thought that she fancied Dick, I mean it's obvious that she's completely besotted with Jules because she has been so weird since she broke up with her. I can't see why she has become so determined not to go back, only forward to something else, it's making her so unhappy. I found some old photos we took when I was looking through my desk the other day. It was when we went to Whitby and Sandsend. I still have the shirt I bought in Shepherd's Purse. It made me remember when she made me buy those red dungarees, and I ended up blowing a huge amount of money on a jacket and some boots too. But I wouldn't be without those things, or Sarah. I realised that I missed her and the closeness we used to have. Just my suspicious, jealous nature. I've even taken to writing this diary up in the library because I was so paranoid that she'd been going through my things.

I see that I have been fooling myself a lot about how I want the world to be, ignoring how it is. Dick doesn't love me. My God, I can't believe that I just wrote that, that I have admitted at long last that our relationship is just never going to work. Whatever or whoever he wants, it isn't me. I'm tired of making excuses and blaming myself for what he's doing. I've been stuck to him ever since Freshers' Night for God's sake. I never even had the chance to see what I could be. I just kept on, in my own pig-headed way, refusing to see what must have been so obvious to everybody else right from the start. I'm worth more than this. All those lines and lines of pointless poetry bemoaning my fate, what a waste of time. I need to burn them all right away, that's for sure. I feel embarrassed that I could be so adolescent about it all. As if the first guy I went to bed with was really going to be my one and only soul mate forever. Far better to do what Sarah did, try a few out to see what works.

But then I'm back to Sarah and how she can't see what works for her, either. I've got to do something about all of this. It's so unbelievably stupid to throw away a friendship for a relationship that's not any good anyway. I'm going back to the room right now, I want to tell her that I'm sorry, try to make it up to her, get back to what we had. Maybe we'll even go out and get pissed tonight, to celebrate my new freedom. Because that's the other thing I'm going to do, straight after, I'm going to tell that shit Dick where to stick it, or rather where not to! It's over, and all I can feel is relief. Isn't that weird? I've spent so much time around him for nearly two years and I don't even feel sad. He never knew me, not really, and I never knew him either, just some image of who I wanted him to be.

So, it's time for action. I was going to meet Stefano in the coffee bar, but I can't be bothered now, I'm going straight back to sort everything out. Tomorrow really will be the first day of the rest of my life! At last!

Sarah and Suzanne   May 1979

Ending

"What the hell are you doing?" said Suzanne. Sarah knelt on the floor beside Suzanne's desk, a sheaf of paper in her hand, other pieces scattered about her on the floor. She'd just been trying to put them back into order, having found the pieces she needed, and hadn't been able to stuff them all back into the drawer in time when she had heard Suzanne's key in the lock. Five minutes later and she would have got away with it again.

Sarah couldn't think of anything to say. She gazed helplessly at the evidence scattered all around her. Suzanne came into the room and shut the door. "You've been reading my poetry," she stated it as a fact, not a question. "You slimy toe rag, you've been reading my poetry. How dare you?" Her words were delivered in a calm, fierce whisper. Sarah looked down, unable to meet Suzanne's blazing eyes. "Look at me, you shit!" Suzanne ordered. Sarah meekly did as she was told.

Even in the midst of the skin tingling horror of what was happening, a sense of relief was starting to creep in around the edges. Her body, which had been tense for so long with the stress of deception was starting to relax, she could feel her eyelids growing heavy, she just wanted to lie down and go to sleep until whatever was coming was over. "Don't you dare close off on me until I've finished," Suzanne hissed. "What's the matter with you, are you on something?" Sarah shook her head. "Come on, spit it out, what exactly are you doing?"

With Suzanne towering over her, Sarah started to flap her hands around in a vague effort to put the poems back into some kind of a neat pile. "I'm stealing your poems," she said. She couldn't think of any lie that would sound convincing so she was just left with the truth. "I've been doing it for months now. I haven't been able to write since, since December," she stumbled. She still couldn't admit that her break up with Jules had anything to do with her behaviour. "I've been handing them in to Professor Ellis as part of my project on creative writing. Been getting really good marks too," she added, although she didn't know whether that made it all better or worse. "I meant to ask you, but you weren't here," her voice trailed off. During her recitation Suzanne's eyes had widened and she'd sat down on her bed, shaking her head as though to rid herself of the troublesome words she was hearing.

"So you've not only been reading my poetry, going through my private things, my really private things," Suzanne's voice was a sharp, hoarse grating, "but you've been handing them in as your own, so that you could scrape through your degree without doing any sodding work, so you could just keep on screwing around, riding on my back, you scheming little shit. I bet that was why you moved in with me in the first place!" Sarah could only shake her head in her turn, as though she could stop hearing Suzanne's words as easily as shaking off droplets of water, coming up for air after a deep dive.

"That wasn't how it was, how could it be," she struggled to find what she knew was the lack of logic in Suzanne's argument. "I didn't know about the poems then anyway!" She felt as though she was barely keeping her head above the surface, treading water desperately, gasping for breath and grasping any passing phrase.

"Well, I'm going to make you pay for this," Suzanne was forcing her words out through rigid clenched teeth. "I'm going to report you to Professor Ellis, to the Dean, to the department, everybody. You'll be chucked out on your ear without any bloody degree, and serve you right. You sad excuse for a human being. And I thought you were my best friend!" Suzanne's words and their implications slowly filtered into Sarah's consciousness. Her mind had been spinning off on its own, she realised that she had not foreseen what Suzanne might do if she found out. She had only thought in terms of their shattered friendship, even though it had been left in rags by their mutual hostility of the past few months. She had expected an outburst, that she might have to move out, that Suzanne would stop talking to her for a while, but never this.

Still kneeling, she started to crawl over to her friend, reaching out, "Suzanne can't we talk about this, I'm sorry, please don't do this." She touched Suzanne's leg lightly. "Please don't get me thrown out, I couldn't stand it."

Suzanne's leg jerked, her body convulsed. "Get your hands off me, don't touch me, you dyke bitch," she spat. "You should have thought about that before you started rooting around in my underwear. I bet that gave you a real thrill too, didn't it?" Both women stared at each other, the words that could not be taken back hanging between them.

Then Suzanne was gasping for air, her chest rising and falling in panicky waves, faster and faster, as her throat started to constrict and her asthma started to kick in. She started to scrabble around for her bag, which she had dropped on the floor when she had come in. She gestured at it, waving Sarah to get it for her. Sarah had witnessed her friend's attacks before now, but none that had come on so quickly or so violently. She leapt up automatically and grabbed the soft tapestry bag, started towards her friend then stopped in the middle of the floor, clutching it to her, her hands like claws clenched around it.

Suzanne's face which had showed a momentary relief as Sarah had fetched the bag with her inhaler, now changed to an expression of puzzled panic. "You said you'd get me chucked out," Sarah said slowly.

Suzanne shook her head violently, realisation breaking over her. "Nnn, nnn," she gasped.

"You said you'd report me to everybody," Sarah continued. "I can't have that, Suzanne." Sarah turned and deliberately sat down on her own bed at the other side of the room, still holding the bag. "I can't let you, I'd never live it down," she went on. "Everyone would know. It would kill my parents."

Suzanne had finally seen that Sarah was not going to give her the bag. Her breath was coming in short, shallow rasps as she fought her body to gain the air to save it. Her face was tinged with blue, her eyes starting to widen and bulge. She still couldn't really believe it, Sarah could see that in her friend's eyes. Suzanne tried to rise from the bed, to come to where Sarah held the life preserving inhaler and epi-pen, but this just made her erupt into sharp coughing barks. She sank back again, her eyes closed with the effort of survival, trying to suck air in against the swelling tissue in her throat.

Sarah sat frozen on her bed, watching Suzanne as she weakened. Minutes passed. Suzanne's hands fluttered and twitched on the bright blue blanket they had bought together, one Saturday at the open market behind Coney Street. Sarah left the bag on her own bed and walked over to Suzanne. Already her eyes had started to film over. She sat on the edge of the bed, took Suzanne's hand in her own, stroked the wet hair from the sweat soaked forehead. "Frnnd," erupted with a final effort from Suzanne's lips as her eyelids drooped and she started to sink into unconsciousness.

"I'm sorry," Sarah said. "I'm so sorry, Suzanne. I just couldn't let you do it." She stayed by her friend as Suzanne's oxygen gradually ran out, her breaths becoming shallower and shallower until the tortured gasping finally stopped. The room was suddenly quiet. Sarah could even hear her own breathing, making the contrast with the still body of her friend even more marked. She laid her cheek against the cooling hand before placing it gently onto the bedspread. She stood and walked over to Suzanne's bag and picked it up, her knuckles white where they gripped the cloth. "I'm sorry," she repeated to herself. "I couldn't let her do it." It was done, it couldn't be undone. Sorry wasn't really good enough.

Sarah walked back to Suzanne's body and tipped out the contents of the bag on the floor, pushing the inhaler under the bed with her foot, leaving the bag upended next to it, as though Suzanne had managed to reach it in her desperate scrambling but knocked the vital medication out of reach. She stood up and looked at her dead friend, keeping back the beginnings of remorse and regret in her own body. She reached down and stroked Suzanne's still warm and soft face once more, as though attempting to break through the ice wall that she was building to insulate her from any emotions.

Sarah opened the desk drawer where all the incriminating poems were stored. If anyone looked through Suzanne's papers after her death there might be an outside chance that some link could be made to the work she'd been submitting under her own name. Scooping them all up, she transferred them to the bottom of her own wardrobe. She checked around to see if there was any evidence that she had been in the room that night. Luckily she had not made herself visible by cooking in the communal kitchen, intending to grab something to eat at the late night snack bar. Most of the others on the corridor were either away or in their respective boyfriends' and girlfriends' rooms. She stuffed a few minimal essentials into a shoulder bag which would get her through an overnight somewhere, anywhere. She needed an alibi.

Her eye was caught by her draft assignment. Shit, she had forgotten what she had been doing when Suzanne had interrupted her. If Suzanne had come back only five minutes later, she would never have known and she would still be alive now. The difference between life and death didn't seem enough.

Sarah bundled up the poems and her other papers. She'd have to neaten up her draft and copy out the poems she had selected in her own handwriting, then she could submit them. She stuffed them into her shoulder bag, along with an assignment cover sheet and an envelope. She could go up to the library, it would be good to be seen.

She didn't want to be spotted coming out of here though, so she opened the sash window and stepped through it onto the top of the walkway that ran underneath, closing the window as far as she could after her. She stood outside for a second looking back into the room. She could just see the toe of Suzanne's boot, dangling off the end of her bed. She shook off the remembrance of the events of the past hour, lifted the strap of her bag over her shoulder and crept silently to the edge. There was no one coming along the lit pathway which ran underneath the canopy so she eased herself off the edge, swinging for a moment by her hands before dropping onto the concrete paving. She turned and slipped through the bushes which ran alongside, making her way to the archway in the wall which had once circled Heslington Hall to keep the riff raff off the manor grounds. Crossing the dual carriageway she made her way through the deserted science block, through Alcuin College and up to the Library.

The next day she would enter the room after making sure that she was seen in the snack bar at the college coming from the other side of the campus where she had spent the night with an old girlfriend who had been pleasantly surprised to receive a return visit. Not that she had managed to enter into the sex which was the price of her bed for the night with any enthusiasm. She managed to fake a convincing reaction of surprised horror, screaming for help, rushing into the corridor in a suitably hysterical condition.

Sarah   Now

Confession

I can't connect at all with the person who felt that hiding the handing in of an assignment with plagiarised and stolen material was worth taking a person's life for. I can't imagine now what made me take that road. Even a twenty-year-old has a well developed sense of right and wrong and more than an inkling of what might be considered an over reaction. I can still remember all the events of that night in crystal detail. The hurt anger in Suzanne's face when I told her what I'd been doing, the violence of her flinch from my touch when she called me a dyke. There was a tiny drop of spit at the side of her mouth, I could see she was trying not to cry. I felt something then, I can even feel it now so many years later, a sharp stab of loss and hurt that we had grown so far apart that she could believe what she said about me. At the same time, a scalp twitching fear that she meant to do what she said, my brain making the lightning connections with images of the consequences of what she threatened. My throat dried up, I had to swallow repeatedly to make my pleadings audible. I can remember leaping up to get her bag as she started to go into spasm, I knew that I had to get the inhaler to her as quickly as possible. I can still feel the rough tapestry of her bag clenched in my hands, the raised pattern against my fingertips.

After that, nothing, no feeling at all until I cried at my dad's funeral two years later. Yet I can recall every one of the items that fell out of the bag after I tipped it on the floor when she was already dead, my escape plan piecing itself together. A gold pen, a packet of tissues, her contraceptive pills, a black Rimmel mascara, a lipstick, Very Berry. Her purse, a black diary, a sheet of white paper with her timetable of lectures and seminars written on it. And of course the inhaler, which I kicked under the bed. If I close my eyes I can see them all, as if I'd taken a photograph of the crime scene. But no feelings.

Maybe that was why it was so easy and inevitable that I got together with Dick eventually. He was the only one I could talk to about Suzanne, about how I felt now she was gone. I could even go as far as telling him that I felt responsible for her death, the official line because I had not been there, rather than the truth. It was comfortable to be with him, he didn't seem to want or expect anything from me emotionally. It took me a long time to realise that he'd fallen in lust with me, I'd thought he was still grieving for Suzanne, that he regretted being such a shit to her. He seemed to feel enough guilt for the two of us, but then he owned up that he had never loved her in the way she had seemed to expect, that he hadn't had the same idea about their relationship as she had. He seemed surprised to find out that Suzanne had known all about his infidelity too. For a man who seemed so adept at listening to women it was a revelation that he had understood us so little. Thank goodness he improved on that score over the years.

I used Dick as a shield against any emotional involvement. I could hide behind his friendship to get by on my course, to do the minimum that was required to get a reasonable degree. When we did eventually fall into bed, I could satisfy my body's craving without having to release any of my locked up feelings. The fact that he was living in Leeds after he'd graduated and already working meant that we could have a semi-long distance friendship and relationship rather than the hothouse of being together on campus.

I couldn't even tell him that I loved him until after my father died, when the tears I cried at the funeral washed away the carefully built dams. Dick didn't seem to mind, he was content to take whatever I would give, he was understanding about what losing Suzanne should have meant to me. When he asked me to move in with him I agreed because I had no other options and I didn't want to go back to live with my parents.

Strangely enough the time we were together when I didn't love him, when he was more like a friend who I went to bed with than a lover, meant that when I could love him I found that the emotion ran much deeper than any I'd had before. I'd come to like him for the things we had in common, our shared interest in music and theatre and dance, for our enjoyment of cinema as well as old films and reading the Sunday papers in bed. Being together was as natural as breathing, we could even cook a meal together in the tiny kitchen in his house without one of us having a tantrum about how I was making the pasta sauce or how he was using every single pan in the house. Having always been looking for a mythical Mr Right, I now found that I was living with him.

He helped me through the pain of finding that my Dad had cancer, through the roller coaster of hoping that he could beat it and coming to terms with the fact that it was eating him alive. Dick drove me to the funeral and held me upright while the tears poured down my face during the whole service and afterwards at the crematorium. So it was only right that he should be on the receiving end of the overflow of all those overdue feelings when I could let go of that tight drawstring of piano wire which was keeping them all in check.

I still have a need to tell him the truth that I have kept from him now for over twenty years, even though my sensible, self-preserving brain tells me that it would serve no purpose to risk so much. Buddha said, "tell the truth", with two conditions. Is it kind and is it necessary? It would be neither of these to let Dick know that all the years of our marriage, the children and the love we share are based on murder and lies, that the house we live in is bought in part with the proceeds of that horrible night. The only necessity is my own compulsion to free myself of the burden of sole knowledge of what happened, and to fulfil my own need for expiation of my sin by losing everything I love.

You'd think I'd have grown up by now.

Sarah   Now

Truth

The house is quiet. Dick and Sarah are asleep upstairs, the result of that bottle of champagne they drank to celebrate their wedding anniversary, followed by a marathon sex session, starting in front of the open fire and proceeding up the stairs, along the landing, into the bathroom. Then opening another bottle to drink while they lay in the huge corner bath, playing Pink Floyd's *Dark Side of the Moon* loudly on the stereo and wallowing in nostalgia and patchouli oil. Then more sex, abandoned due to exhaustion, before collapsing on their king size bed with its crisp white Liberty cotton bedlinen.

Sarah wakes with a start at about one in the morning to find the lights still blazing, with a need for a pint of water to rehydrate her throat. She tries to go back to sleep after switching the lights off and carrying a glass back to bed, but lies awake staring at the patterns of leaves and street lights on the ceiling, listening to the clock strike two and three.

At last she gives up, grabs her thick blue towelling robe and shuffles on sheepskin mules to pad downstairs. Automatically she goes into the kitchen, puts the kettle on. While she is waiting for it to boil she looks out of the kitchen window at the dark garden, that will start to become visible as the night moves towards dawn. She has a picture of herself walking out onto the lawn bare foot, feeling the mud and the dew-wet grass between her toes, smelling the brown smoky leafiness of autumn that signals the descent into winter. For a moment she almost does it, she even has her hand on the doorknob, but no, she shakes her head, the kettle boils and clicks off. What is she thinking of? She is over forty now, a wife and mother, she can't wander around her garden at half past three in the morning without her slippers on. She makes the tea and carries it through to the lounge.

The open fire they'd lit last night to drink and screw in front of is still smouldering. She stirs the embers with the poker and adds a few scraps of kindling and a small log. The flames start to curl round the edges of the wood, sharp spikes of orange and yellow flickering up. She leans back on the cream leather sofa, an extravagance she bought with some of the royalties from her first book. The kind of sofa that should only be bought by people with no children, who would protect it from the scuffs and knocks and stains of old jam sandwiches it bears. It symbolised the fantasy nature of the book for her, she thought she should buy something rather superficial and out of place as that was how she felt at the time.

It's wonderfully comfortable, she tucks her feet up under her on the wide cushions.

Sarah breathes in the stillness of the house. Zanne is home from college for the summer break but is staying at her boyfriend's flat tonight. No sneaking around fucking in parked cars and under hedges for her. Sometimes Tom stays here when Zanne is around, Sarah is quite used to finding him unexpectedly frying bacon in her kitchen. How like her daughter to go all the way to university in Oxford to meet a man from Bradford. Martin is sleeping over at his friend Owen's, an opportunity for an all out brain-numbing festival of computer consoles, beer and junk food. When her children were younger, the quiet of the house if they were away had a tenseness about it, she could never really quite let go, she always felt an underlying sense of unease until they were back. Now she finds she can enjoy it at last.

She finishes her tea, puts her mug down on the tiled coffee table. The fire is crackling nicely. She knows what she has to do. Sarah goes across the lounge into the annex that serves as her space. She hasn't really needed to use it until recently, but Dick insisted that she have it when they moved to this house.

"You're a published poet," he'd said, "it's important that you have a space to write in."

Once again she kept her secret unspoken, accepted that, "Yes, a writing space would be good." She'd gone along with it, choosing pale blues and greens, deep yellow rugs, a chair for the desk that would support her weak back. She'd refused the computer though, insisting on a typewriter, claiming artist's eccentricity to avoid committing her copying to disks and hard drive.

She unlocks and opens the bottom draw. There they all are, crumpled sheets of lined foolscap, covered in a handwriting that is clearly not her own. Most of them have been used now, they have served their purpose. Still she keeps them here in this locked drawer. What for? Proof of her guilt?

She takes out the pile and carries it back into the lounge, setting it down beside her on the flame orange hearth rug that Dick and she brought back from Petra. It was made to adorn a bedouin tent, not some suburban living room in Leeds. She takes the top sheet off the pile and reads it. Yes, this was one of the first she used, probably still at university. She feeds it into the fire, where the paper takes a long moment to catch light before it starts to blacken and curl. She repeats the routine with the next sheet and the next.

Looking at them she is struck by the pencil marks, the crossing out, the words transposed, lines replaced, marks she was not conscious of making. As she goes through the whole pile, reading each one, marking it in time and space and where it was published, this one in a magazine, that one in *Granta,* that one in the first book, she realises that these poems were far more her own work than she ever realised. When she comes to the finest of them all, *Breathe,* the one that won the prize, the one that she thought Suzanne wrote about Dick, she realises that she has been deceiving herself for all these years. This is not even about the man who is sleeping upstairs in her bed, there is hardly anything of the original left, these are not Suzanne's words but her own, an expression of her love for her daughter. She reads it, hesitates, feels her breath catch. This is the one that is the most hers, the most real. Suzanne could never have known the feeling she gets when she looks at her namesake child. She exhales, then drops it into the fire and watches the paper burn and the smoke blow up her chimney.

Sarah goes back into the office and takes out the contents of the other locked bottom drawer, reams of snowy white paper pocked with lines of black type. This is her story, right from the start. Her childhood, what she can remember of it, growing up fat and then thin. All those characters dancing on the page. Johnny Manfredson and his friend Ged. Going to university. Dick and Suzanne and Jules. Smelly Ellis. Why she took her friend's work and used it as her own, how that led to Suzanne's death. Starting her relationship with Dick, their life, their marriage, their children. All overlaid and washed in the colour of her guilt. Sarah starts to read it, something she has not done before. She'd only been conscious of the contents of each page as she scrolled it out of the typewriter and placed it underneath its predecessors in the desk.

She starts at the beginning and keeps going right until the end. She looks up as she finishes the last page. She is back in the lounge, at some point she must have carried all the paper through here and settled back onto the sofa, spreading the sheets around her as she read. They cover the rug and the sofa, so many dirty snowflakes telling the story of her life. The clock strikes again. It is 6am. Dick will be stirring soon, to shower and shave and dress for work.

She needs a minute to digest what she has read. She knows it is the best thing she has written, better than any of the work of Suzanne's, better than the poems she made out of them. It's prose, but that wouldn't be a problem with something this good, she knows Cynthia would pass it on to the relevant editor.

The fire is still burning, the embers glowing hot and red surrounded by an acre of blackened ash. She gathers up all the paper and puts it back into order, then sits back on the rug and starts to feed each sheet into the fire, just like the stolen work she destroyed earlier in the night. This time it's a quicker process, because she's already read it. She is grateful for her insistence on a typewriter. This is the only copy and it can never be repeated.

At last it is done, transmogrified into the smuts floating out on the morning air. She stretches out, stiff from kneeling, the bedouin pattern etched deeply into her knees and shins. Sarah goes over to the large French windows and draws back the gold velvet curtain to reveal the wet grey Yorkshire garden. Mist has come down in the night, she can't see half of the dank green grass which vanishes into the grey. Shrubs and flowers droop under the weight of water. It's raining and dull. Yet she feels light and transparent, like a crystal reflecting the sun's rainbow onto the walls of her house. She is balanced between sky and earth, resting lightly on the ground, her head brushing the clouds.

She has been awake half the night but she feels bright and alert, ready to start living without the paper weight she has been carrying around with her all these years.

She makes another cup of tea for herself and one for Dick, and carries them both up to bed to tell him what she has done.

0-595-28230-X

Printed in the United Kingdom
by Lightning Source UK Ltd.
111519UKS00002B/1-3